EDA BLESSED II

···

MILTON J. DAVIS

MVmedia, LLC
Fayetteville, GA

MVmedia, LLC
PO Box 143052
Fayetteville, GA 30214
www.mvmediaatl.com

Publisher's Note: This is a work of fiction. Names, charac-ters, places, and incidents are a product of the author's imagination. Locales and public names are sometimes used for atmospheric pur-poses. Any resemblance to actual people, living or dead, or to busi-nesses, companies, events, institutions, or locales is completely coincidental.

Book Layout ©2017 BookDesignTemplates.com
Cover Art by Stanley Weaver, Jr.
Cover Design by Uraeus

Ordering Information:
Quantity sales. Special discounts are available on quantity purchases by corporations, associations, and others. For details, con-tact the "Special Sales Department" at the address above.

Eda Blessed II/Milton J. Davis. -- 1st ed.
ISBN 978-1-7372277-1-7

Contents

Contents

To Charles R. Saunders. Sword and Soul Forever.

NGISIMAUGI

The Mikijen recruits filed into the human circle again, each armed with a sword and jambiya. The humid, hazy sky blurred the morbid scene under its watch. Omari pushed his sweat soaked braids back from his face with his bruised right hand. Bare-chested drummers pounded out a martial rhythm on the djembes hanging from their shoulders as the senior Mikijen clapped their hands in time and sang. For three months the new conscripts endured the Mikijen training, two hundred souls dwindling down to the ten standing in the blood-stained sandy circle. The day began with twenty. The others were either dead, dying or crippled. This was not a test of who could pass. It was a test for survival.

"What are you waiting for?" Kamada Hodari shouted. "Finish it!"

Omari glared at the Mikijen commander. There would be no mercy from him or any of the others. He was surrounded by survivors of the same ritual. There we no favorites, no friends.

Omari's anger almost cost him his life. The attacker was almost upon him when he turned. The fool yelled as he brought his sword down, certain of his victory. Omari reached up, grabbed the man's wrist then twisted, throwing the man on his back. He drove his sword into his throat then snatched it free.

Omari head jerked up as he crouched. Two warriors ran toward him, swords and jambiyas at the ready. Omari didn't wait for them; he spun and fled. Just before he reached the barrier he turned about, throwing his jambiya at the closest man. The jambiya sank into the startled man's eye and he fell where he stood, his hands clutching the knife hilt as he died.

Omari and the second man fought a vicious duel, their skills equally matched. He blocked and slashed, fighting of the fatigue threatening him with each blow. His opponent fared no better. Omari's defense was failing when the man grimaced and arched his back. He fell to the left, revealing the conscript that ambushed him. Omari prepared himself, knowing he would not survive this day.

"Enough!" Kamada Hodari shouted.

The muwanis fell silent, the drummers' hands stilled. Omari looked around the fighting circle. Only five of them stood. The others lay dead or dying.

Hodari strode into the circle. His eyes met Omari's and the Kamada smiled. Omari couldn't tell if it was pride or some other emotion the kamada expressed and he didn't care. His legs trembled and his entire body ached.

"Muwani!" Hodari said. "What do you see before you?"

"Mikijen!" the others shouted.

Hodari exited the circle. The drummers played a different rhythm and the muwani rushed the survivors. Omari was swamped by smiling faces, his body pummeled by welcoming hands, his ears filled with victorious ululations. It was all too much. The muwani were lifting him off his feet when he passed out.

* * *

Omari dipped his fingers into the warm beeswax on the tiny table in his room. He massaged it into his loose beard, careful to make sure every hair strand was sufficiently oiled. He wiped his fingers on the cotton towel on his lap, then began braiding. The process relaxed him as it always did since he decided to stop shaving. It was the one thing that took his mind off what a shithole his life had become.

Insistent knocking on the door of his tiny pleasure house room interrupted his peace.

"Go away!" he shouted.

"That's no way to treat you new family!" someone shouted back.

Omari scowled "My family's dead."

The lock jiggled then the door swung wide. Three drunken Mikijen crowded the open space, all with silly grins on their faces. One of them, a stout dark-skinned man with yellow eyes pointed his stubby finger at Omari.

"How adorable!" Lephelo said.

"Let me do it!" Gahiji said. The thin bald man reached for Omari's beard and Omari punched his hand.

"Leave him alone," Kago said. The muscular man staggered into the room the placed a bottle of palm wine on Omari's table.

"Come outside when you're done," he said. "We have something for you."

"What?" Omari asked.

"Your last test," Kago said.

Omari stopped braiding his beard. "I thought I was done with tests."

"You are," Lephelo said. "But you're still not one of us. Not until you get this."

Lephelo unfastened his shirt then pulled it down to his waist. He turned his back to Omari revealing his tattoo, the ngisimaugi. The kraken's dark body occupied most of Lephelo's back, the tentacles rising up to his shoulders then extending down his arms to the back of his hands. The black ink shimmered with flecks of blue. The specks were what made the tattoo special, giving the Mikijen their healing abilities and near immortality. It was kipande, the remnants of Daarila's axe, a mineral that blessed and cursed.

"Today is the day you get yours," Kago said.

Omari stopped braiding his beard.

"Why today?"

"Because I say so," Kago replied. "You've had long enough to heal. It's time we made you a real muwani."

"Or you could refuse, and we'll kill you where you sit."

The lightness was gone from the trio's faces. Omari was tempted to call them on their threat. He could see nothing good coming from his conscription; might as well get it over with. He felt no sense of accomplishment from surviving Mikijen training, no satisfaction enduring an ordeal that killed so many others. But Omari the street rat was a survivor. He knew that as long as he was alive, the situation could always get better. He stopped braiding his beard, picked up the bottle of palm wine then drank until it was empty.

"Let's get this tattoo," he said.

Omari finished his beard then followed his new 'friends' down the narrow hallway then into the bright afternoon sunlight. They had come to the mainland to celebrate his passing over. To his surprise Kamada Hodari paid for the celebration. The new muwani did not celebrate together. After three months of literally trying to kill each other, there was no bond between them. Instead, each was adopted by a separate *taapo,* a group of senior muwani tasked to teach the new recruits the things training could not provide. Omari did not get to choose his taapo. Kamada Hodari made the decision. As far as Omari was concerned, he made a bad choice.

He followed his new cohorts out of the city and into the bush. Omari's anxiety grew the further they went. Had he endured three months of torture to be killed in the woods? He sized up each man, playing out in his mind how he would take them. Then there was the other option; he could run and pray to Eda they were too old to catch him.

The road ended at a wide expanse. At the center was a large circular hut crowned by a conical palm leaf roof.

"Okeyo!" Kago shouted.

The hut door shook then was pulled inside the house. A pack of wild dogs burst through the entrance, running headlong toward Omari and the others. Omari turned to run, but Kago caught his arm.

"If you run, they will chase you and kill you," Kago said. "Be still."

The dogs surrounded them, jumping and yipping but not attacking. Omari sweated and trembled but the others showed no sign of fear. After what seemed like eternity, Okeyo emerged from the house. The tall, broad-shouldered man wore a plain kanga, his chest exposed. Dozens of gris-gris necklaces jangled with his footsteps.

"Dek cen! Cet cen!" Okeyo shouted, his basso voice filling the space.

The wild dogs broke their circle then melded into the bush.

Okeyo approached Kago and the men shook wrists.

"Kago. It's been a long time."

"It has."

Okeyo ambled to Omari. "What is your name, muwani?"

"Omari Ket."

"Where are you from?"

"Sati-Baa."

Okeyo looked at Kago.

"You bring me a city boy?"

"He survived the training," Kago replied. "He'll survive this."

Okeyo looked Omari up and down.

"Come with me," he said.

He turned away walked toward the house. Omari followed for a few strides before he realized the others weren't coming with him. He turned to look at Kago.

"You're not coming, too?"

Kago shook his head. "This is your journey."

Lephelo grinned. "We'll be back, for you . . . or your body."

"My body?"

The trio shared a knowing glance among themselves then walked away. Omari stared at them for a moment, then looked at Okeyo who waited.

"Make up your mind," Okeyo said.

Omari shrugged. "As if I had a choice."

Omari followed Okeyo into the house. The man's possessions were against the wall except for a bed in the center. Opposite of the door was a libation altar.

"Sit on the bed while I gather my tools," Okeyo said.

Omari went to the bed and sat. He scanned the room. The items along the wall suggested Okeyo was a sonchai, but there were other items that said different.

Okeyo went to a cart then rolled it to the bedside. He returned to the cart, pushing a black iron kettle filled with an equally black liquid. Okeyo made one more trip, carrying a medium sized square box that seemed heavier than it should be. He grunted as he placed the box near the kettle.

"What are you doing?" Omari asked.

"Preparing the ink," Okeyo replied. "We are waiting."

"Waiting for what?"

His question was answered by the sounds of yelping. Okeyo ambled to the door and opened it. The wild dog pack rushed into the house, the animals surrounding the man and jumping for his attention. The last dogs to enter dragged a carcass inside. Okeyo went to them and shooed them away. He lifted the dead springbok onto his shoulders then carried it to the altar. Placing the body before the shrine, he lit the wax candles then prostrated.

Omari could not understand his words but the dogs did. They fell silent and lay on their bellies as Okeyo continued to pray. Though he could not translate, there was a cadence to the words that captured his attention. His eyelids became heavy; he felt his body swaying in the rhythm. Then it stopped. Omari looked up to see Okeyo staring at him, his eyes wide. The tattooist faced the altar and prostrated again.

"So be it."

Okeyo took the knife from his waist belt then cut into the springbok. He stood, walking back to the bed, his hand clutching a bloody object. Omari tried to glimpse it but Okeyo dropped it into the ink too fast.

"Chamo," he said.

The dogs jumped to their paws then trotted to the springbok carcass. They dragged it from the house.

Okeyo opened the heavy box and the faint blue light of kipande filled the space. He dipped a spoon into the substance then dumped it into the ink. He then scooped a second spoonful. He was about to add it to the ink then hesitated. He looked to the altar.

"Are you sure?" he said aloud.

His head jerked as if struck before he opened his eyes and added the second spoonful to the ink. Okeyo picked up an ink-stained stick then stirred the concoction, whispering as he mixed the ingredients. Omari watched, his throat tightening.

After an hour, Okeyo ceased mixing. He gave Omari another long look then got up from his stool and went to his shelves, returning with a small gourd.

"Drink this then lay on your stomach, your arms at your side."

Omari took the gourd then smelled the contents. The aroma was pleasant and soothing.

"What it is?" he asked.

"It will help you relax," Okeyo said.

Omari shrugged then drank. He felt the effects immediately. He lay on his stomach then closed his eyes.

*　*　*

Omari dreamed of Sati-Baa. Sati-Baa when he was a boy; Sati-Baa before the bacillus plague. He ran the narrow streets, dodging through crowds of merchants, laughing with his friends and picking a purse or two along the way. He broke away from his friends, taking a narrow street to a tangle of small huts, one of which he called home. Mama and baba sat at the one table, talking as always. He interrupted their discussion with hugs then dropped his illicit bounty on the table top. Baba grinned then rubbed his head. Mama frowned then scooped the cowries from the table and added them to her collection gourd. Omari sat at the table and mama brought him a bowl of sorghum.

He felt a prick on his back, then another, and another. The world went black and Omari fell in darkness.

He screamed but no sound came from his mouth. His arms flailed, his hands reaching for anything to stop his descent. After what seemed an eternity a speck of blue light appeared below him, growing rapidly as he fell. The light engulfed him and his falling ceased.

Omari felt firmness under his feet as his vision cleared. He stood on the precipice of a mountain, looking down into valley surrounding a large body of water. Everything within the depression radiated with the same blue illumination that swallowed him.

"The Cleave," Omari said.

"We are here," a strange voice answered.

Omari looked right and left. There were others with him, but he could not make out their features.

"Why are we here?" he asked.

He was answered with darkness.

* * *

Omari woke to insistent voices. He tried to move but could not. He opened his eyes; his sight was blocked by what looked like a thin fabric. His body was wrapped, his arms folded across his chest. He heard Kago's voice as he fought to free himself.

"How did this happen?" Kago said.

"As it sometimes does," Okeyo replied.

"You know that, Kayo," Lephelo said. "I knew he was going to die."

"What did you do different?" Kago asked.

Okeyo said nothing. There were sounds of struggle.

"What did you do?!?" Kago shouted.

"I gave him more," Okeyo said.

"Why in the Cleave did you do that?"

"The ancestors demanded it."

Omari wriggled on the table.

"Kago!" he said.

"Did you hear something?" Lephelo asked.

"Kago!" Omari said louder. "Get me out of this shit!"

"He's alive!" Okeyo said.

"No thanks to you," Kago replied. "Cut him out."

Omari lay still while Okeyo cut him free. He sat up then glared at Okeyo.

"What did you do to me?" he asked.

"What I was told to do," Okeyo replied.

"Enough of this," Kayo said. "He's alive. I guess you didn't test him."

Okeyo shook his head.

"I will," Lephelo said. He pulled out his jambiya and stabbed Omari in the stomach.

"Wha . . ."

Omari fell back on the table, his stomach burning. Moments later his back became warm, blue light radiating from beneath him. The pain in his gut subsided. Omari dared to look down. To his amazement, the wound healed before his eyes. He looked up at Kago, who smiled at him.

"Congratulations, muwani," he said. "You're officially one of us. Now put on your clothes so we can leave this place."

Kago and the others went outside. Omari stood, his eyes on the stomach wound until it disappeared. He saw a mirror leaning against the wall and went to it to look at the ngisimaugi. Okeyo joined him.

"It is yours until you leave the Mikijen . . . or die," Okeyo said.

"I can die?" Omari said.

"Yes," Okeyo replied. "A wound to the heart will do it. Decapitation as well."

"That makes sense," Omari replied.

"If you receive too many wounds at one time as well," Okeyo said.

Omari nodded. He ambled back to the table and put on his clothes. He was walking to the door then stopped.

"I heard you tell Kago you put more kipande in my tattoo. Why?"

"Because the ancestors demanded it," Okeyo said.

"What do they have to do with this?"

"Everything."

Okeyo put his hand on Omari's back then guided him to the door.

"Goodbye, Omari Ket," he said. "May Eda bless you."

"I hope so," Omari replied.

His new companions gathered beyond the house, chatting as they waited for him. Omari took a deep breath, then stepped out into his new life.

TO THE EAST

"Omari."

"Hmm?"

"Omari!"

"What?"

"Wake up."

Omari touched the hand shaking his shoulder. It was rough with callouses. His eyes went wide, and he jumped up from the bed, swinging wildly.

"Ow!"

Omari kicked. He felt his foot smack against flesh.

"Shit! Somebody grab his ass!"

Multiple arms wrapped around Omari then pushed him down on the bed. He headbutted another assailant before someone bashed him on the head, taking the fight out of him. He collapsed onto the straw mattress.

"By the Cleave, Bakari!"

"What? He headbutted me!"

Hearing Bakari's name cleared Omari's head. He blinked his eyes then focused on his assailants. Bakari frowned, rubbing his bulbous bleeding nose. Abedi glared at Bakari with his golden eyes, his bald head beaded with sweat. Juba held back a laugh as he pressed down on Omari.

"What in Daarila's name are you doing here?" Omari said. "Where's Akina?"

"We paid her and sent her on her way," Abedi replied.

"Paid her?" Omari managed to laugh despite his throbbing skull.

Abedi's eyes went wide. "You mean she wasn't . . ."

"No, she wasn't," Omari said between chuckles.

"And she took the money anyway!"

"Serves you right," Omari said.

His friends released him, and Omari sat up then stood on shaky legs. He groaned as he picked up his clothes and dressed.

"You owe me a stack," Abedi said.

"I don't owe you shit," Omari replied. "You should have asked. What are you doing here?"

"We came to get you," Bakari said, still rubbing his nose. "Cleave! I think its broken. You broke my nose!"

Omari ignored Bakari and looked to the window. It was still dark.

"Get me for what?"

"We're going on a safari," Abedi said. "One only a chosen few can take."

"And how do you know I want to go?" Omari asked.

"Because it pays eight stacks up front, eight when we return. Plus, you get to make whatever side deals you wish once we reach our destination."

Sixteen stacks! It was more money Omari had opportunity to make since he was banished from Sati-Baa and forced to serve in the Mikijen.

"Where are we going, and when do we depart?"

"We depart tonight," Abedi answered. "As to where, I can't say. I can tell you this; once we get there, you'll be glad you came."

Omari shuffled to the corner of his flat and retrieved his sword and jambiyas. He'd paid good money for the room; it was in the better part of Mombisa, providing a relatively safe place for his trysts. He gave the room one long look then shrugged.

"Okay," he said. "Let's go."

Abedi led Omari and the others out of the hostel and into the deserted streets. Instead of heading for the Mikijen barracks, they took a road leading to the outskirts of the port city.

"Where are we going?" Omari asked.

"To the rendezvous," Abedi said.

"I thought this was a Kiswala safari," Omari said.

"It is, but it isn't," Abedi replied.

Omari stopped.

"Abedi, what are you getting me into?"

"A lot of stacks," Abedi replied. "I thought you'd be interested, but maybe I was wrong. If you don't want to go, now's the time to leave. Once we reach the rendezvous there's no turning back."

Omari looked at Bakari and Juba.

"Do you two know where we're going?"

Both shook their heads.

"I've served Abedi for a long time," Juba said. "He's never steered me wrong. Whatever it is can't be any more dangerous than anything else we've done. Besides, I don't see why you're worried. You're the lucky one."

Omari folded his arms. "I'm not lucky. I'm blessed. Still, I don't know, Abedi."

"You don't know about sixteen stacks?" Abedi frowned. "I guess I overestimated you, Ket. I took you as a gambler."

Abedi stuck out his hand and Omari shook it.

"May Eda continue to bless you," Abedi said. "See you in six months."

Abedi, Juba and Bakari continued down the road. Omar watched them for a minute as he reconsidered. Sixteen stacks was a lot of money.

"You can't tell me where we're going?" he called out.

"No," Abedi called back.

"Sixteen stacks?" Omari shouted.

"Sixteen," Abedi shouted back.

"Shit."

Omari trotted to catch up with the trio. They strolled in silence for a few more strides until they reached a place in the road marked by a large acacia tree. Abedi reached into his bag and took out four masks. They were simple black hoods that covered everything but their eyes.

"Why the masks?" Omari asked.

"The members of the expedition are to be anonymous to each other until we're on the water," Abedi said. "That way no one will be able to share who took the safari because everyone will be committed at that point."

"This doesn't sound good," Omari said as he put on his mask.

"Sixteen stacks," Abedi replied.

"Sixteen stacks," Omari repeated.

The men secured their masks.

"Now what?" Omari asked.

"We wait," Abedi answered.

Omari strolled to the acacia and sat down against it. He folded his arms across his chest then dozed off, still tired from a vigorous night with Akina. He slept a moment before Juba jostled him.

"Wake up. They're here."

Omari stretched and rubbed his eyes. A wagon had come, hitched to two bulls. The bare-chested driver wore a mask and a white loincloth. as well. Omari and the others climbed in and they set off down the road. They traveled for an hour before the driver guided the wagon into the bush. The way became rough as they weaved through bushes and trees until the foliage cleared, revealing a hidden path. They followed the path until the plants gave way to an open beach. Anchored off the shore was a bahglah, a large dhow used for long voyages. Piles of supplies were stacked high on the sands, masked laborers loading them into waiting boats which ferried the goods to the dhow. The driver guided the wagon into the surf to a canoe waiting to take them to the ship.

"Whose dhow is this?" Omari asked.

"You keep asking questions I can't answer," Abedi replied. "Be patient. Everything will be revealed once we're under way."

Omari watched his companions climb into the boat, his hands on his hips.

"Come on, Omari,' Abedi said. "You've come too far now. If you try to leave now, we'll have to kill you, and we really don't want to do that."

Omari shrugged then climbed into the boat.

There was a slight chop on the water, bobbing the boat on the dark waves. They eased beside the dhow. Omari and the others climbed the cargo net onto the deck. The laborers hurried about, loading cargo into the hold, and preparing the sails for launch. A lone figure paced before them, issuing orders when needed. By the shape Omari could tell it was a woman; whether she was nahoda or someone else he did not know. He nudged Abedi.

"Who is that?" he asked.

Abedi glared and Omari raised his hands.

"I know, I know. Everything will be revealed when we're under way."

The hooded woman looked in their direction. Abedi went to her immediately.

"These are your men?" she said.

"Yes, malkia," he answered.

Malkia. Whoever the woman was, she was a Kiswala of noble blood, Omari thought. The fact that a Kiswalan was taking part in this safari raised its importance tenfold.

"This is all?" she said, disappointment clear in her voice.

"They are enough," he said.

"Every year you bring fewer. I think your trying to rob me, Abedi."

"It's the other way around, malkia," Abedi retorted. "You give me less money and expect the same results."

"Mikijen are cheap these days," the malkia said. "There are more than enough of you since we've fought no wars in years."

"You get what you pay for," Abedi said.

"Or not," the malkia replied.

She waved her hand. "Enough of this. Take them below and keep them there until I send for you."

"Yes, malkia," Abedi replied.

Abedi stomped to Omari.

"Come on. Let's get below."

Omari and the others followed Abedi below deck to their barracks. It was a wide room with ten hammocks, more than enough space for the four of them. Abedi took the hammock closest to the port hole; Omari took the hammock closest to the door.

"How long do we have to stay down here?" he asked.

"Until we're in open water," Abedi answered. "Our destination is only known to the malkia."

"A monopoly? That's smart," Omari said.

"It is. It's the reason she's one of the richest merchants in Kiswala."

"What about us then?" Bakari asked. "We won't know the route, but we will know the destination."

"We're Mikijen," Abedi replied. "It's a good chance all of us will be dead within a year. And this is your only journey. You'll make enough stacks to leave the service if you wish or live like mansas until you're broke."

"How many safaris have you taken?" Omari asked.

"Six."

"What makes you special?" Juba asked.

"For one, I can be trusted," Abedi replied. "As for the other . . ."

Abedi grabbed himself between his legs and the others laughed.

"So, she loves you?" Omari asked.

"I don't know, and I don't care," Abedi replied. "This is our time together. We enjoy ourselves and when we return to Kiswala we go our separate ways."

"And you're okay with this?" Juba asked.

Abedi shrugged. "I'm a Mikijen. I know my place."

Abedi's expression was stern, but Omari detected sadness in his voice. His mind drifted back to Sati-Baa and Aisha. Their relationship was complicated, but there was no doubt that they loved each other. He knew he would never see her again, but there were times he still thought of her. He wondered if she was still making the best of her life in the streets or if she had finally found comfort in some rich merchant's bed. He hoped for the latter, for she deserved it.

Omari stored his possessions, climbed into his hammock, and slept. The smell of roasted goat woke him a few hours later and he joined his companions for the simple meal. They spent three days below deck, cleaning their weapons, playing oware and annoying anyone that did not have the sense enough to avoid them. On the morning of the fourth day Abedi shook him awake.

"Time to go topside," he said. "No masks."

"Finally!" Juba said.

The Mikijen walked single file to the steps then onto the deck. Omari winced when the sun touched his eyes as did the others. His vision cleared and he took stock of their circumstances. They were in the midst of the ocean, with no sight of land in any direction. The baharia busied themselves with the continuous duties needed to keep a dhow afloat and functional on the open sea. This was the most boring part of any sea safari for the hired muwanis. With nothing to guard and no one to fight, they might as well remain below.

"Why are we on deck?" Juba asked.

"Because the malkia demands it," Abedi replied.

"So, what are we to do? Protect everyone from flying fish?"

As if on cue, a massive school of flying fish surrounded the dhow. The baharia immediately went to work, casting huge nets and trapping hundreds of fish.

"Catch fish," Abedi replied.

Omari and the others stripped down to their loincloths then joined the crew in catching the flying fish landing on the deck. It was not unusual for the mercenaries to help the baharia with duties during a long voyage, but Omari hated it. It was bad enough he became a Mikijen against his will and having to perform mundane chores for free made it worse. He filled his bucket with the flailing fish then carried it to the baharia cleaning and smoking them for storage. Some would be eaten later.

Omari managed to glance at the rear of the dhow. The nahoda steered vessel deftly, following the swarming school, his eyes focused on their moves. The malkia stood beside him, but her attention was on the baharia and Mikijen gathering the fish. Her eyes lingered on Abedi, then shifted to Omari. She smiled then nodded; Omari did the same before getting back to the work. The malkia was Abedi's woman, but it didn't hurt to have her attention. He might be able to use it to his advantage down the road. He glanced toward Abedi and saw the man watching him. Omari nodded then continued to pick up fish. This might get complicated, he thought.

The school of airborne fish finally dispersed. Juba and Abedi washed off and put on their uniforms. Omari and Bakari remained in their loincloths.

"Here's the deal," Abedi said. "The malkia expects us to oversee everything on the dhow until we reach our destination. Since there's only four of us, we'll divide the day into four shifts. I'll take the first shift; Juba will take the second. Bakari, you have third shift. Omari, you'll take fourth shift.

"The night shift," Omari groused.

"Just like home," Abedi said. "Low man gets the shit shift. You two get below deck and get some rest. Juba, you're up."

Juba nodded then walked away, his hands clasped behind his back. Omari and Bakari headed for the stairs that led below deck.

"Omari, wait," Abedi said.

Omari turned. "What is it?"

Abedi placed his hand on Omari's shoulder.

"Be careful. The malkia is not one to be toyed with."

"I have no intentions . . ."

"Don't lie to me, Ket," Abedi said. "I saw how you looked at her, and how she looked at you."

"I would never violate your relationship with her," Omari said.

Abedi laughed. "Good try. This will be a long safari. The malkia is rich and attractive. The longer we're at sea, the better she'll look."

"Like I said, I won't go near her."

"But what if she comes to you?" Abedi asked.

Omari opened his mouth to speak and Abedi shushed him.

"Don't make promises you won't keep. Just remember my words."

There was nothing Omari could say. He shrugged then went below. He found their barracks, hopped in his hammock and was asleep as soon as his head touched the netting.

He awoke among snoring and darkness. He donned his clothes then slipped onto deck. He met Bakari on his way back.

"Kill anyone?" he asked.

Bakari laughed. "I wish I could kill this boredom. This is unnecessary."

"I agree, but the malkia makes the rules."

Bakari patted his shoulder as he passed on his way below deck. Omari began his shift, walking along the bulwark to the bow. He stopped, gazing into the darkness toward the invisible horizon.

"There is nothing to protect out there, Mikijen."

Omari turned toward the woman's voice. The malkia strolled toward him, holding a lantern which luminated her face. She stopped before him.

"Omari Ket, is it?"

Omari nodded. "That is my name."

"I am Tishala Imamu. This is my dhow and my safari."

"The Imamu are a powerful family," Omari said. "I have heard your name spoken often."

"This safari is the foundation of our power," she said. "The goods we bring back from our destination can't be found anywhere in Ki Khanga."

"So, this voyage is important," Omari said.

"Very," Tishala replied.

She set her lantern on the bulwark then leaned on it, her forearms resting on the top. Omari stole a glance at her profile and smiled.

"Tell me about yourself," she said. "Where are you from?"

"Sati-Baa," he replied.

"I've been there," she said to Omari's surprise. "Fascinating city. Nothing like it anywhere else in Ki Khanga."

"If you say so," Omari said. "I'm sure I'm not as well traveled as you."

"Why did you leave?"

"I had no choice," Omari answered. "It was either that or a death sentence."

Tishala turned to look at him. Omari expected a shocked expression; instead, he met a curious gaze.

"What did you do? Kill someone?"

"I dishonored a very important person," Omari said. "At least that was the charge."

"And you say you didn't," Tishala said.

"It doesn't matter now," Omari replied. "I'm here on your dhow keeping your goods safe."

"You're not one to dwell in the past, I see."

Omari shrugged. "What good will it do? I live in the moment."

"You don't miss your family?"

"I have no family," he answered. "I have no siblings and my parents died when I was ten during the bacillus epidemic."

Tishala's eyes went wide. "How terrible!"

Omari shrugged then spat into the sea. "It was Daarila's will."

"I assume Abedi warned you about me," Tishala said.

"What do you mean?" Omari replied.

"Don't lie. He told you to be wary of me. He tells every new person he brings."

"He noticed me looking at you," Omari confessed. "I take it you share a relationship."

"We do no such thing," Tishala replied. "Abedi is a good leader, that is all. There have been times that I have asked him to go beyond his duties. He has no right to claim a relationship with me, even for the simple fact that he is a Mikijen, and I am Kiswalan. Do you understand?"

"I understand very well," Omari said. "The woman that had me sentenced to death was very much like you. The moment I did not 'serve her needs' I was disposable."

Omari walked away.

"I didn't mean it that way," Tishala said.

"Yes, you did," Omari replied. "It's late malkia. You should get some sleep, and I have my rounds."

If Omari had any intentions to share a bed with Tishala, he dismissed them after hearing her words. He was smart enough not to get in the same situation again, especially when the man he answered to was involved. Six months was a long time, but he would manage. It wouldn't be the first time.

Another week of boring duties passed by before a change in their routine appeared on the horizon. Omari rested was relaxing the cabin, playing a game of oware with Abedi when Juba stuck his head into the room.

"Come see!" he said.

Omari and Abedi followed Juba to the upper deck. A cluster of buildings broke the horizon unlike anything Omari had ever seen. They seem to float on water.

"What is this?" Omari asked.

"Mjiwahari," Abedi replied. "The floating city. We'll dock here for a few days for a bit of trading and to replenish supplies."

"Where's the land?" Juba asked.

"There is none," Abedi replied. "At least not visible. The legends say that there was once an island here. But when Daarila struck the world with his Axe, a massive wave consumed the islands, sweeping away most of its inhabitants. Those that survived tethered their homes and buildings together and constructed air bladders and stilts to support them. The Kiswala trade wood and labor with them for seafood and other items."

"Labor?" Omari said.

Abedi glanced at him. "You'll see."

One of the baharia climbed to the top of the highest mast with a shell horn. He blew a series of bursts that were answered. The bahari waved to the nahoda and he steered the dhow to Mjiwahari.

They came upon a massive sea gate that opened upon their approach, allowing them into an artificial harbor. A crowd of bare-chested people waited as they docked, their eyes wide with curiosity.

"They look as if they've never seen other people before," Juba commented.

"They don't get visitors often, and when they do, they rarely allow them into the harbor. These waters are infested with pirates, and Mjiwahari is one of the few worthy targets on the open sea besides another dhow."

"They looked rather frail," Omari said.

"Don't let their appearances deceive you," Abedi warned. "The baMjiwa are formidable fighters. How else to you think they have been able to thrive out here for so long? Some of them serve as mercenaries on other dhows, and a few have become pirates. You'll do best to respect them, or you might find yourself at the bottom of the sea, ngisimaugi or no."

A commotion behind them caught their attention. Armed baharia led a line of chained people onto the deck. The haggard looks on their faces and blank stares said more than any words could convey.

"Sit!" one of the baharia shouted. The prisoners complied, sitting cross-legged on the deck.

"Who are they?" Omari asked.

"Does it matter?" Abedi asked.

"It does to me," Omari said. "I'd like to know who we're serving."

"Kiswala prisoners," Abedi said.

"That doesn't tell me anything," Omari replied.

"You are a curious one Ket," Tishala said.

The malkia walked up to them, dressed regally as always.

"They are enemies of the Kiswala council that have been exiled," she continued. "It is against our customs to spill the blood of our own, so they were given a choice. Die by drowning or come to Mjiwahari to live out their lives as slaves."

"Not much of a choice," Omari said.

"Those who choose death are more respected," Tishala said.

"That only matters to those who make the rules," Omari replied. "As long as one is alive, circumstances can change."

Tishala smirked. "Spoken like a true survivor."

Tishala turned her attention to Abedi.

"I need you to escort these prisoners to the stockade while I meet with *mwenye* Khamisi. Omari, you'll come with me."

Omari cursed under his breath. He glanced at Abedi, who frowned at him before responding to Tishala.

"As you wish, malkia," he said.

Abedi gestured at Juba and Bakari, who followed him to the seated prisoners.

"Get up," Abedi ordered. The prisoners responded, a few of them looking at the Mikijen with disdain. Omari understood their anger; there was a time they were giving the orders to the Mikijen.

Abedi escorted the prisoners down the gang-plank to the docks; Tishala, Omari and the others followed. The baharia mingled among the baMjiwa while the Mikijen, the prisoners, Tishala and Omari proceeded into the city. The buildings were connected by wooden planks that were steadier than Omari thought they would be. Abedi and the others broke away, following another route while Tishala and Omari continued toward the center of the city where the mwenye resided. His home occupied the center of the man-made island, a wide brightly painted two story structure swarming with people. Omari placed himself between the malkia and the increasingly dense throng.

"Which way, malkia?" he asked.

"Continue in the same direction," she said. "We will be greeted soon."

After a few more moments shouting voices cut through the din.

"Make way! Make way!"

The people separated, revealing soldiers dressed in leather armor and metal helmets carrying tall spears and short swords hanging from their waists. A dark brown woman with a golden band around her thick hair came forward, bowing before Omari and Tishala.

"Welcome, malkia," the woman said.

"Thank you, Kiojah," Tishala said. "It's good to see you are still in command."

"Until the day I die," Kiojah replied. She gave Omari a hard stare.

"Where is Abedi?"

"He's taking the prisoners to the stockade," Tishala said. "This is Omari Ket."

Kiojah nodded sharply. Omari sensed she was not pleased to see him.

"Follow me please, malkia," she said. "Mwenge Khamisi is anxious to meet with you. He has some interesting news to share."

"That could be good or bad," Tishala said.

"I'll let you decide," Kiojah replied.

They trailed Kiojah and her warriors to the mwenye's lair, the throng quickly getting out of their way. Omari noticed a few of them glaring at Kiojah, a sign that she was not well liked. A path opened, revealing Khamisi and his entourage. Tables of food were laid out below a stage where the mwenye sat with his consorts and bodyguards. He looked down on his sycophants while five drummers, two flautists and a kora player soothed the crowd with their hypnotic music.

"Is this for you?" Omari asked Tishala. The malkia laughed.

"This is every day for Khamisi," she said. "The man is richer than the richest Kiswalan. He controls the shipping lanes for spans, supplying almost ever dhow heading to and from the East. He also provides protection from pirates, which he charges an enormous price.

"What will you pay him?" Omari asked.

"I hope the prisoners are enough," she replied.

Khamisi turned their way and his eyes brightened.

"Tishala!" he shouted. "Everyone, Tishala is here!"

The entire party looked at them then responded with a chorus of praises that seemed rehearsed. Khamisi began waving his hands at those sitting at his table.

"Make room for my special guests!" he ordered.

The people surrounding him grabbed their plates and moved aside. Kiojah led them up the platform. Tishala sat beside Khamisi; the mwenye offered his cheek and she kissed it.

"I'm so happy to see you, Tishala," Khamisi said. "It's been too long."

"Stop exaggerating," Tishala replied. "It's been as long as it's always been."

"But I miss you so much!" Khamisi said. "You're the only visitor that brings me information of Ki Khanga."

Khamisi's eyes drifted to Omari.

"Oh my! He's a handsome one," Khamisi said. "Who is he?"

"His name is Omari Ket," Tishala replied. "He serves Abedi and the Mikijen."

"Is that all he serves?" Khamisi asked with a knowing grin.

"As Malkia Tishala said, I serve the Mikijen," Omari answered.

Khamisi looked shocked. Omari felt a nervous pang in his gut that remained until the mwenye laughed.

"Take a seat, Omari Ket," Khamisi said. "I like you."

Omari looked to Talisha for permission and she nodded her head. He sat in the seat beside her.

"Bring my guests food!" Khamisi said.

Servants hurried from the table. Khamisi pushed his plate aside the placed his elbows on the table, resting his head on his intertwined fingers.

"Although I'm glad to see you Talisha, I wish you'd come under better circumstances."

"What is going on here?" she asked.

"Not here, your destination," Khamisi said.

Talisha's eyes narrowed in concern.

"What have you heard?" she asked.

"I'm afraid there's been a war, a very nasty one," Khamisi said.

"Are you certain?" Talisha asked.

"Very," Khamisi answered. "We received a ship of refugees three moons ago. The stories they shared were terrible."

Talisha fell silent. Omari could imagine what she was thinking. This safari was essential to the wealth and prosperity of her clan.

"Who controls the harbor?" she finally asked.

"No one knows," Khamisi replied. "The land is in chaos. It's best you postpone your safari."

"You know I can't do that," Talisha said. "It would ruin me."

"In that case, can I make a suggestion?" Khamisi asked.

Talisha's eyes narrowed. "What do you have in mind?"

"Sail to the East with my mercenaries. Take over the harbor and hold it until you can claim your goods."

"How many mercenaries can you spare?" Talisha asked.

"One hundred, with two dhows," Khamisi said.

"And how much will that cost me?" Talisha asked.

"Half of your cargo and control of the harbor," Khamisi said.

Talisha winced. "That's a steep price."

"It is," Khamisi admitted. "But what choice do you have?"

The food arrived, interrupting the negotiations. The server sat a plate before Omari that had him confused and hungry at the same time. A large slice of meat filled his plate, surrounded by shellfish and sea grass.

"It's anu," Khamisi said. "It is a delicacy from the sea. Once you taste it, you'll be spoiled for anything else."

Omari cut into the fish steak then ate. He closed his eyes and moaned.

"This is amazing," he said.

"Only sex is better," Khamisi replied. "And that depends on who you're having sex with."

Omari's eyes drifted toward Talisha. The malkia returned his gaze, cutting into her anu with a smile on her face.

Talisha finished half of her anu steak before picking up the conversation.

"You have everything you need to claim the harbor," she said. "Why do you need my assistance?"

"We don't know the way," Khamisi replied. "And we have been afloat on this platform for so long we don't have the skills to secure a land base."

Khamisi finished his anu then washed it down with palm wine. His servants brought him another plate.

"You know I am a man of my word," Khamisi said. "We've done business for a long time. You can trust me on this."

"I can," Talisha said. "I need time to think, Khamisi."

"Take all the time you need," Khamisi said. "Or should I say all the time you can afford."

Khamisi's revelation seemed to dampen Talisha's mood. She was ready to leave as soon as they finished their meals. Omari was disappointed; Khamisi's entertainment was good and he saw at least one woman whose eye contact and gestures suggested an interesting conversation and maybe even more. Instead, he found himself trailing the malkia back to the dhow.

Abedi and the others were waiting.

"How is the mwenye?" he asked.

"Fat and mirthful as always," Talisha said.

"And Kiojah?"

Talisha grinned. "Good. She was disappointed not seeing you."

Abedi nodded.

"We have a problem," Talisha said. "It seems our destination is embroiled in a war. You should have brought more Mikijen."

"How was I to know?" Abedi said.

"I know," Talisha said. "You of all people know we have to continue to see what we can salvage. Khamisi has offered the use of his mercenaries."

"Those scavengers?" Abedi spat.

"We don't have a choice," Talisha said. "The plan is to sail and claim the harbor long enough to get our cargo. Khamisi wants to establish an outpost."

"That will make him insanely wealthy," Abedi said.

"Exactly. The Kiswala will not be happy."

"What will we do?" Omari asked.

"What Khamisi wants, for now," Talisha said. "In the meantime, we'll prepare to set sail. I'll need you and Omari to inspect Khamisi's mercenaries. He said he can spare one hundred."

"I can inspect them myself," Abedi said.

"Take Omari," Talisha ordered. "Khamisi likes him."

"As you wish malkia," Abedi said.

Talisha walked away to her cabin. Abedi looked at Omari with a frown.

"Remember when I told you to be careful? You're done a poor job of it."

"I've only done what I've been told," Omari replied.

"Well, you're deep into it now."

"I'm only following orders!" Omari said.

Abedi grunted then walked away. Omari shrugged; there was no way around either Abedi or Tishala. He retreated to his cabin, taking refuge in his hammock until the evening meal. He thought of eating with the Mikijen but decided he didn't want to be bothered with Abedi's accusing stares. He stood in line for his fish stew, then sat with the baharia. Omari took a spoonful of the stew and grimaced. Compared to the anu he'd eaten earlier, this was swill.

"So, one trip with the malkia and you're too good to sit with the rest of us?"

Juba ambled up to him with his bowl and sat beside him.

"I didn't need the scrutiny," Omari replied.

Juba ate a spoonful of his stew and moaned in pleasure.

"This is delicious."

Omari handed him his bowl. "Eat up."

Juba poured the contents into his bowl.

"You can't blame Abedi, you know," he said. "He's been Tishala's favorite for some time, even in Kiswala."

"He can't blame me either," Omari replied. "I didn't ask for any of this."

"You never do," Juba said. "At least I've never seen you do it."

Omari smiled and Juba laughed.

"Maybe you should wear a mask," Juba continued. "Or let someone hit you in the face with a sword. It might leave an ugly scar."

"I'll bet Abedi would be happy to oblige," Omari said.

"With enthusiasm," Juba replied.

"I'll turn down Tishala's requests to accompany her from now on," Omari commented.

"You can't do that, she's the malkia," Juba said. He finished his stew, licking the bowl clean before standing.

"I'm going to get more stew," Juba said. "You coming?"

"No," Omari replied. "I think I'll stay here for a while."

Omari spent the night on deck, falling asleep while gazing into the star-studded sky. A stiff boot to his side woke him the next morning. He opened his eyes to Abedi walking away to the gangplank.

"Come on," he said. "We have mercenaries to inspect."

Omari gathered his gear then followed. He caught up to Abedi at the first market, where he stopped to buy bread and fish to quell his morning hunger. Abedi glanced back at him with a frown.

"There's food waiting for us where we're going," he said.

"You didn't tell me," Omari replied. He wrapped a piece of bread around the fish and ate.

He was finishing his meal when they reached the Khamisi's compound. The grounds were empty except for the mercenaries. They milled about, exchanging boasts and insults. Kiojah was among them, sharing a few words as well.

"Kiojah!" Abedi called out. "Are you in charge of this rabble?"

Kiojah turned to them. A wide smile came to her face when she recognized Abedi. The smile dimmed a bit when her eyes fell on Omari.

"What took you so long?" she said. Abedi and Kiojah shook arms then hugged. She looked at Omari with narrow eyes.

"Ket," she said.

"Kiojah," Omari replied.

"This is your army," Kiojah said as she swept her hand. "They're better fighters than they appear."

"You don't have to convince me," Abedi said. "I'm happy to have them with us."

"Come, let's get you some food," Kiojah said.

Kiojah led them to Khamisi's mess tent. The cook gave them bowls of a spicy fish soup that went well with Omari's bread. Omari ate while Kiojah and Abedi talked.

"So, what's really going on in the East" Abedi asked.

Kiojah glanced at Omari then back to Abedi. "It's okay," he said. "Omari's a Mikijen first."

Omari nodded as he drank the last of his soup.

"I hear it's chaos," she said. "The mountain tribes have been at war for years. One of the tribes was pushed out and decided to make the harbor town their new home. It was a massacre."

"Daarila's beard!" Abedi cursed.

"Exactly," Kiojah said. "We have to secure the harbor town."

"Why is Khamisi concerned about this?" Omari asked.

"He is allies with the Kiswala," Kiojah replied. "Securing the harbor town keeps him in their good graces. It's also a way to please some of the inhabitants here. Some of us are tired of living on this giant raft."

Abedi finished his soup.

"When will your dhows arrive?"

"Tomorrow morning."

Abedi stood and Omari did the same.

"We will leave at first light," Abedi said. "The sooner we set out, the better."

"They'll be there," Kiojah said.

"You're not coming?" Omari asked.

"No," Kiojah replied. "I'm Khamisi's top ranking warrior. This place would slip into chaos without me."

"So, who's leading the mercenaries?"

"I am," Abedi replied. "They will do as Kiojah tells them."

Kiojah nodded in agreement.

"Let's get this over with," she said.

Omari and Abedi followed Kiojah to the mercenaries. She took a small horn from her waist belt, put it to her lips and blew three sharp notes. The mercenaries formed four lines and fell quiet. Omari was impressed. They had some discipline.

"Listen up, fish shit!" Kiojah shouted. The mercenaries groaned and laughed. "As I shared with you earlier, you have been chosen to go on vacation with the Kiswala. You'll be paid a stack if you return, and you get to keep all the loot you can carry."

Omari leaned to Abedi.

"We didn't agree to that," he whispered.

"Minor detail," Abedi replied. "Keep quiet."

Kiojah gestured for Abedi to join her.

"This is Abedi Okoro," she said. "He will be your commander. Abedi is a skilled warrior, almost as good as me."

The mercenaries laughed again.

"He is a fair and experienced commander," Kiojah continued. "I vouch for him with my life. Follow his orders and you might just survive to spend your pay."

Abedi stepped forward. "I can't say I'm happy to have you under my command, but we'll make it work. Meet us at our dhow at first light. May Eda bless us all."

The mercenaries responded with half-hearted praise then dispersed.

"They're all yours," Kiojah said.

Abedi and Kiojah shook.

"Will you return tonight?" Kiojah asked.

Abedi grinned. "You know I will."

"I'll be waiting," Kiojah replied then winked. She looked at Omari with narrow eyes.

"Ket."

"Kiojah."

Kiojah marched away. Omari and Abedi set out for the dhow. He wasn't going to ask about that exchange between Abedi and Kiojah; it was none of his business.

"Those mercenaries will forget Kiojah's orders as soon as this city sinks below the horizon," Omari said.

"You don't have much faith in them, do you?" Abedi replied.

"Of course, I don't," Omari said. "We're mercenaries too, remember?"

"We're a much better breed," Abedi said. "Besides, they're being well paid and will get more once the town is secured. It's a better offer than any scheme they might come up with. Just work, and if you survive, you'll get paid well."

"Let's hope you're right," Omari said.

"I am," Abedi replied.

Omari and Abedi went their separate ways as soon as they reached the dhow. Omari was full, so he spent the rest of the day patrolling the deck and working with the baharia. He watched as Abedi left the dhow for his rendezvous with Kiojah and smirked. This dhow was full of secrets, he thought.

Once again, he chose to spend the night on deck, and once again the malkia decided to seek him out. Omari had removed his uniform and donned the calf length pants of the baharia. He wore no shirt, his muscled torso and ngisimaugi exposed. He was finishing off a bottle of the local spirits, a bitter concoction that made him purse his lips but delivered the necessary punch.

"Omari."

"Malkia."

Tishala gathered her dress then sat on the deck beside him. She gestured to the bottle and Omari handed it to her. Tishala took a sip then grimaced.

"I've always hated this brew," she said.

"It does what it's supposed to do," Omari replied.

"I have better in my cabin," Tishala said.

"And Abedi is gone," Omari replied.

Tishala frowned. "As I told you before, Abedi has no claims on me."

"I'm not sure I want to be a part of this game you two play," Omari said.

"I didn't take you as a man with scruples."

"I'm not," Omari confessed. "But we're on a safari, and I answer to Abedi. When you fight with warriors, you want to make sure they are with you. The way you do that is to show loyalty."

Tishala stood.

"It's your choice," she said. "My offer stands."

Tishala ambled away. Omari watched her until she disappeared below deck. He finished his spirits, then looked again where Tishala had been.

"Daarila's beard!" he cursed.

He tossed the bottle overboard then made his way to Tishala's cabin. When he reached it, the door was unlatched and slightly open. Omari pushed it open; Tishala stood before him naked.

"The longer you stand there with your mouth gaping, the less time we have," she said.

Omari hurried out of his pants.

* * *

Omari was awakened by the arriving mercenaries. He had returned to the dhow deck after his tryst with Tishala, sleeping under the stars. He shed his baharia garb and put on his uniform. The other Mikijen emerged from below deck, led by Abedi. The commander cut his eyes at Omari and grinned.

"Ket," he said. "Are you trying to make good with the Malkia by beating us on deck?"

"No," Omari replied. "I just can't deal with the stink."

Abedi and the others laughed. Omari fell in with them and they left the dhow to meet with the mercenaries. They were greeted by a tall warrior with skin like onyx wearing leather pants and a vest

festooned with talisman. A baldric holding a curved
sword hung from his narrow shoulders; a host of
daggers circled his waist. The man grinned, exposing bright perfect teeth.

"Which one of you is Abedi?" the man asked.

"I am," Abedi replied.

The man extended his arm and Abedi
grasped his forearm.

"I am Komi," the man said. "Consider me the
commander of these waterdogs."

"Good," Abedi replied. "Where are your
dhows?"

"They should be here soon."

"Excellent. We set sail as soon as they get
here."

Tishala and her bodyguards appeared. Omari
held back a smile as the previous night's events sur-
faced in his head. Tishala didn't look his way. She
did share an unpleasant glance with Abedi.

"Are they ready?" she asked.

"Yes, Malkia," Abedi answered.

"Good."

She pivoted then walked away.

"Let's get underway. We waste time."

The Mikijen followed the Malkia back to
their dhow. An hour later the mercenary dhows appeared, accompanied by a small fishing fleet. The
mercenaries were not supplied with abundant provisions; they would survive on the bounty of the sea
along the way. By noon, the fleet was on its way.

After three weeks of open waters and favorable winds their destination loomed on the horizon.
Abedi, Tishala and Omari stood at the bow of the
dhow, Abedi scanning the shore with his spyglass.
Tishala had come wearing a Shuru uniform, the
garb of the Kiswala personal guard. A scimitar hung

from her shoulder in a jeweled scabbard. Her forearm was adorned with a wrist knife with a jambiya and a machete secured to her waistbelt.

"I see no signs of life, not a single person," Abedi said.

"What about the buildings?" Tishala asked.

"Lots of damage," Abedi replied. "Whoever attacked this place ransacked it."

"The Cleave take them," Tishala said.

"Will what we seek still be available?" Omari asked.

"Our goal does not lie at the harbor," Tishala said. "What we came for is located in the interior. The problem is we need experienced guides to take us there."

"And they may be dead," Abedi said. He turned to Omari.

"You'll lead the landing party. Take Juba with you. Go to the mercenary dhow and tell Komi you need 25 of his best fighters."

Omari held his anger in check. Abedi's orders were appropriate. As junior warrior it was Mikijen protocol that he be assigned the more dangerous tasks. Still, he felt Abedi's reason was more personal. He nodded and was about to find Juba when Tishala spoke.

"Why Ket?" she asked. "He's never been here before. You know the harbor."

"His job is to secure the docks, nothing more," Abedi replied. "You made me commander because I make good decisions. Is there any reason you should doubt me now?"

Tishala looked at Omari, a hint of worry in her otherwise stern countenance.

"Go," she said.

Omari bowed then trotted to the bulwark where the boats were stored.

"Juba!" he shouted. "You're with me."

Juba ambled over to him with a frown on his face.

"First to go; first to go," he said, uttering the Mikijen phrase.

"As always," Omari replied.

They helped the baharia lift the boat over the side then climbed in. The baharia lowered the boat onto the calm waters and the Mikijen rowed to the mercenary dhow. Komi stuck his head over the side.

"What's the word?" he asked.

"We need twenty-five of your waterdogs to secure the docks," Omari replied.

Komi disappeared, yelling out names. Moments later landing boats were heaved over the side, splashing onto the water. Knotted ropes were flung over the sides and the mercenaries clambered down into the boats. Komi was with them.

"Lead the way, Mikijen," he said.

The landing team rowed to the docks. Mercenary bowmen loaded their bows and scanned the shore as Omari and the others climbed onto the wood docks. They tipped to the nearby ruins, inspecting each one before moving into the harbor town and establishing a protected perimeter. Omari returned to the docks, waving in the dhows. The mercenary dhows responded, but the malkia's dhow remained at a distance. Instead, Tishala and the Mikijen arrived by boat.

"Search the rest of the village for any survivors," Tishala ordered.

"I doubt if there will be any," Abedi replied.

"Search anyway," Tishala said. "We need to be sure."

The warriors fanned out into the village, finding the same morbid evidence. The village had been sacked and burned months ago, with no signs of recent human habitation. There was nothing out of the ordinary until they reached the outskirts of the village.

Omari was the first to spot them, tall poles topped with skulls.

"Shit," he said.

Juba joined him and they went to inspect them.

"I don't need to know the language to know what this mean," Juba said.

"True," Omari replied. "We'll be receiving visitors soon. Let's get back and tell the others."

Omari found Abedi assisting the malkia set up a large tent.

"You might not want to do that yet," he said.

Abedi approached him.

"What's going on?"

"Juba and I found a row of skull tipped poles at the outskirts of the city. This place is either cursed or off limits. Either way I think will be getting visitors by tomorrow if not tonight."

"We'll place the bulk of our forces just behind the perimeter," Abedi said. "Everyone else needs to be prepared to evacuate if the attack is too large to handle."

"We need to reinforce it," Tishala commented.

"We don't have time to dig a moat," Omari said.

Komi sauntered up the group.

"We can fill the space with brush," he said. "That's faster than digging."

"How will that help?" Abedi replied. "They'll just push it aside."

"Not if it's on fire," Komi replied. "We'll soak the wood with fish oil. One flaming arrow and we'll have all the time we need."

"That's a good plan," Tishala said. "However, we can't abandon the harbor completely. We need to reopen it so we can reach our contacts in the interior."

"We don't have enough people to do that," Abedi said.

"We can't abandon the harbor," Tishala said, her voice reflecting her resolve. "We'll have to reach out to a local clan and form an alliance."

"Find the one who has suffered the most," Omari suggested. "They'll most likely be happy for our help."

"First things first," Abedi said. "Let's survive the night. Then we can make other plans."

"Agreed," Tishala said.

"Omari, you're in charge of securing the perimeter," Abedi said.

Omari nodded.

"Let's get to it!" he shouted. As he took out his machete and ambled to the forest, he glanced at Tishala. This time she didn't hide her worry. Omari nodded his head and winked. Tishala gave him a smile before leaving with Abedi and the others.

Omari and the others set about gathering enough branches and small trees to create the barrier. Juba and Komi stood watch until the pile was complete. Komi sent a group of his warrior back to the dhow for fish oil. They returned a few minutes later with the rancid concoction, pouring it liberally over and around the branches. After a brief inspection they retired to the cover of the damaged buildings as the sun settled into the western horizon.

Omari's nose wrinkled as the wind blew the fish oil smell in their direction.

"Daarila's beard!" he said. "I hope who's ever out there will hurry up and come so we can set this on fire."

"Don't wish the worst," Juba said. He pulled his metal spiked glove over his right hand then up to his elbow. "These might be our last moments alive. Enjoy the company."

"Have you seen yourself?" Omari teased. "How can I enjoy that?"

"Your attitude stinks like that fish oil," Juba said. "You should go find the Malkia and spare me."

Omari's eyes widened. "What have you heard?"

"Let's just say that the dhow is small, and the walls are thin."

"Cleave!" Omari said. "That means Abedi knows."

"Abedi always knows," Juba said. "But what can he do about it? We serve the Malkia in any way she sees fit."

"It's not like that," Omari said.

"Okay," Juba replied. "Whatever you say."

"I'd cut off your head if I didn't need you," Omari retorted.

"Good thing I'm needed," Juba said.

Their jibing was interrupted by the thunk of an arrow hitting the wall near Omari's head.

"Here they come!" Omari shouted. "Light the brush!"

A volley of flaming arrows sailed from the ruins. As they descended toward the brush, they revealed a horde of warriors scaling the barrier. Cries ran out as the arrows fell into the brush, igniting the oil.

Omari unsheathed his sword and jambiya.

"It's going to be a long night," he said.

Juba swung his sword then threw a few punches into the air with his mailed fist.

"Longer for some than others."

"Damn them to the Cleave," Omari said.

"To the Cleave," Juba replied.

The stench of burning flesh mingled with the fish oil odor, making Omari's stomach queasy. The archers finished off the warriors that managed to make it across the blazing barrier. Omari and the others knew the respite was temporary. Once the branches burned down the mysterious attackers would come in force. But they would not meet them in the open. The plan was to ambush them from the buildings, thus slowing their advance. The warriors would be forced to check every structure or risk being struck down from behind. Omari watched the fire slowly reduce, the light diminishing. As the flames transformed to embers a roar rose from the bush. Moments later the warriors charged through the ashes and smoke.

Omari and Juba waited for the warriors to enter the village. A group ran down the road leading to their position and Juba nodded before leaping into the open, smashing his armored fist into the face of the first man. Omari was close behind him, driving his jambiya into the throat of the warrior behind Juba's victim. The Mikijen fell into a coordinated defense, the actions of veterans that had fought together many times. They held back the wave as the waterdogs joined them. A desperate fight developed in the dark, the attacking horde stifled by the determined resistance of Mikijen and waterdogs.

The sharp bark of a familiar horn cut through the grunts and curses of the battle.

"Push them back!" Omari shouted.

He pressed forward, driving back the warriors before him step by step. They slowly forced the attackers back into the open; the archers releasing their arrows into the rear, adding confusion to the melee. The attackers finally broke and ran back into the bush.

"This is not over," Omari said.

Komi appeared, a wicked gaze on his forehead.

"I don't think we can stand another assault," he said. "We lost many warriors."

"Let's pull back to the docks," Omari decided. "We can't hold the harbor until we can establish reinforcements."

Komi called out to his men and they began the evacuation. Omari and Juba lingered behind, their eyes on the bush. Omari glanced at Juba; an arrow protruded from his rib cage.

"You need to get that out," he said.

"It's okay for now," Juba replied. "My ngisimaugi is at work."

"Yeah, but if you wait too long, you'll have an arrowhead in your ribs forever."

Juba grinned. "Just another story to tell."

A wave of yells came from the bush.

"Here we go again," Omari said.

Omari and Juba ran through the village toward the dock. They were met by Abedi.

"What are you doing?" he asked. "We have to hold."

"You do it," Omari said. "We stopped one wave; we won't hold back the next."

"The malkia demands it," Abedi said.

"Then tell her to lend a hand," Omari replied. "We're mercenaries, remember? We don't get paid if we die. Besides, I'm sure you passed the waterdogs on your way to ask for the impossible."

"Cleave!" Abedi said. "You're right. We'll have to pull back to the dhows. Juba, let the malkia know of our plans. Omari, help me make sure no one is left behind."

Juba nodded then hurried away. Omari followed Abedi, the cries from the unknown warriors growing louder.

"Abedi, I don't think this is a good idea," Omari said.

"It's not," Abedi replied.

Omari saw Abedi's sword too late. He dodged the swing for his throat, but he couldn't avoid Abedi's jambiya. The blade plunged into his chest.

"The head or the heart. Isn't that what they say?" Abedi said.

Omari yanked the knife from his chest. He swung as he fell, driving the blade into Abedi's thigh. Abedi yelled in pain.

Omari struck the ground, his back hot as his ngisimaugi worked to heal the fatal wound. He grimaced as he lifted his head, watching Abedi hobble away as the voices behind him grew louder. He laid his head down then whispered to Eda as he was swallowed by darkness and betrayal.

* * *

Omari opened his eyes. He lay where he fell, his clothes damp from the morning dew. Sounds from the nearby bush reached his ears, confirming he was still alive. He remained still, listening for voices or any signs of movement that would let him know he was not alone. Satisfied he was, he rolled onto his back. His chest ached from Abedi's stab; his shirt stained with blood. He flashed hot with anger as the moment played in his mind. Abedi had apparently missed his heart. Otherwise, he would have died.

Omari stood; his legs wobbly. He stumbled toward the docks, his balance improving with each step. His chest still pained him, so he slowed his pace. As he neared the dock, a terrible sight greeted him. The dhows were gone. He eased himself down and sat.

"Cleave," he whispered. "Daarila take them all!"

If they had sailed back to Kiswala without him, he was doomed. He knew nothing of this land or its people. If he was lucky the people who attacked the village would return and kill him quickly; if he wasn't, a worse fate probably waited.

"Enough brooding," he said to himself. "Time to get about surviving."

Omari walked back to where he was stabbed. His weapons were gone, probably taken by their attackers. He pulled up his right pants leg then smiled; at least his ankle knife remained. He could fashion a spear from a tree limb, and maybe even construct a small bow and arrows. He laughed; he could barely make a toothpick. A spear would be enough.

Omari scavenged the nearby buildings, seeking anything he could use to increase his chances of survival. He found a few pots, utensils, and other small items, but nothing of significance. He decided to make his camp near the dock's edge and close to the forest. Both afforded a reasonable escape, although he would prefer a dash into the bush than jumping onto the ocean. With his camp secure, Omari settled into his unknown predicament.

He was two weeks into his involuntary exile when he saw the first signs of life. A large canoe carrying ten warriors approached the docks from the south. Omari abandoned his camp before they saw him, melting into the bush. The warriors seemed to be searching for something, or rather someone. They held strange tube-like objects in their hands, with long sticks clinched between their teeth. One of the men took the stick from his mouth then called out.

"Mikijen!"

Omari moved deeper into the bush, his hands tightening on his spear. They knew he was here, and they knew he was alive.

"We are not here to harm you," the man called out in perfect Trade Speak. "We are the people Malkia Tishala was seeking. We need you as much as you need us."

Omari contemplated his situation. This man knew the Malkia. If what he said was true, there was no reason for them to be hostile. But it could be a ruse to draw him out. But why would they want to fool him? He had nothing of value, except his knowledge, and that would only be valuable to someone trading with the Kiswala.

"You need not fear the others," the man continued, "because they fear you. They say you are the man who rose from the dead. That is why we came. Only a Mikijen could do such a thing."

Omari scratched his chin. There were ten of them. They carried short swords and those metal tubes. Worst that could happen is they would kill him; the best outcome would be he will kill them all and take their boat. He shrugged them emerged from the bush.

"My name is Omari Ket," he said.

The man at the bow of the boat grinned.

"Hello Omari Ket. I am Fanamby."

The oarsmen steered the boat to the dock. The others made room for Omari to board.

"We are happy to have found you," Fanamby said. "Where are the rest?"

"They're gone," Omari said.

"When are they returning?" Fanamby asked.

"I don't know," Omari replied.

Fanamby's face bunched. "That is not good. That is not good at all."

"I agree," Omari replied.

"We will take you to our city," Fanamby said. "Our Njaka will wish to speak to you."

Omari nodded. Now that he was in relative safety, he allowed himself to embrace the fatigue that nagged him ever since his revival. He slept soundly until the boat jarred, knocking him from his dreamless sleep. The others were climbing out of the boat onto the wooded shore. Fanamby sat beside him, a broad smile on his face.

"We must walk from here," he said. He reached into the leather pouch tied to his waist belt and took a shriveled root.

"Chew this," he said. "It will give you energy for the journey."

Omari looked at the root with skepticism. Fanamby laughed. He broke the root in half then popped it in his mouth.

"It's safe," he said. "We are not here to hurt you, Mikijen. We are your friends."

"That's what I thought about someone else," Omari replied. He took the root from Fanamby, put it in his mouth and chewed. A brief bitter bite was immediately overtaken by a rush of heat that dispersed throughout his limbs. He stood up straight, feeling like he could run a thousand lengths.

"What is that?" he asked.

"Tika," Fanamby replied. "It is what your people seek from us. You have not experienced it?"

"No, I haven't," Omari said. Now he knew the secret of the Kiswala nobles' vibrant energy. This root was worth stacks, and Tishala was the single source. That explained why her clan never traded with the people of Ki Khanga. They made their fortune off of their own.

Omari joined the warriors on the shore. The oarsmen pulled the canoe from the waters then lifted it onto their shoulders. Fanamby took the lead and they entered the bush, following a narrow trail that forced them to walk single file. Omari continued to chew on the root, fascinated by its effect. The enhanced energy also made him extremely hungry. His saviors carried no provisions, but he observed them plucking various leaves and fruits from the surrounding plants and eating them as they made progress. Omari did the same, making sure he took them from the same plant. Most were bland but filling. After a few more lengths his hunger was sated.

They stopped to rest at midday. Fanamby came to sit beside him. He handed Omari a sword and sheath.

"The last part of our journey will be dangerous," he said. "Our city is under siege. Bwambale has united the hill clans and is determined to claim our land. We have resisted, hoping for help from the Kiswala. It seems that will not happen."

"I don't think so," Omari replied. "We did not hear of what was happening here until we reached Mjiwahari. Even then, we did not come prepared for a war."

"The Njaka suspected as much, but still we hoped," Fanamby said. "We have you, which means we still have hope."

"I'm one muwani," Omari said. "I don't know what you expect me to do."

"You have the mark," Fanamby said. "With your help, our plan might succeed."

Omari knew what 'the mark' meant. This did not sound good.

"What's your plan?" he asked.

"We will kill Bwambale," Fanamby replied. "He is the knot that holds the ropes together. The other clans either fear him or love him. If he dies, the hill clans will fight among themselves. We can then defeat them one by one and reclaim the harbor."

"This Bwambale," Omari said. "I'm sure he is well protected."

"He is," Fanamby said. "But we have someone that can get us close to him. Once the deed is done, all will be well."

"And our chances to survive?" Omari asked.

"Slim, but with you they are better," Fanamby replied. "Your mark will help us."

"It only works for me," Omari said.

"That is enough," Fanamby replied.

"Why should I volunteer for this one-way mission?" Omari asked.

Fanamby's smile faded. "Because our Njaka would be very disappointed if you refused, as would I."

The other warriors and the oarsmen looked at Omari, their faces stern. He could probably fight himself out of this situation, but then what? Everyone would be hunting him.

"Shit," he finally said.

Fanamby's smile returned and the others looked away. "Thank you for deciding to help us."

They continued their trek, following the road until just before nightfall. The warriors and oarsmen were more observant as the sun set, their eyes darting back and forth. Omari did the same, although he had no idea what he was looking for. As darkness overtook them, Omari heard rumbling in the distance.

"There is a storm coming," he said.

"No," Fanamby replied. "Our city is under attack. Bwambale had decided to try to breach our walls in darkness again. He will fail."

"What does the rumbling have to do with his attack?"

Fanamby lifted the metal tube hanging from his shoulder.

"When *upungufu* blinks, *radi* speaks."

Omari was confused.

"What does that mean?"

Fanamby chuckled. "You will see. We must hurry now. The attack will cover our arrival."

Fanamby and the others took pouches from their waists then poured a portion the contents into the tube. They took the sticks he had seen them with earlier and stuck them into the corners of their mouths. Once they were done, they ran toward the rumbling. Omari stayed as close as he could, following their footsteps so not to crash into a tree or some other object as they dashed through the darkness.

They reached an open field. Omari saw flashes of light in the distance as the rumbling grew louder. The walls of the besieged city came into view. Hundreds of warriors filled the grass field, loosing arrows and throwing spears at the warriors on the wall. They were answered by bright flashes and explosions. Dozens of warriors fell with each explosion. Omari looked at the tubes his cohorts carried then grinned.

"I want one of those," he whispered.

The warriors veered away from the battle, plunging back into the woods. They traveled few more lengths then stopped before a large bush. As Fanamby knelt by the bush, the silence was shattered by a war hoop. Omari spun around to see a warrior charging him, his sword held high. Omari sidestepped the man's chop then shoved him back as he drew the sword Fanamby had given him. The man charged him again and Omari stabbed at him, the sword striking the man's breastplate. Other warriors swarmed from behind Omari's adversary and a desperate melee took place. Omari finally struck down his attacker by chopping off his head. He picked up the hapless warrior's sword then continued to fight with both blades against the others.

One of their attackers backed away then ran.

"Don't let him escape!" Fanamby shouted. "He will tell the others of our passage!"

Omari and two of Fanamby's warriors sprinted after the man. Omari quickly distanced his cohorts, whether because he was faster or still under the influence of tika, he didn't know. He caught up with the man then drove his sword through the man's back. The man yelled then arched before falling to the ground. Omari stood over him to make sure he was dead, then trotted back to the others. The large bush had been moved aside, revealing a tunnel entrance. Everyone climbed into the hold; the last people remaining were Omari and Fanamby.

"Go," Fanamby said. "I will close the entrance."

Omari took his time. Once he entered the tunnel there was no turning back. He shrugged then followed the others climbing down a crude ladder into utter darkness. Omari saw the flash of a flint stone; moments later a torch blazed in a warrior's grip. Three more torches were lit before they proceeded down the tunnel. The sounds of battle faded the further they trudged. The appearance of another ladder marked the end of the tunnel. Fanamby climbed the ladder then tapped a distinct rhythm on the cover. Moments later the cover slid aside and Fanamby climbed out. Omari followed the third man out. As he emerged his eyes met those of a tall woman standing beside Fanamby. A column of twisted dreads rose from her narrow head. Her painted face and brown leather dress covered with gris-gris identified her as a sonchai. Her dark eyes narrowed as she focused on Omari, and he felt his ngisimaugi respond. The woman smiled, revealing sharpened teeth.

"You found a Mikijen," she said. "I am pleased."

Fanamby frowned. "I could care less about you," he said. "It was the njaka's wish that we find him and bring him here."

"Because of my advice, fool." The woman shoved Fanamby away then strode to Omari. The others filed by Omari, heading for the ramparts to join the battle still raging beyond the city walls.

"I am Diamonda," the woman said. "I felt your presence when your people arrived."

"You mean the Mikijen," Omari said.

"No. you," Diamonda replied. "Take off your shirt."

"Why?" Omari asked.

"Take off your shirt!" Diamonda shouted.

Omari stripped off his shirt without thinking.

"Why did I do that?" he asked himself.

Diamonda stepped behind him. She ran her calloused hands over his ngisimaugi, and the tattoo responded. It was a feeling Omari had never experienced before, an energy that was strange yet not unpleasant.

"This is very good," Diamonda said.

"What are you talking about?" Omari asked.

Diamonda grabbed his wrist.

"Welcome to Vatasoa," she said. "You will meet the njaka tonight. The sooner we begin the better."

Omari yanked his hand away.

"I'm not going anywhere until you explain to me . . ."

"Silence!" Diamonda shouted.

Omari's mouth closed. Omari felt a shiver of fear pass through him. He'd never met a sonchai that could control a person's action with their voice. Diamonda grabbed his wrist again.

"Now, shall we try this again?" she said.

Omari followed Diamonda through the streets of Vatasoa. The city exhibited all the signs of a city under siege. Inhabitants peeked through the cracks of shuttered windows, a few brave enough to stand in their doorways to watch them pass. Omari knew their pain; he'd been on both sides of long sieges and knew well the consequences.

They reached the center of the city, the location of the njaka's compound. Twenty warriors snapped to attention at their arrival, relaxing when they recognized the sonchai. They cleared the way then opened the gate leading into the compound.

The njaka's compound contained several white walled one-story buildings. A woman emerged from the central building, her dress and appearance indicating she was a person of power. The frown on her painted face revealed her annoyance.

"What are you doing here so late, Diamonda?" the woman asked.

"We are under attack and you ask such a question?" Diamonda replied. "The njaka should be at the ramparts lifting our warriors' spirits."

"The njaka does as she pleases," the woman said. Her eyes strayed to Omari.

"Is this the one?" she asked.

"Yes, he is, Rindra," Diamonda said. "Now you know why I am here."

Rindra turned and walked away.

"Follow me."

Omari and Diamonda followed Rindra into the njaka's abode. Inside was a large open area, the walls lined with the wealth of the ruler. Stacks of shining metal shared space with finely woven reams of cloth and gourds filled with glittering jewels.

Omari noticed two large ceramic pots emitting a faint blue glow from their lids; kipande.

The njaka paced before her throne, her hands clasped behind her back. She wore a white dress decorated with flowers which fell from her broad shoulders to her sandaled feet. A baldric hung from her left shoulder, holding a long sheath that held a wide sword. Her beaded braids reached just below her ears. She stopped pacing as they neared, her pleasant face marred by a frown.

"How is the battle going?" she said with a deep resonant voice.

"It goes well," Rindra replied.

"I should be there," the njaka commented.

"It is not your place Toavina," Rindra said. "You are our njaka. You have warriors that fight for you."

The njaka pulled her sword from its sheath. Omari was impressed. This was no display weapon; this was a sword that could cleave warriors in half.

"I don't need anyone to fight for me," she said. Toavina turned her attention to Omari and Diamonda.

"This is the one?" she asked.

"Yes," Diamonda replied. "He is stronger than I suspected."

"Bring him closer," the njaka demanded.

Omari followed Diamonda to the njaka. He had no idea how to honor her, so he prostrated as was the custom in Kiswala.

"Get up," Toavina said. "There is no need for that. What is your name?"

"Omari Ket," he said.

The njaka eyed him curiously before sheathing her sword then taking a dagger from her waistbelt.

"Give me your arm," she commanded.

Omari knew what was coming next. He extended his left arm. The njaka grasped his wrist then ran her dagger across the inside of his forearm. Omari winced then waited as his ngisimaugi warmed and his wound healed. The njaka smiled.

"How soon can we begin?" she asked Diamonda.

"Begin what?" Omari asked.

"As soon as we can gather the others," Diamonda replied. "I have everything we need."

"Begin what?" Omari asked louder.

"Good," the njaka said. "I'll have the prisoner brought to you at first light. The others will need rest from tonight's battle."

"Begin what?" Omari shouted.

"Silence, Mikijen!" Diamonda shouted back. Her strange nyama fell over him, forcing his mouth shut. The njaka smiled at him.

"Your gift will end this war and open the harbor again," she said.

Omari could do nothing but nod his head and glare at Diamonda.

"You may leave," the njaka said.

Rindra escorted them out of the compound. Vatasoa's warriors gathered in the streets, some drinking in celebration, others looking thoughtful and relieved. The sonchai found Fanamby and his warriors drinking from gourds with the others, laughing and boasting. Their energy diminished when Diamonda cleared her throat. Fanamby lowered his gourd from his lips.

"What is it, Diamonda?" he asked.

"I have spoken to the njaka," Diamonda said. "We will begin tomorrow morning. You and your warriors should rest tonight. There will not be much of that after the ceremony."

"We will," Fanamby said. "Sleep well, sonchai."

"Sleep well," Diamonda replied.

Fanamby and the others continued drinking. Omari looked at them longingly then followed the sonchai to her abode. Her home was small and cramped, filled with elixirs, talisman, gris-gris and other items essential for a sonchai. Diamonda cleared a sleeping cot in the corner opposite hers then gestured for Omari to sit.

"I'd rather be out celebrating with the others," Omari said.

Diamonda looked puzzled. "Why? You did nothing. You are not even Vatasoan. Besides, you more than anyone else needs rest. Tomorrow will be very tough for you."

"And if I refuse?" Omari said.

"You can't," Diamonda replied. "Now lay down and go to sleep."

Omari attempted to resist Diamonda' s command. He gritted his teeth, struggling with all his might not to stretch out on the cot. Diamonda witnessed his defiance and laughed.

"Save your fighting for tomorrow," she said. "Sleep!"

Omari flattened on the cot like a board, closed his eyes, and slept.

* * *

When Omari woke the next day, he felt refreshed. It took him a few minutes to realize he was naked, his body covered with patterns painted on his skin.

"What in Daarila's Beard is this?" he exclaimed. He reached for the patterns on his stomach.

"Don't touch it!" Diamonda warned. "If you do, I'll have to start over."

Omari stood, looking at the images in anger.

"Sit down," Diamonda said. "I'm not finished."

"You've painted everything," Omari said as he looked at his crotch. "Everything."

"There is one more thing left to do," she said.

Diamonda opened the ceramic jar she carried under her arm then stuck her hand inside.

"Close your eyes," she said.

Omari closed his eyes. Diamonda pulled out a handful of ashes from the jar and threw them at Omari, covering him with them.

"You can open your eyes now," she said.

Omari coughed as he fanned away the ashes.

"Come with me," Diamonda said. "The ceremony is about to begin."

Omari followed Diamonda out of her hut. They returned to the njaka's compound. This time the gates were open and the guards expected them. They nodded to the sonchai and Omari as they passed, their eyes lingering on Omari's nude ash covered body. A group of people waited for them; a circle of drummers, their djembes hanging off their shoulders, the njaka and her councilor, both dressed in matching simmering green dresses and golden headwraps, and Fanamby and his warriors, naked and powdered like Omari.

There was another person in the circle, one Omari had never seen. He too was naked and powdered; except he lay on the ground unconscious.

Diamonda led Omari to the circle then gestured for him to stand beside Fanamby.

"Who is that?" Omari asked, nodding at the man on the ground.

"That is Iasimanana, Bwambale's son," Fanamby replied. "He was captured during the last attack. He is a great warrior. He managed to climb our walls and enter the city. He killed many of our warriors before I subdued him."

Omari caught the pride in Fanamby's voice.

"Why is he here?" Omari inquired.

"After we are bonded, he will lead us to Bwambale," Fanamby said. "Then we will kill them both."

Omari's eyes went wide, matching his fear. "Bonded?"

"Quiet!" Diamonda said. "The ceremony is about to begin."

Diamonda joined Rindra and the njaka. She nodded her head, and the drummers played a soft, pulsing rhythm. Omari's heartbeat matched the tempo and his breathing slowed. He watched through heavy lidded eyes as Diamonda knelt before a small square stone. The njaka and Rindra placed offerings on the stone, which Diamonda pounded with a small hammer while reciting words in Vatasoan. Omari did not understand what she said, but he felt the effects. His eyesight expanded; he viewed the ceremony from every angle.

Diamonda fell silent. She reached into her pouch, taking out a small vial and pouring its contents over the offering. She lit the stone with a flint and a huge flame burst before her. For a moment Omari thought it had consumed the women, but when the fire and smoke cleared, they were revealed untouched. Diamonda gathered the ashes from the fire into a gourd. She approached Omari.

"Hold out your arms," Diamonda said.

Omari obeyed. The women went to each warrior with small brushes in their hands. They painted glyphs on their arms with the ash and an ink Omari was familiar with. It was the same ink used by the tattoo masters of Kiswala, a concoction infused with kipande. As Rindra and the njaka decorated his arms, Omari felt a connection forming between himself and the others in the circle. The last person to receive the symbols was Iasimanana. The symbols drawn on his arms were different. Omari felt himself connect to the man, but the bond was not as intense.

The women returned to the circle. Diamonda swept the warriors with her intense eyes then nodded. The drummers ceased playing and Omari emerged into full consciousness. He studied the patterns on his arms then those on the others. He sensed familiarity between them now, a bond that reminded him of the emotions he felt for his friends when he ran the streets of Sati-Baa as a boy. His eyes met Fanamby's and they nodded. Then he experienced warmth from his ngisimaugi, and he realized what Diamonda had done. She had connected them with the ashé of his tattoo.

"You are siblings now," Diamonda announced. "Daarila's curse has bonded you for this task, one that will lead to the destruction of Bwambale and his vexatious alliance. Who knows destruction better than The Axe Wielder? No one. We use his power for our freedom, and we ask Eda to forgive us for what we must do."

Diamonda walked to Iasimanana who was still unconscious.

"This one has been tethered to you," she said to Omari and the others. "He will lead us to his father, and you will strike them both down. We will pray for your safe return, yet we know that whatever happens, your loved ones and your ancestors will honor you."

The njaka stepped forward.

"Go," she said. "Do what you need to do to prepare. You will know when the time comes."

The warriors dispersed, going their separate ways. Omari remained; he had nowhere to go, and he was not about to spend what might be his last moments crammed into Diamonda's hut.

"Mikijen."

Omari turned to see Fanamby smiling at him.

"Come with me. We'll clean off this dust and you will eat with my family."

"There's something else I wouldn't mind doing, since I might be dying," Omari said.

Fanamby laughed. "That I cannot help you with. But I can assure you that if we return, there will be quite a few who will be willing to give you a proper homecoming."

"I guess that will have to do," Omari replied. "Lead the way."

Fanamby took Omari to his home. It was a modest home as was most of the houses within the gates, built with whatever was available. A small woman dressed in a calf length dress and braided hair emerged from the house, a baby on her hip and holding the hand of a small girl. The girl let go of her mama's hand and ran to Fanamby.

"Baba!" she shrieked.

"Tandra!" Fanamby scooped the girl into his arms and she hugged his neck. Fanamby's wife walked up to Omari, inspecting him before speaking.

"You are the Mikijen?" she asked.

"Yes," Omari replied.

"Will you protect my husband and make sure he comes back alive?" she asked.

"I can't promise you that," Omari said.

Fanamby's wife looked to her husband.

"At least he does not lie," she said.

Fanamby frowned at his wife. "Be nice, Marevaka."

"I'll be nice when this is over," she replied.

She turned her attention back to Omari. "I assume my husband had brought you here to feed you?"

Omari grinned. "Yes."

Marevaka turned and walked back into the house.

"There is enough . . . this time."

Omari turned to Fanamby.

"Are you sure this is okay?"

Fanamby nodded.

"Marevaka is always this way with strangers. She'll be singing by the time you leave."

Fanamby gestured for Omari to enter. The house was as simple on the outside as it was inside; three sleeping cots, a small table, a few chairs, and a fireplace. An iron pot hug over the fire, the contents slightly boiling. It smelled delicious.

"Here," Marevaka said. She handed the child on her hip to Omari. Omari took the child like it was precious glass. The boy grinned then grabbed his nose. Omari pinched the boy's nose and he giggled.

"Do you have a wife and children?" Marevaka asked.

"No," Omari replied.

"Beloha likes you," Fanamby said.

"And I like him, too," Omari said. "As long as I can give him back."

Marevaka and Fanamby laughed. Marevaka filled their bowls with stew and they ate, talked, and played with the children. By the end of the day Omari could see why Fanamby was willing to risk his life to kill Bwambale. He had a family to protect. Instead of taking one of the family's cots Omari found a soft space outside to sleep. He settled into his space and his mind went back to the moment Abedi stabbed him. His mood darkened and he made himself a promise. He would survive what as to come not to make sure Fanamby saw his family again, but so that he would see Abedi again and kill him.

* * *

The morning came and the warriors gathered. Omari sensed that Iasimanana would not be joining them. He felt the man was far away, and the way the others looked at him let him know they sensed it, too. They gathered at the gate, forming a ragged line. Diamonda, Rindra and the njaka arrived a few minutes later, surrounded by their bodyguards. The councilor inspected them, nodding her head in approval. Omari did not wear his Mikijen uniform; instead, dressed as the Vatasoans, a kilt that fell to his knees and no shirt, exposing his ngisimaugi. Talisman ringed his neck and gris gris, his sword, machete and daggers circled his waist. Diamonda went to each man, giving them an additional bag to attach to their belts.

"What is this?" Omari asked.

Diamonda grinned. "Always with the questions. It is your tika bag. Chew it when you need it, but not too much. It can harm as well as help."

Omari took the bag then secured it to his belt. He was tightening the knot when the njaka began to speak.

"Our future is in your hands," she said. "The viper must be slain for the nest to die. The ancestors see you through our eyes, and they love you through our hearts."

Fanamby raised his spear.

"Vatasoa!" he shouted.

"Vatasoa!" the others responded.

The gate opened. Omari swayed as an image filled his mind, the vision of Iasimanana resting in his father's hut, surrounded by family. Bwambale stood before his son, a proud look on his face. Omari switched his attention to the open field before him. His ngisimaugi warmed and footprints glowed in the grass.

"Do you see this?" he asked Fanamby.

"What?" Fanamby replied.

"Only you can see Iasimanana's path," Diamonda said. "Your tattoo is the source of everyone's power, the connection between you and Bwambale's son. It will end when you take his life."

"Let's be about it then," Omari said.

He ran from the fortress and the others followed. Their brisk pace took them across the grasses quickly and into the bush. Omari focused on the foot trail, ignoring everything else. When fatigue found him, he reached into the tika bag for a root. The others did the same. They did not stop for food or rest.

Soon they found themselves in Bwambale's territory. The pursuit slowed as the war party avoided patrolling warriors. Omari's hands itched to hold his sword, but he resisted the urge. There would be plenty time for that. For now, they had to find Bwambale's camp.

It was dusk when they came upon the outpost. Bwambale's siege city sat atop a steep hill surrounded by the encampment of his allies. One narrow road wound up the summit, and a wooden palisade surrounded the camp on the crest. Omari, Fanamby and the others squatted within the brush, studying their objective.

"It is well defended," Fanamby said.

Omari nodded as he chewed more tika root.

"Do you think we can fight our way through?" Omari asked.

Fanamby shook his head. "Even with your healing ashé, it would be impossible."

"Then how do you expect us to get in?" Omari asked.

Fanamby grinned. "We will wait until nightfall, until most in the camp are asleep. We'll follow Iasimanana's prints. Once we are inside, we must act quickly."

"No swords. Only daggers," Omari said. "We must be silent."

"Yes," Fanamby agreed. "If we are lucky, we will be out of the camp before anyone discovers our deed."

Darkness settled on Bwambale's encampment but still they waited. It was only when the camp had settled into slumber did they begin. Bwambale was so confident of his strength he did not post a night watch. If all went as planned, he would not live to contemplate the error.

Omari led the infiltration, still following Iasimanana's footsteps. They worked their way to the base of the hill then began the steep climb. Omari focused on making it to the summit, assuming his cohorts would keep pace. When he reached the palisades, he stopped and looked behind him. Everyone was with him. Fanamby reached into his tika pouch and took out two roots. Omari and the others did the same. He chewed and renewed energy surged throughout his body.

"We are ready," Fanamby said.

Omari sprang to his feet and ran toward the palisades. He crouched then jumped, clearing the wooden barrier by a few feet, and landing in a crouch. He waited to make sure his cohorts were with him before relocating Iasimanana's steps. What had been a singular trail was now a puzzle.

"What is wrong?" Fanamby asked.

"His footprints are everywhere," Omari said. "I don't know which tent he's in."

"It doesn't matter now," Fanamby said. "We're not here for Iasimanana; we're here for Bwambale. And his tent stands before us."

Fanamby gestured ahead. Bwambale's tent was an elaborate thing, three times as wide as the others and twice as high. A banner crowned it; the details indistinguishable in the darkness. Omari nodded, stood to full height then sprinted toward the tent.

"Hey!" someone shouted.

Omari head turned toward the voice. A lone warrior stood, holding his spear in the guard position.

"Intruders!" he shouted "Intruders!"

Omari veered toward the man then threw his dagger. The warrior deflected the knife then attacked, stabbing at Omari's gut. Omari spun to his right, then barely evaded the spear butt swung and his head. He drew his sword then slashed the warrior's thigh. He finished him with a slash across the throat.

The others were almost to the tent when the flap flew open and Bwambale's guards poured out. The camp woke as a melee broke out. Omari took advantage of the distraction, hurrying to the backside of the tent then slashing it open. He entered to see Bwambale and Iasimanana standing at the ready behind their guards. Omari scowled; Bwambale held Omari's Mikijen sword and jambiya. Omari rushed up then drove his sword through Bwambale's back, the point emerging from his gut. Iasimanana spun to see his father falling to the ground with the mortal wound. His face was still frozen in shock when Omari slit his throat. Omari stabbed them again to make sure the deed was done, then he took his sword and jambiya from Bwambale's hands. He took another tika root from his bag, stuck it in his mouth, and attacked Bwambale's guards from the rear. In moments they joined their leader in death.

Fanamby smiled at Omari.

"Are they dead?" he asked.

Omari nodded then stepped aside so the others could see.

"Now comes the hard part," he said.

Omari and the Vatasoans ran for their lives. Spears and arrows whizzed by them as they made for the trail leading down the hill. Omari felt a dull ache; he did a quick inspection of his body to see what caused the pain but saw nothing. He looked at his cohorts; one of the warriors had an arrow sticking from his shoulder. Diamonda's bond meant he would feeling the pain of the others, an experience Omari would rather not have. But he could do nothing about it. He only hoped he could bear the suffering.

They cleared the palisade and charged headlong down the hill. Omari winced from a sharp pain in his back. He looked back to see a warrior sprawled on the ground, a spear protruding from his back. The ngisimaugi warmed, but it was to no avail. Enemy warriors fell upon the hapless man and hacked him to pieces, Omari feeling every blow.

Although the summit camp was in full alarm, the base camp still seemed unaware of what had occurred. Bwambale's personal guard pursued them down the hill and into the main camp, their yelling awaking the warriors. Omari glanced from left to right, grimacing as he watched warriors emerge from their tents, take up arms and join the pursuit. He took another tika root from his pouch, stuck it into his mouth and chewed. Seconds later he ran faster.

The bush was a welcomed sight. Omari and the others plunged into the darkness and continued running. Their adversaries followed, although not as many as they feared. Bwambale's death was having the effect the Vatasoans desired. While many of Bwambale's followers pursued Omari and the Vatasoans, most rushed to the Bwambale's camp. The further they traveled, the fewer their pursuers. By dawn Omari and the others strolled across the grass moat to Vatasoa. The cheers of the inhabitants on the ramparts greeted them with the sunrise. The gates were opened, and the entire city turned out to celebrate.

Omari was exhausted. It took all his energy to put one foot in front of the other. He was jostled about as the Vatasoans met their returning warriors, showering them with praise words, hugs, and kisses. The crowd parted before him and Diamonda appeared, a satisfied grin on her face.

"Your ashé worked," he said. "But it almost killed me."

"Almost," Diamonda replied. "I sense it was you that took Bwambale's life. The njaka is very grateful."

Omari smirked. "How grateful?"

"Don't be vulgar, Mikijen," Diamonda snapped. "You are alive because of us."

"And you're victorious because of me," Omari retorted.

"You will be rewarded," Diamonda said. "All of you. You will receive land, wealth and a high station among us."

"I don't need that," Omari replied. "I just want to go home."

"You will," Diamonda said. "The winds will change, and your people will return. Our root is valuable to them. Now come and rest, Mikijen. You have earned it."

Diamonda took his hand and led him through the crowd. Omari found his eyes swaying with the sonchai's hips. Diamonda looked over her shoulder and smirked. She was more attractive than he'd thought before. He took a tika root from his bag and chewed. He had a feeling he would need it.

* * *

Omari was cleaning his sword when Diamonda entered the house. He greeted the sonchai with a smile. She answered with a somber look.

"The Kiswala are here," she said.

Omari stood and went immediately to his chest. He opened it and took out his Mikijen uniform.

"So, you are leaving?" Diamonda asked.

Omari hesitated. He put down the uniform, went to Diamonda and they embraced.

"You always knew I would," he said.

"I hoped to change your mind," she replied.

They kissed, then Omari went back to undressing.

"Do you really want me to stay?" he asked.

"No," she said. "You would get in my way. There are so many things I haven't done because of you."

Omari stripped down to his loincloth.

"I did nothing," he said. "You're the one with the commanding voice."

Omari was reaching for his uniform when Diamonda's arms wrapped around his waist. He felt her breasts press against his back.

"Then I command you to please me one last time," she said.

Omari twisted about in her embrace then lifted her off the floor.

"How can I refuse?" he said.

* * *

The harbor was filled with merchants waiting anxiously for the Kiswala dhows to dock. Omari stood in the background, dealing with a mix of emotions. The excitement of finally being able to return to Ki Khanga was dampened by the anger building inside. That anger spilled over as the gangplank was extended and the Mikijen appeared. The first person down the gangplank was Abedi.

Omari yanked his sword free then pushed his way through the throng. There were a few complaints until the Vatasoans realized who he was. By the time he reached the dock his path was clear. Omari didn't recognize the other Mikijen with Abedi; he'd recruited a new group as was his way. It didn't matter. The man he waited for had come.

Abedi looked at him in confusion for a moment. His raised eyebrows let Omari know he'd been recognized. Abedi smiled then ambled toward Omari, his new cohorts close behind him. Omari reached into his pouch for a tika root. He stuck it in his mouth then chewed.

"Omari!" Abedi said. "I didn't expect to see you. I hope our . . ."

Omari's blade flashed across Abedi's neck. There was a moment of hesitation before his head toppled from his neck. His body soon followed it to the ground. The other Mikijen looked stunned then pulled their swords. Omari braced for their attack then was overwhelmed by a familiar yell. He turned to see Fanamby and the other Vatasoan warriors running to his aid.

"Stop! I beg of you!"

Tishala stood on the bow of the dhow. She tried but failed to hide her shock of seeing Omari alive.

"Let us use cooler heads," she managed to say.

"Yes, let us."

The crowd parted for the njaka. Accompanying her as always were Rodina and Diamonda. The njaka stopped beside Omari and looked at Abedi's body.

"This is the one that tried to kill you?" she asked.

"Yes," Omari replied.

"So, you have your vengeance."

"Yes," Omari said.

The njaka smiled. "Good. Take your place behind me."

Omari fell in behind the njaka, as did the other warriors. They followed her to the docks where she met Tishala.

"It is good to see you, Toavina," Tishala said. "I worried for you and your people. I see my worrying was not necessary."

"You were concerned about your tika supply," the njaka said. "Still, it is good to see you. I have someone that belongs to you."

Omari stepped forward, his hand on the hilt of his sword. He saw the fear in Tishala's eyes, and he grinned.

"Don't worry," he said. "My quarrel is settled."

"Abedi said you were dead," Tishala replied. "I had no reason to doubt him."

"Actually, you did," Omari said. "But that doesn't matter now. Safe passage back to Ki Khanga is all I require now, and you owe me that."

Tishala lowered her head. "I do."

The njaka stepped between them.

"Omari was instrumental in us reclaiming this town," she said. "He is a man of high standing among us, yet he wishes to return to your homeland. I hope you will give him the respect he deserves."

"I give you my word," Tishala replied.

The njaka embraced Omari, to his surprise.

"Farewell warrior," she said. "May your seas be calm, and your journeys many."

Diamonda stepped forward with a carved wooden box.

"A gift from your cohorts, and from me," she said.

Omari took the box then opened it. Inside was a hand cannon. He closed the box then tucked it under his arm before kissing Diamonda.

"Thank you," he whispered. He then turned his attention to the others. "Thank you all. I will never forget you."

He closed the box then faced Tishala.

"With your permission, I would like to retire to the dhow. I want to be sure I don't miss our departure again."

"You may go," Tishala said.

Omari began to walk away but Tishala grabbed his wrist.

"It is really good to see you, Omari," she said.

Omari pulled his hand free.

"It's a long safari back to Kiswala," he said. "I hope to see as little of you as possible. Be sure to stay clear of me. Once we're home you will never see me again."

Sadness filled Tishala's eyes. "I understand, Omari."

She looked to the confused Mikijen who awaited her orders. She pointed at Omari.

"This man is you kamada now," she said. "If you wish to be paid, you will do as he says."

The Mikijen cut their eyes at Omari as they nodded. Omari sized the men up; they were not happy to have to answer to him, but they would obey if only to make sure they were paid.

"Let's check out the cargo," Omari said. As he ambled up the gangplank a smile came to his face. The truth was his life would be better if he remained in the east, but home was home. He couldn't wait to return.

THE ESCORT

Omari Ket lay naked on the warm sand, his dark brown skin contrasting with the white grains supporting his muscled frame. He gazed at the fading stars as the sun peaked over the eastern horizon, its muted light riding in on the gentle waves. Omari stretched, yawned then reached out for his clothes. Instead of grasping the rough fabric of his Mikijen uniform, his fingers clutched grit. Omari sat up then looked to where his clothes should have been. They were gone.

"Cleave!" he uttered.

He stood and dusted the sand from his back and buttocks. Taking one more look at the ocean, he turned then walked into the seaside town of Geda, his destination the Mikijen outpost. People he passed during his nude stroll responded with a variety of expressions, but Omari ignored them all. He was not a modest man. What drew their attention almost as much as his body was the giant kraken tattoo covering his back and running down the back of his arms to his wrists. The ngisimaugi was the symbol of the Mikijen and the source of their amazing healing abilities. It was something not often seen, and the villagers made quite the commotion as they observed it and his other endowments.

The Mikijen outpost occupied the town center. The guards on the walls, Damu and Sadeeki, saw Omari approaching and laughed as loud as they could. Sadeeki gestured with his spear.

"Look! We're being attacked!" he yelled.

"His weapon doesn't look very impressive," Damu said.

Omari bent over, picked up a rock then threw it. It bounced off Damu's head.

"Hey!" he shouted. Sadeeki hid behind his shield while he laughed.

"Open the damn gate," Omari said.

Sadeeki disappeared from the ramparts. Moments later the piercing squeal of the opening gate doors cut through the usual morning din. The post *kamada*, Dalila Fuli, blocked the entrance, her arms folded across her chest, a frown on her face. Omari performed an exaggerated bow.

"My apologizes, Kamada Fuli," he said. "It seems you've caught me unprepared."

Fuli strode to Omari until their noses almost touched.

"Where is your uniform, Mikijen?" she asked.

"I lost it on the beach," Omari replied.

"It's coming out of your pay."

Omari groaned, turned around and walked away.

"I'll find it," he said.

"Come back here, *soli*!" Fuli shouted.

Omari returned. Dalila sighed.

"We'll send someone to look for it later," she said. "It's a Mikijen uniform. The fools who stole must know no one will buy it. Get to the quartermaster and get another uniform. I have an assignment for you."

Omari followed the kamada into the post. A gauntlet of Mikijen waited, laughing and jeering at him as he passed. He responded with lewd hip thrusts. Halfway through the courtyard, Fuli stopped and called for silence.

"You've had your fun, now back to your stations!" she ordered.

The muwanis dispersed and Omari continued alone to the quartermaster. After receiving a new uniform then stopping by his bunk for his weapons, he hurried to the kamada's office. The commander sat at her desk shuffling though a pile of parchments.

"Sit," she said without looking up.

Omari dropped on the stool before the desk. Fuli pushed the documents aside then looked directly into Omari's eyes.

"*Bazoli* Chane has planned a safari into the hinterlands. He needs an escort and has chosen you to lead it."

Omari's eyes went wide. This was not good. "Why?"

"The ironwood cargo is late. The bazoli has sent numerous messages to our contacts but has received no response," Fuli answered.

"No, not that," Omari said. "Why did he choose me to lead the safari?"

"I don't know," Fuli replied. "He usually doesn't get involved in such details, but this time he insisted. Maybe he saw you naked and was impressed. I have no idea."

"Someone he knows has," Omari whispered.

"What?" Fuli asked.

"Nothing."

The kamada returned to her parchments.

"Pick your muwanis. You will meet the bazoli at his compound at first light tomorrow."

Omari left the office and returned to his bunk. He fell asleep until he was summoned for guard duty. Despite his rank, everyone did duty and chores. As he paced the ramparts, he mulled over the bazoli's summons. Did he know? If so, their safari wasn't going to be pleasant. But if he really did know, why go through the charade? Just have him reassigned to a shithole town or send him to Aux.

By the time Omari's shift ended he was aggravated. He marched into the mess hall then stomped his foot for attention.

"I'm forming an escort to accompany bazoli Chane to the hinterlands. I need twenty muwanis. Sadeeki, Duna, Kadira and Adea are coming with me."

Kadira's eyes widened then narrowed as she glared at Omari. She was not a Mikijen, but a Haisetti archer that had come to the outpost looking for work. She and Omari had a history together, which was why she chose Geda.

"The rest who wish to go submit your names in my box. I'll take the first sixteen," Omari finished.

The muwanis hurried from the mess hall. A safari meant extra pay, a rare opportunity for a post like theirs. Omari strolled over to Kadira and Adea. Sadeeki and Duna came and sat with them.

"What's the plan, boss?" Duna said.

"We'll divide the muwanis into two groups," Omari said. "Duna, you'll lead the vanguard; Sadeeki, you'll take the rear. Kadira, Adea and I will tend to the bazoli."

Kadira looked up from her bowl of stew then wiped her mouth with her sleeve.

"I didn't come here to work like this," she said. "If I wanted to get killed, I would have gone to Mali."

"I'll make it worth your while," Omari replied.

"With stacks?"

Omari laughed. "Yes, with stacks."

"Should I bring my bow?" she asked with a grin.

"No," Omari replied. "I'll have my hand cannon."

Kadira snorted with laughter "Then I should bring my bow."

The others covered their mouths as they laughed.

"That's settled then," Omari said. "We'll leave at daybreak."

* * *

Omari stirred from a fitful sleep. He tossed his blankets aside and cursed as he dressed and armed himself. The morning was not going to go well. He still worried about bazoli Chane choosing him to lead his expedition. As he left his room to join the others at the stables, he pushed his worries aside. Whatever the reason, he would soon find out.

His cohorts were waiting when he arrived. They mounted their horses then rode from the post to the bazoli's massive compound. The Kiswalan merchant had become wealthy despite Geda's isolated location. Kenja pearls were prized throughout Ki Khanga, and those from Geda's bay were the most valuable due to their size and symmetry. Chane did an excellent job managing the trade, and the enormity of his compound reflected his success.

He was also pure blood Kiswalan as was his wife
Barika, both boasting a lineage that reached as far
back to when Kiswalans still lived on the Aux mainland.

Chane's compound guards rode out to meet
the Mikijen. Their leader, Bakari, was a former Mikijen, one of the few who had survived his inden-
tured servitude. Despite their shared experiences he
cared little for the mercenaries. He met Omari with
a curt nod.

"I don't see why the bazoli asked for you,"
Bakari said as he maneuvered his horse beside
Omari. "My muwanis are more than equal to
yours."

"You'll have to take that up with the bazoli,"
Omari replied. "I'm just following orders. This is
not a contest as far as I'm concerned. To be honest,
I'd rather be back at the post. Better your muwanis
die than mine."

"It's your attitude that makes you unsuitable
for this safari!" Bakari said.

"Like I said, I could care less," Omari replied.
"But I can assure you the bazoli has nothing to fear.
We are Mikijen. You more than anyone else should
know what we're capable of. Now leave me alone
unless you have good news to share."

Bakari scowled at Omari then spurred his
horse away. He led the Mikijen through the compound gate and into the courtyard surrounding
Chane's impressive home. A servant emerged from
the veranda carrying a wrapped bundle. He stopped
before Omari and offered the bundle to him.

"The bazoli will be with you momentarily,"
he said. His eyes narrowed as he focused on Omari.

"This is for you," he said.

Omari took the bundle then opened it. It was his uniform.

"Oh shit," he said. This was going to be a terrible safari.

The servant returned with Chane's horse. The bazoli exited from his home wearing a simple shirt and pants, practical clothing for the long journey. He was not alone. Walking beside him was his daughter, Jina. Omari suppressed a smile as the events of the night came back to him. Their eyes met and Jina grinned. If Chane noticed their reactions, he did not reveal it.

The servant knelt beside Chane's horse then got down on his hands and knees. Chane stopped before the servant, looking at Omari.

"Get up," he ordered the servant. The man clambered to his feet then shuffled away.

"Ket," Chane said. "Assist me."

Omari climbed from his mount. He sauntered over to Chane then offered his hand. Chane scowled.

"That is not the way a servant helps his master onto his horse."

Omari was confused for a moment until he saw Chane's servant smirk.

"You expect me to . . ."

"Of course," Chane said.

Omari looked at his muwanis. Sadeeki and Kadira shook their heads vigorously; Duma shrugged and Adea covered her mouth to hide her grin. Omari took a deep breath then turned to face Chane, forcing a smile on his face.

"As you wish, bwa," he said.

Omari ambled to the bazoli's horse, dropped to his knees then placed his hands on the ground. The bazoli dropped his sandaled left foot hard on

Omari's back, causing him to grimace. As Chane
lifted his right leg to mount his horse, Omari stood.
The bazoli was thrown off balance and he tumbled
over the horse and onto the ground.

Omari rushed to the other side of the beast
and extended his hand.

"I apologize, bazoli," he said. "I am not used
to helping one such as yourself mount his horse.

"Get away from me!" the bazoli shouted. "It's
not enough that you . . ."

Chane looked at his daughter then fell silent.

"Shida!" Chane called out.

Shida, the bazoli's servant, hurried to his
side and helped him onto his horse. Another servant handed him his weapons.

"You'll have no need of those," Omari said.

"I don't travel without them," Chane said.

"I hope you're good with them," Omari said.
"I don't want you injuring any of my muwanis pre-
tending to be a swordsman."

"I'm very good," Chane said.

"I doubt it," Omari replied.

Omari returned to his muwanis and mounted his horse.

"Duma, take us out," Omari ordered.

Duma rallied his muwanis then led the way
out of the compound. Omari, Kadira and Adea
flanked the bazoli; Sadeeki and his muwanis
brought up the rear. Kadira pulled alongside Omari
then leaned closed to him.

"He doesn't like you. Why?" she asked.

"That night I came naked from the beach?"
Omari said.

"Yes?" Kadira replied.

"I was with his daughter," Omari said.

Kadira closed her eyes. "By the Cleave, Omari."

"It was her idea, not mine," Omari said. "I met her at the market. She said she wanted to see the moonrise and she needed someone to protect her since her guards had already returned to the compound. She said she would pay well."

"And did she?"

Omari frowned. "No. I wanted stacks. She had other intentions. We sat on the beach and drank palm wine most of the night. At some point I passed out. When I woke up, she and my clothes were gone."

Kadira rolled her eyes. "So, you want me to believe she took off your clothes by herself and you fell asleep before anything happened?"

"I took off my clothes . . . I think," Omari said. "But I'm sure nothing happened."

"I know you, Omari," Kadira said.

Omari chuckled. "Yes, you do."

Kadira smiled. "Let us not go there. I believe you because you have never been silent about your escapades. But please do not anger Chane any further. Our pay depends on it."

"I'll try not to," Omari said. "It depends on what he does next."

"No, Omari. It depends on how you react," Kadira said. "He's a bazoli and a Kiswalan. No matter what happens or how it happens, he's right."

Kadira sighed. "I still wonder how you became a soli."

"Everyone in front of me is dead, that's how," Omari said with a smile.

"Well, let's make sure no one gets promoted during this expedition, okay?"

Omari laughed. "I'll try."

The expedition rode through the town then into the bush, traveling until dusk. Duna guided them to a decent clearing where they set up camp and prepared for darkness. Chane's servants pitched an elaborate tent for him then prepared his food as the bazoli practiced with his sword. Omari observed him as he cleared a spot for himself to sleep for the night. Chane moved as if he had some experience; but swinging a sword was very different from fighting with one. Chane suddenly looked at Omari.

"Shit!" Omari said as he looked away, hoping the bazoli didn't notice.

"Ket," he said. "Come and bring your sword."

"I must make sure my muwanis are prepared for the night," Omari said.

"I'm sure this is not their first time on a safari," Chane said. "Come. I need the practice."

Omari sighed as he picked up his baldric, slinging it over his shoulder. When he looked up, Kadira and Sadeeki stared him in his face.

"Go easy on him," Sadeeki advised.

"I will," Omari replied.

"We mean it," Kadira said.

"The both of you are overstepping your rank," Omari said. "The bazoli wishes to practice and I will oblige him."

Omari sauntered to the bazoli then nodded.

"I should tell you . . ."

The bazoli charged Omari, swinging his saber with practiced skill. Omari dodged and sidestepped as he attempted to draw his own sword, cursing as he did so. When he finally freed his blade and tossed his baldric aside, the momentum shifted quickly. Omari went on the attack, driving the bazoli back then circling around him to prevent him from escaping. The bazoli's eyes were wide with fear; Omari suspected the man thought he was going to kill him. Omari considered it after that sudden attack which was meant to kill or at least maim him. But as Kadira said, they needed the stacks. He backed off, allowing Chane to regain the advantage. He feinted, blocked, and dodged until he tired the bazoli out.

"You have some skill," Omari said.

"Nothing compared to you," Chane admitted. "For a moment I thought you meant me harm."

Omari smiled. "You are bazoli. I would do no such thing."

"If only you had been kinder to my daughter," Chane said.

"I did nothing to your daughter," Omari replied.

"Then why did she come home in the middle of the night crying with your clothes?"

"She was embarrassed."

Omari saw Chane's fingers tighten around his sword hilt.

"Embarrassed? How?"

Omari lowered his head then pinched the bridge of his nose before answering.

"She was embarrassed because I got too drunk and fell asleep before anything happened," Omari finally said.

"And if you had not fallen asleep?" Chane asked.

"You would have reason to be angry with me."

Chane let go of his sword then stabbed at Omari with his finger.

"You should know your place, Mikijen!"

Omar shrugged. "I do. It's your daughter who needs this speech, not me."

"We will settle this when we return to Geda," Chane said.

Omari didn't answer. He walked back to his bed, took off his weapons and tried to sleep. This was going to be a long safari.

* * *

The morning brought clouds and drizzle, a sign of the approaching rainy season. After a quick meal, the travelers broke camp and continued their safari. Duma sent two riders ahead to scout the trail as the others settled into the monotony of the road. The clouds cleared and the sun emerged, burning away the dampness. A thick fog covered the road and haunted the bush, making it hard to see.

Omari was nodding off on his horse when he heard shouting. A rider emerged from the fog ahead. It was one of the riders Duma sent ahead. Fear gripped the rider's face and there was blood on his uniform.

"Watu wa mchanga!" the rider shouted "Watu wa mchanga!"

Chane rode up beside Omari.

"Sand people?" he said. "That's impossible. We're too far south for their like to . . ."

The bush around them exploded with ululation.

"Swords!" Omari shouted. "Defensive formation!"

The Mikijen riders maneuvered their horses into a circle as metal spears streaked from the woods. A few riders were hit and fell from their mounts. Sand muwanis burst from the bush covered in white cloth and leather armor; their curved swords held high to behead the fallen. They were experienced in fighting Mikijen and knew that decapitating the mercenaries was one of the few ways of keep their ngisimaugi from healing them. However, they were unprepared for the fury of the Malian war horses. The beasts leapt between their wounded riders and their assailants, beating the attackers back with their hooves and their bodies. Omari was about to ride into the fray until Chane called out.

"No, Omari!" he said. "Your duty is to protect me!"

"That's what I'm about to do," Omari said. "A dead person isn't a threat to anyone."

The watu we mchanga running toward the bazoli jerked stiff as an arrow pierced his forehead. Kadira appeared moments later, reloading her bow.

"He's right," she said to the bazoli. "We'll handle these bandits!"

Another cry rose from the bush, one that was not of human origin. Omari spun in his saddle in time to see a hulking mass rushing toward him. He was bringing down his sword when the thing jumped then slammed into him, knocking him from his horse. He blacked out for a moment; when his eyesight returned the thing had Chane on its shoulder and bounded away into the bush, the watu wa mchanga close behind. Shida lay dead, his head a few feet from his body. The attack was apparently a distraction to claim the real price; bazoli Chane.

Omari's commanders gathered around him as he sat up.

"What was that?" Sadeeki asked.

Duma helped Omari to his feet. Omari took a long look at the beast fleeing with Chane. He walked to his horse.

"We're done here," he said.

"Omari, we have to go after them!" Duma shouted.

Omari watched the creature carry Chane deeper into the bush. He shrugged.

"He's a bazoli! It's our duty to protect him!" Sadeeki said.

The beast hopped up a hill that rose over the bush canopy, carrying Chane as if he was a child. Omari did not move.

"We can't let this happen!" Adea argued.

Kadira jumped from her horse, marched up to Omari and stood beside him, her bow in her hand.

"Whether we deliver the wood or not, if we return without Chane, we don't get paid."

Omari turned into the bush. The beast had halted at the crest of the hill. It threw Chane to the ground, tilted back its head then let out a piercing cry.

"Can you hit it from here?"

Kadira loaded her bow then pulled back the bowstring as she raised the bow then let the arrow fly. The arrow struck the creature in its thigh. It howled as it tumbled out of sight, dragging Chane with it.

"Good shot," Omari said. He swept his eyes over others.

"Mount up!" he ordered. "Let's go get our pay."

"What about the wood shipment?" Kadira asked.

Omari looked at her with a frown.

"What do you want me to do? Save the bazoli or find the wood?"

"We can do both,' Kadira said. "Send Duma and his muwanis ahead to find the shipment. The rest of us will go after Chane."

"I don't like it," Omari said. "We're spitting our forces."

"We'll locate him and whoever has him," Kadira said. "If we're at a disadvantage we won't attack until Duma joins us. If it is still too dangerous, we will send word back to Kamada Fuli for reinforcements.

"It's a good plan," Omari said.

"I know," Kadira said.

Omari looked at the others.

"You heard her. Let's go."

Duma gathered his muwanis then rode ahead. Omari and the others left their mounts with two muwanis. The rest followed Omari and Kadira into the bush.

"I'll take two muwanis with me and take point," Omari said.

"I should do that," Kadira said. "You're the soli."

Omari laughed. "You and I both know who's really giving orders here. Everyone else does, too."

Kadira grinned "Well, since you mentioned it."

"I never wanted the responsibility in the first place," Omari said. "To the Cleave with Chane."

"He may already be there," Kadira replied.

"Let's hope for the sake of our stacks he's not. The watu we mchanga probably know we're pursuing them. They'll set up an ambush. Maybe we can flush them out."

"What if they let you pass then ambush us?" Kadira asked.

"Let's hope they're not that smart."

"How will you let us know if they do ambush you?"

Omari swung his hand cannon around from his back.

"You'll know," he said. He turned his attention to the other muwanis.

"Jaramogi, Asafa," Omari called out.

The two muwanis stepped out from the others.

"Come with me," Omari said

The trio trotted ahead of the others until they could no longer be seen.

"Stay vigilant," Omari said. "They'll be expecting us."

Omari sheathed his sword then took out his hand cannon. He loaded it earlier, stuffing the iron barrel with gunpowder and lead shot. The weapon was useless at a distance, but at close range it was devastating, not to mention loud. The bush was a perfect environment for it. Omari stuck a matchstick in the corner of his mouth then continued into the bush.

Asafa took the lead for he was the best tracker. He picked up the wounded beast's spoor and they increased their pace. They stopped once to eat, then continued their hunt. The bush thickened, forcing them to push through thorn bushes and other painful obstacles that didn't seem to deter the beast they followed. The greenery eventually relented, the low trees and vines thinning until they reached an open patch of grass. They walked into the opening before they realized what they were doing.

"Back!" Omari yelled.

It was too late. A hail of spears rained down on them from cover on the other side of the grasses. Two spears struck Asafa, one in his shoulder and the other through his left thigh. Jaramogi managed to avoid the first spear that reached him, but the second grazed his scalp, sending him spinning to the ground. Only Omari remained standing to face the charging horde of watu wa mchanga. He took the matchstick from his mouth, holding it over the strike patch on the fuse of his hand cannon. He heard Jaramogi moan as he regained his feet.

"Take Asafa into the bush," Omari said without looking back.

"I'll stand with you," Jaramogi said.

"No need," Omari replied. "Kadira and the others will be here soon. Now take Asafa into cover and pull those spears out of him!"

Omari dodged more spears as he struck the matchstick. The watu wa mchanga were only a few strides away when he lit the powder. The blast sprayed the muwanis with shot, knocking the closest into those behind them and sending others to the ground in pain. Omari didn't wait for the smoke to clear; he attacked the dazed warriors with his sword and jambiya, wreaking as much havoc as he could before the sand bandits recovered from shock. Half of the mchanga were dead or wounded before the others fought back. Omari went on the defensive, blocking, and dodging spear thrusts and sword swings. There were too many for him to mount any attack. All he could do was defend himself and pray to Eda.

A sword hack meant for his thigh was blocked by Jaramogi's sword. The muwani pressed his back against Omari's and they battled the mchangas relentless assault. Omari suffered small cuts as his arms became fatigued but continued to fight on.

"Eda, where are you?" he whispered.

He was answered by an arrow that whizzed by his ear and sank into the forehead of the mchanga in front of him. Mikijen erupted from the bush and attacked the mchangas mercilessly. The bandits attempted to flee, but Mikijen blades and Kadira's arrows cut them down. Omari didn't realize how tired he was until Jaramogi stepped away. He collapsed onto his back, laboring for breath.

Kadira appeared over him, a stern look on her face.

"Get up," she said. "We have to move."

"You go ahead," Omari replied. "I'll catch up."

"You're not safe alone," she warned.

Omari sat up. "I'll manage. How's Asafa?"

"He's still recovering," Kadira said. "His wounds were deep."

"I'll stay with him," Omari said. We'll come when his wounds allow him to move."

Kadira nodded.

"To me!" she shouted. The other Mikijen gathered around her then they jogged across the grass into the bush.

Omari took a swig from his water gourd before standing and staggering to Asafa. The man sat against a small tree; his wounds bandaged. Omari could see the glow emanating from around the neck of his shirt, indicating the ngisimaugi was hard at work.

"How much longer?" Omari asked.

"Ten more minutes at least," Asafa replied.

The two rested, drinking water and eating rations as the sounds of the bush returned. Asafa finished his food then stood.

"I'm ready," he said.

Omari came to his feet. His wounds had healed, and his energy returned. No matter how many times he experienced it, he was always in awe of the ngisimaugi's healing powers.

The two Mikijen set out to find their cohorts. Kadira made sure their trail was easy to follow. The path led to a small rise crowned with tall ironwood trees. Omari and Asafa were about to ascend the hill when a familiar whistle caught their attention. Kadira emerged from hiding and waved them over.

"What's going on?" he asked.

"There is a camp just over that hill," Kadira said. "More mchangas are there, as well as more of those beasts. I'm sure Chane is there, too."

"What do they want with him?" Omari asked.

"Ransom, no doubt," Kadira replied. "They know the Kiswala are particular of their own."

"What if it's something else?" Omari asked.

Kadira tilted her head. "Like what?"

Omari shrugged. "Those creatures are not natural. They probably belong to a sonchai, maybe one who likes to make pets of Kiswala highborn."

"Whatever the reason, we need to get him out," Kadira said.

"They'll send more muwanis soon to find out what happened to the others," Omari said. "We'll set an ambush for them. You and I can circle the hill and wait outside the camp. As soon as the mchanga leave we can enter the camp and find Chane."

"What about the beasts?" Kadira said.

"I'll expose myself," Omari said. "When they attack, you take them out with your bow."

"You have a lot of faith in me," Kadira replied.

"You're a Haisetti. I've never seen you miss. I'm told you don't know how."

Kadira beamed. "The Haisetti who missed are dead."

"Exactly," Omari replied.

Omari and Kadira gathered the others and shared their plan. Soon afterwards they set out, skirting the base of the hill while staying far enough away from the camp so not to draw attention. They worked their way to the rear of the camp where they found a large hut constructed from local trees with a thatch roof. Three beasts patrolled the shelter, pacing back and forth while occasionally fighting amongst themselves. Omari took out his sword and jambiya then laid them before him; Kadira loaded her bow and waited.

A voice called out from the hut in a language Omari did not recognize. Moments later a person emerged of the likes Omari had never seen. The person's body was wrapped in an indigo-colored robe that glittered like the night sky, with fabric of the same color wrapped tightly around their head, leaving only eyes their exposed. It was those eyes that captured Omari's attention. They blazed blue with the familiar hue of kipande. Whoever was swathed in those robes was surely a sonchai, but one Omari was not familiar with. The beasts fell to their bellies then crawled to the sonchai's feet. The person knelt the patted the beasts' heads like they were pets, speaking softly to them. The beasts regained their feet then turned toward Omari and Kadira.

"Shit!" Kadira said.

The creatures bounded toward them. Kadira loosed an arrow while Omari scrambled to load his hand cannon. Instead of packing the barrel with shot, he shoved in a single slug.

Kadira's first arrow bounced off the lead beast's head. Her second arrow penetrated its stomach, but it broke the arrow off and continued to charge. The third arrow bit into its leg and it stumbled.

"Shoot the legs!" Omari yelled.

"I don't need your advice!" Kadira yelled back.

Kadira loosed more arrows with uncanny precision. The beasts' legs bristled with arrows, yet they still hobbled toward Kadira and Omari. Omari didn't have time to light the cannon; he dropped it then picked up his sword and jambiya. Her arrows spent, Kadira drew her sword, and the duo sprang from their hiding place. They pounced on the beasts, beheading them. After dispatching the creatures, they faced the sonchai, who looked at them with a blank expression. It raised its hand and its eyes glowed.

"Down!" Omari shouted.

He shoved Kadira into the grass then followed. Blue light engulfed them, searing heat flashing across Omari's back. His ngisimaugi deflected the brunt of the bolt but his nose filled with the smell of his burned flesh. The grass and trees around them blazed; Omari lifted Kadira from the grass and pulled her into the open as he picked up his hand cannon.

The sonchai strode toward them, his eyes glowering. He raised his hands again, but Omari was faster. He raised his hand cannon, lit the powder and fired. The slug smashed into the sonchai, blowing off his right arm. The wounded sonchai let out an unnatural scream that caused Omari to cover his ears and close his eyes. When he opened them the remaining beasts and mchangas were running to the sonchai's aid.

"Let's go!" Kadira shouted.

Omari and Kadira sprinted into the bush. The beasts and mchangas chased them, closing the gap with every step. Omari glanced back then grimaced. If they could only make it back to the others . . .

A Mikijen war chant greeted them as they rounded the hill. Their cohorts advanced in formation, joined by Kamada Fuli and the full Mikijen garrison. Omari and Kadira turned to face their pursuers as their comrades surged by them. Although greatly outnumbered, the beasts and mchangas attacked. They met the full fury of the Mikijen and were brutally decimated.

Omari and Kadira collapsed onto the ground exhausted. Omari watched the kamada shout out orders to secure the area before marching up to him.

"Where's Chane?" she asked.

Omari climbed to his feet then gestured. "Follow us."

Omari and Kadira led Fuli and the others into the camp. The sonchai lay dead, the ground around him stained with purple blood. Kamada knelt beside the corpse then stuck her finger in the ichor. She rubbed her fingers together; the liquid turned blue.

"Daarila's axe!" she whispered. "What are you doing here?"

Omari was puzzled by the kamada's words.

"What do you mean by that?" he asked.

Fuli didn't answer. She pushed by Omari then entered the hut. Moments later she reemerged, a stunned look on her face.

"Is Chane inside?" Omari asked.

"Yes," Fuli replied. "He's dead."

Omari stepped toward the hut, but Fuli raised her hand to stop him.

"I just want to . . ."

"No!" Fuli shouted. "Obey my order and stay where you are!"

Kamada's intense eyes swept the Mikijen.

"Bring all the bodies and pile them near the hut. When you are done gather enough straw and wood to make a bonfire. We'll burn everything."

"Even bazoli Chane?" Kadira asked.

Fuli glared at Kadira.

"Everything."

The muwanis did as they were ordered. Omari and Kadira exchanged glances as they worked. Something was not right. Once the fire was at full blaze, the Mikijen marched back to Geda and retired to their outpost. Omari was grateful to be back. He went to bath house, stripped off his clothes then scrubbed the battle filth from his skin. Afterwards he returned to his room and waited to be summoned by the kamada for an assessment of the safari, but that never happened. Days passed but still the kamada did not ask for a review. Finally, the curiosity became too much. On a bright morning three weeks after the safari, Omari entered the kamada's office. She was working as always and didn't notice Omari enter the room. He cleared his throat for attention. Fuli raised her head then looked into Omari's eyes.

"Ket. What do you want?"

"It's about the safari."

Fuli put down her quill, giving Omari her full attention.

"What about it? The trade route was reestablished, the ironwood flows, and you were well paid. What else is there to discuss?"

"You didn't ask for a report," Omari said.

"There was no need," Fuli replied.

"Why not?" Omari said. "What were those beasts? And I've never seen a sonchai like that in my life!"

Fuli sighed. "In two weeks, a fleet of transport dhows will arrive from Kiswala. You and every Mikijen here will be reassigned. Once you are relocated, you will not speak of what you saw in the camp. Do you understand?"

"Kamada, why is this happening?"

"You didn't answer me, Soli Ket. Do you understand?"

Omari's eyes narrowed. There was more to this. Much more.

"Don't pull rank in me now, Fuli. I've been a good muwani," Omari said. "I've done more than enough to deserve an answer. What was it?"

Fuli rubbed her chin.

"I can't say. Just hope that you never see its likes again. Now get out of my office."

Omari bowed and did as he was told. Kadira was waiting for him.

"Well, what did she say?"

"Nothing, except we're all being reassigned."

Kadira gasped. "Why?"

"She won't say."

Kadira scowled. "I'm going in! I'm Haisetti; I don't answer to her."

Omari grabbed her arm.

"No, let it go," he said. "If Fuli is this adamant about being quiet, I don't think I want to know."

"So just let it go? Just like that?"

"Yes," Omari replied. "Be glad we're still alive."

He walked by Kadira. She hesitated then followed.

"Besides, you'll be leaving soon. We have stacks and only a few days to spend them. What do you say you and I go to the bath house and make some bad memories?"

Kadira grinned then wrapped her arm around his waist.

"Let's do it," she said. "I'll give you something to talk about at you next outpost."

"I'll give you something better."

Kadira winked then grabbed Omari's butt.

"We'll see."

Omari did the same.

"Yes, we will."

They laughed as they sauntered toward the gate.

LITTLE THIEF

Omari gripped the galloping warhorse's reins and prayed to Eda. The beast charged down the narrow trail as if Daarila himself was after them and in a sense, he was. Omari dared to look back. A sigh of relief escaped his dry lips when he saw the road was empty, at least for now. The Yedah garrison had at least twenty minutes, maybe thirty minutes at the most. It wasn't enough time, but it was all they would get.

He crashed into the open field between the bush and the outer walls. The sound of drums echoed off the trees behind him, alerting those on the wall of his approach. The gates swung wide and a team of Mikijen carrying the narrow bridge for crossing the thorn bush moat jogged out. They dropped the bridge and Omari's horse slowed just enough cross then picked up speed as it dashed into town.

It took all of Omari's strength to rein the horse still, and then it reared, almost throwing him. He jumped off the beast as soon as it calmed.

"Damned war horse," he shouted.

Kamada Russom trotted up to Omari, his eyes intense. The tall, lean commander had only recently taken over the post, replacing the elder Kamada Mosi. Unlike most Mikijen, Russom did not wear a turban. Sweat beaded on his bald head as Omari saluted him.

"Are they coming?" he asked.

"Yes," Omari replied.

"How many?"

"Too many. A thousand, maybe more."

"Then we have no choice," Russom said. "We'll evacuate all Kiswala merchants and citizens. I'll need you to take a platoon and set up an ambush on the road. We need more time."

Omari cursed under his breath.

"Kamada, I was thinking since I risked my life to locate the Basala, I would be assigned something less interesting."

Russom's eyes narrowed.

"What are you saying, Mikijen?"

"I'm saying that I've risked my life once today," Omari replied. "I'd rather not do it again."

Russom spat. "You have no shame, Ket."

"No shame? I was the only one who volunteered to go on reconnaissance!"

Russom laughed. "I chose you because you were trying your best not to be seen. Besides, you're a good muwani when you choose to be."

"So, do I help with evacuation?"

Russom turned and walked away. "Choose your muwanis for the ambush. Leave as soon as you can."

"But the Basala are almost here!" Omari said.

"Then you need to hurry."

Omari stomped off to the Mikijen barracks. He chose thirty muwanis; twenty sword wielders, five archers and five spearmen. They mounted then galloped out of the town, following the road, and advancing as far as they dared. Omari raised his hand for everyone to dismount.

"Archers and spearmen, I want you in the middle of the road with me," he ordered. "The rest of you take cover in the bush, ten on either side. Take the horses with you. As soon as you see the Basala advance falter, attack. Do not hesitate. If you do, you'll have so many holes in you your ngisimaugi won't save you. Understand?"

The muwanis nodded, although his words weren't needed. Most of the muwanis he chose were veterans, and those who weren't could follow orders.

"Spearmen, I want you up front," Omari said. "Archers, take position behind the spearmen. I don't want them to see you until it's too late."

The Basala war song reached their ears. The sword wielders disappeared into the bush. Omari loaded his hand cannon as he talked.

"When I raise my sword, I want you spearmen to open a gap so the archers can step forward. Throw your spears as they loose their arrows. Understand?"

Everyone nodded. Omari paced back and forth, his stomach a nervous knot. He had no idea if his plan would work, but it was the best he could come up with in such a short time. The Basala war song grew louder as they drew near, then suddenly it fell silent. A loud voice called out and the war song changed. A few minutes later the Basala appeared, shields joined together, their spears jutting from the gaps.

"Daarila's breath!" Omar exclaimed. "Archers forward!"

The archers ran forward as the spearmen made room.

"Spearmen, clubs!" Archers, send them a volley but aim your arrows over the vanguard!"

The archers released their arrows. They soared over the front ranks, landing among the muwanis in the rear. The war song was shattered by the cries of wounded muwanis.

"Aim your next volley at the front ranks," Omari said. "Spearmen, wait for my signal then throw your clubs low."

The archers released a second volley. The Basala front ranks raised their shields to deflect the arrows.

"Spearmen, now!" Omari shouted.

Omari and the spearmen threw their war clubs, striking the front ranks in the legs. The muwani fell in pain, grabbing at their injured knees and shin. The Mikijen threw more clubs as the archers loosed more arrows. The swordsmen held their positions. When they were out of clubs, Omari swung his hand cannon about.

"Attack!" he yelled.

The swordsmen charged from the bush, slamming into the Basala from both sides. Omari and the spearmen ran forward, Omari lighting his hand cannon on the way. They were a few feet from the Basala when the gun discharged, sending bronze shot into the Basala and opening a gap where the dead and wounded attackers once stood. Omari tossed the cannon aside, unsheathed his sword and jambiya and jumped into the gap. He hooked a Basala shield with his jambiya then yanked it aside. The muwani's eyes went wide as Omari plunged his sword into his ribs. The man dropped to the ground and Omari leaped over him to the next muwanis. As the Mikijen cut into the Basala ranks, the archers continued to send arrows over their heads into the Basala rear. The Basala could take no more; they broke ranks and fled down the road away from the town. The Mikijen pursued them for a time then broke off.

Everyone knew there was no time celebrate victory or loot the Basala bodies. They returned to their horses then rode back to Yedah. The bridge was already in place and the gate open. Within the walls, chaos reigned. Mikijen gathered Kiswalans, escorting them to the waiting dhows. The indigenous folk gathered their belongings and families, fleeing to their boats if they had them, or into the bush if they did not. Kamada Russom met Omari as he dismounted.

"We beat them back," Omari said, "but it won't take them long to regroup and return with a larger force."

"Good," Russom said. "I knew you could do it."

Omari answered with a scowl. Russom shook his head.

"Send your wounded to the dhow," Russom ordered. "The rest of you sweep the Kiswala houses and make sure we have everyone."

Omari saluted then set about his task. The Kiswala district was in the center of town and was small in comparison to those in other cities. Omari figured they could check the homes in a short time then head to the waiting dhows with minutes to spare. The first home he inspected was completely bare; the owners had done an excellent job clearing it. As Omari entered the second home, he heard rustling coming from the main bedroom. He pulled his sword before entering.

Someone slammed into him, knocking him to the floor. Omari reached out and grabbed a handful of fabric. There was a yelp, then a sharp pain on his hand. Omari let go then snatched a rungu from his sash. He threw the club low, and it entangled in his attacker's legs. Omari stood as the person fell. He walked up, placing his foot on the person's back. The person turned to look at him with an angry face. It was a boy.

"What are you doing here?" Omari said. "You should be gone."

"Everyone else is," the boy said. "So, it is easier to steal."

Omari almost laughed. He took his foot off the boy's back.

"Get out of the city," he said. "You don't want to be here when the Basala arrive."

The boy stood. He reached Omari's chest; his ebony face filled with naïve confidence.

"I am not afraid of the Basala," the boy said. "Let them come. I'll steal from them, too."

"You don't understand," Omari said. "The Basalans take no prisoners or slaves. Everyone who is not of their blood is killed as an offering to their ancestors."

The boy's stern countenance wavered for a second. He reached into his ragged clothes then pulled out a jambiya.

"I can defend myself," he said.

Omari's hand flashed forward. He snatched the knife from the boy's hand. The boy's mouth dropped open.

"I see," Omari said.

"Give it back!" the boy shouted.

"Not until you tell me your name," Omari said.

The boy tried to take the jambiya from Omari a few times but failed. His shoulders slumped as his head dropped.

"Gakura," he said. "My name is Gakura."

"Okay Gakura. I'll give it back to you if you promise you will leave the city."

"I promise," Gakura said.

Omari flipped the knife, catching the blade. He offered the hilt to the boy.

"Now go," he said.

Gakura snatched the jambiya, grinned, then ran from the house.

As Omari inspected the other homes, he found himself thinking about Gakura. He wasn't much different at the same age, roaming the streets of Sati-Baa, stealing and fighting, doing whatever he needed to do to survive. He wondered if Gakura had parents and siblings. Was stealing for himself or for them? He shook his head clear. That was none of his concern. If the boy was smart, he would leave the town and sneak his way onto a boat. That's what he would have done.

Omari and the other Mikijen completed their inspection then hurried to the dhows. Their departure was none too soon. The Basala war chant rose from the bush at the edge of the clearing and those still in the village cried out in response. Omari reached the dhow deck and gazed back at the town as the people fled for their lives. He found himself inspecting each one, looking for Gakura. As the last of the villagers left the town, Omari scowled.

"That fool," he whispered. He made his way to the gangplank.

"Omari!" Russom shouted. "Where are you going?"

"I'll be back," Omari said.

"We will not wait for you!" Russom warned.

"I didn't ask you to," Omari retorted.

Omari ran to the town. As he neared, the Basala war song grew louder. He entered the town and was disheartened by what he saw. A group of young and old men gathered at the gate, determined to hold the Basala back to give the others time to flee. Gakura was with them.

"Hey!" Omari shouted.

They turned to see him; their eye wide with fear.

"Get out now," he said. "Everyone else is gone. Save yourselves."

The men were about to leave when a hail of spears fell upon them. Omari ran backwards, managing to avoid them. A few of the men were lucky. They ran as fast as they could to the docks. Omari was about to follow.

"Mikijen! Help me!"

Omari spun about. Gakura lay on the ground, a spear in his back. Omari rushed to him, then pulled the spear free.

"I told you leave!" he said.

"I . . . I was going to, but the chief caught me and told me I must fight."

Omari looked at Gakura's wound. It was bad. As he squatted to lift Gakura to his feet the Basala burst through the gate. Omari cradled Gakura in his arms and ran. Spears and warclubs hummed by him but Omari did not look back. His eyes were locked on the dhow.

"You came back for me," Gakura said, his voice weak. "Why?"

"Because no one came for me," Omari replied.

The Basala closed the gap between them. Omari ran faster, breathing hard. He tensed, waiting for a spear to pierce his back but it didn't happen. As he escaped the city, a hail of arrows from the Mikijen dhow fell on the Basala, driving them back into the city. Omari ran up the gangplank and was met by Rossum.

"That was a stupid thing to do Omari," Rossum said.

"I had to go back for him," Omari said, looking at the boy in his arms.

"Why? Do you know him?" Rossum said.

"Yes," Omari replied.

Omari looked down at Gakura. His eyes were closed as if he were sleeping. Rossum inspected the boy.

"You wasted your time," he said. "The boy is dead. Throw him overboard."

Omari stood stunned.

"Did you hear me? Throw him overboard!"

Omari glared at Rossum.

"No."

The Mikijen dhow had sailed a good way from the shore. Omari carried Gakura to where the landing boats were secured. He lay Gakura inside a boat then lowered it to the sea.

"Omari!" Rossum yelled. "What the Cleave are you doing?"

Omari didn't reply. He climbed down into the boat, picked up the oars then rowed south until he was sure he was clear of the Basala. He found a small village and rowed into their mooring. A group of curious fishermen met him; they gasped when they saw Gakura's body.

The eldest of the fishermen approached Omari.

"What do you want, Mikijen?" he said. "We have no wealth here."

"I want you to bury this boy," he said. "His name is Gakura."

"Is he your son?" the man asked.

"No," Omari said. "He is my brother."

The elder summoned two fishermen. Omari gave Gakura to them. He reached into his pouch, giving the elder all his coins.

"Give him a decent burial," Omari said. "Keep what is left for you and yours."

"We will," the elder said. "You have my word on Eda's heart."

"That is all I can ask."

Omari returned to the boat, then rowed toward the horizon.

THE JEWELER

AND THE ROGUE

Omari crept down the mud packed streets of Kunis, a torch in his right hand as he tugged at the collar of his tunic with his left. He cursed himself for not finding a better tailor for his uniform, but his options had been limited. There were very few seamsters willing to counterfeit a constable's uniform, and it came at a high price. He still wasn't sure if it would have been prudent to kill the man, but it was too late now. The plan was in motion. There was no turning back.

Omari entered the merchant district then made his way to his objective. For weeks he'd studied all movement in and out of the compound. He memorized the servants' coming and going, deliveries and market trips. He even knew when the inhabitants relieved themselves. All the scrutiny led to this moment, his window of opportunity. If all went well, he would be a very rich man in a few hours.

Omari did not consider himself a thief. But with the end of the war between Asanteman and Oyo there were plenty of warriors seeking work as bodyguards and mercenaries, making the opportunities for a foreigner with a strange tattoo on his back rather slim. Omari would use the stacks to travel west, where political intrigue and squabbles kept someone with his skills busy and well paid.

He doused his torch then slipped into a nearby alley. He watched as the last of the servants exited the compound, then listened as the gate was locked behind them. The compound's owner was so protective of his wealth that he didn't allow any of his servants to spend the night, not even his bodyguards. He trusted the diligence of the constables to keep him safe. That was his mistake.

Omari had two hours before the real constable would make his appearance. He emerged from the alley as the final servant faded into the darkness. Omari sprinting to the wall. He lifted his tunic and unraveled the rope around his waist. Omari leaned against the wall then lifted his shirt again, this time pulling the grappling hook free that he tucked in the back of his pants. He secured the grappling hook to the rope then threw it over the wall. Omari yanked the rope making sure the hook was secure before pulling himself up then over the top of the wall. He pulled up the rope then used it to lower himself into the courtyard.

Omari ran across the open space to the veranda. The door to the house was easy to open. He tipped up the stairs to the upper level of the home as quietly as possible then tipped his way to the room at the end of the hall. To his delight, the door was unlocked. He opened it then found himself standing face to face with another burglar.

Omari ducked the interloper's wild swing then tackled the man into the treasure room. They grappled on the floor, each reaching for the other's throat. Omari rammed his forearm into his opponent's neck then reached for the dagger tucked in his sash. He pulled the blade free then plunged it into his foe's ribs. The person jerked then gasped as Omari stabbed him a second then third time, pressing him hard until he ceased moving. Omari was standing when firelight washed over him.

"What is this?" a startled voice said. "What is happening?"

Omari turned toward the voice, the bloody dagger in his hand. Kwaku Appiah, jewel merchant and owner the compound stood in the doorway, an oil lamp in his quivering hand. He stared at Omari, a confused expression on his round face.

"Constable, what are you doing in my home? How did you get inside?"

"I . . . uh . . ." Omari began.

Kwaku came closer with his lamp, peeking past Omari to the dead man on his floor. He gasped.

"Efum?"

Kwaku looked to Omari then to Efum, the dead man on his floor. His confused expression gave way to a scowl.

"I should have known!" Kwaku said. "I thought there was something suspicious about him. Always asking about how many jewels I acquired during my safaris whenever I returned. I see you suspected him, too."

"Ah . . . yes. Yes, I did," Omari replied.

"Is he dead?" Kwaku asked.

"Yes," Omari replied.

"Good! Anyone trying to steal from me deserves no less!"

Kwaku spat on Efum's remains.

"I assume you will make arrangements to dispose of his body?" Kwaku asked.

"Yes," Omari answered. "I'll do it right away."

"Thank you. I wouldn't want to wait until the morning. I'll open the gate for you."

Kwaku went to get the gate key. Omari rushed into the treasure room, grabbed a handful of jewels then stuck them into his pouch. He lifted Efum onto his shoulders as Kwaku returned.

"Follow me," Kwaku said.

Omari trailed the jeweler to the gate.

"Thank you again for your diligence," Kwaku said.

"Anytime," Omari replied.

He walked through the gate.

"Constable!" Kwaku called out.

Omari closed his eyes and exhaled before turning.

"Yes?"

"How were you able to enter my compound?"

"Efum used a rope to climb your wall," Omari said. "He left it dangling. That is how I suspected something was wrong. I climbed the rope then followed his trail inside."

"I'm glad you were nearby," Kwaku said. "Will you return in the morning to make sure nothing is missing?"

"Yes, I will," Omari said.

"Good. It will save me a trip to the constable's compound."

"I'll come back at first light," Omari said.

"I will be waiting," Kwaku replied.

"Of course, you will," Omari whispered.

"What was that?" Kwaku asked.

"I said of course you should."

Omari walked into the street with Efum's body. He would have to carry it a way before dumping it in an alley.

"Constable!"

"By Daarila's Beard!" Omari hissed. He composed himself before turning.

"Yes?"

"What is your name?"

"Kofi," Omari replied. It was the only Asanteman name that came to mind.

"Thank you, Kofi. See you tomorrow!"

Omari nodded then hurried away. He had to move quickly before the true constable made his rounds. He slipped into the first alley he came to, thankful for the darkness. He moved from alley to alley like a stray feline until he reached the river. He dumped Efum's body into the waters, hoping the strong current would take it out to the ocean before dawn. Hurrying back to his small hut, Omari lit the palm wax candle on his table then poured out the contents of his bag.

"Cleave!" he said.

There were barely enough baubles to get him to the next town, let alone across Ki Khanga. The night had been a waste; he would have to make do with what he was able to obtain.

But then he remembered Kwaku's words, and a grin came to his face.

See you tomorrow!

If he visited the jeweler the next day, he'd have another chance to get more jewels. It was a risk, but it was worth it. Omari put the trinkets back into the bag, then extinguished the candle. He needed to make best of what little time he had to sleep. The next day would be very eventful.

* * *

Omari waited at Kwaku's gate with his servants. They looked at him with nervous expressions, no doubt wondering why a constable was calling on the merchant so early in the morning. Omari tapped his foot, hoping the true constable did not appear before he was allowed inside. His good luck won out; Kwaku appeared with his keys, unlocked the gate, and let his workers in. He smiled when he saw Omari.

"Constable! You're here early."

Omari shook Kwaku's arm.

"I wanted to make sure everything was okay. Last night must have been a terrible experience for you."

"I've seen worse," Kwaku said. "My profession is full of danger. There's always someone scheming to take what's not theirs instead of putting in a good day's work."

"Indeed," Omari replied.

"Come, join me for breakfast," Kwaku offered.

Omari's stomach growled. "I'd be delighted to."

Omari scowled as he followed Kwaku to the veranda. It was as if the merchant's words were meant for him. His foul mood dissipated when he saw the food spread out on the table. He now knew the reason for Kwaku's full cheeks and plump stomach.

"Sit and enjoy," Kwaku said.

Omari didn't hesitate. Kwaku laughed as he watched Omari eat.

"You have quite an appetite."

"A constable's pay only goes so far," Omari replied.

"I can imagine," Kwaku said. "Which brings me to the real reason why I asked you here."

"How can I help you?" Omari asked with a mouth full of bread.

"I am planning a safari to Ile-Ife in a few days. There is a shipment I need to deliver."

Omari washed down his food with a gourd of water. "Really?"

"Yes," Kwaku said. "I have acquired the services of a security merchant, but I would feel much better if I had someone of true authority and integrity overseeing them. I'm wondering if the constable guild could spare you for a few days."

"I believe it would be possible," Omari said.

"I'll pay you well," Kwaku continued. "It's a route I don't travel often. I'm afraid with the end of the war many warriors have taken to thievery to fill their pockets."

"That's such a shame," Omari said. "I am at your service, bwa Kwaku."

"Excellent!" Kwaku said. "I insist that you stay at my compound until we leave. Will that be a problem?"

"I'll have to let my commander know," Omari said. "I'll leave to gather my things and return . . . if I get permission."

"Outstanding!" Kwaku replied. "Please, eat your fill. I'm looking forward to our safari together."

Omari ate almost everything at the table. The morning guard let him through the gate, and he hurried back to his hovel. This was too good to be true. Kwaku was practically putting the jewels in his pouch. Omari rubbed his stomach on his way back. He hadn't eaten so well in months. It didn't take him long to grab his meager items and stuff them in a bag. He returned to the compound and was greeted at the gate by one of Kwaku's servants.

"Welcome back, Kofi," the servant said.

"Who . . . oh yes, thank you," Omari replied.

"Bwa Kwaku ordered me to show you to your room. Follow me."

The servant led Omari into Kwaku's home and the bedchamber on the first floor. This was a true honor. To be allowed into a merchant's home was as sign of respect and trust. Omari didn't know who was praying for him, but he hoped they continued.

He spent the day lounging around the compound. As the servants became distracted with their duties, he made his way to his objective; Kwaku's treasure room.

The door was unlocked. Omari stepped inside to admire Kwaku's collection. He had never seen so much wealth in one room except in Kiswala. There was so much he didn't know where to start.

"Is everything in order, constable?"

Kwaku stood beside him, his chubby fingers gripping his sash.

"It seems to be," Omari replied.

"I haven't had time to check my inventory," Kwaku said. "For all I know Efum has been stealing from me all along."

Kwaku waved his hand as if swatting a fly then walked away.

"I don't have time now. I must prepare for the safari."

Omari stared at the stacks of jewels, his mouth watering.

"Is there something else, Kofi?" Kwaku asked.

"Ah . . .no. Nothing at all."

"Good. I would like you to meet the guards I hired," Kwaku said. "I've done this many times, but I might as well use your expertise since I'm paying for it."

Kwaku laughed as he descended the stairs. Omari thought of shoving him down the steps then returning to grab handfuls of jewels, but there would be too many witnesses. Instead, he trudged downstairs to meet the guards.

The compound courtyard was filled with the pack animals and servants in preparation for the safari. Kwaku led Omari to a group of armed warriors milling near the gate. Omari recognized most of them as former soldiers, but two of them stood out. They were mercenaries, men he had worked with in the past. They saw him and their eyes widened. Omari shook his head and they responded, looking away.

Kwaku took him to a heavy-set man wearing a leather kilt and leopard skin shirt.

"Kofi, this is Manu," Kwaku said. "He is the commander of these guards. I have used him a number of times and he has served me well."

Manu extended his arm and Omari took it.

"I'm constable Kofi," Omari said.

"I'm familiar with most of our constables," Manu replied. "I don't know you."

"I haven't been here long," Omari said.

"That would explain it," Manu replied. "Kwaku told me you will oversee our safari, although I don't see why this is necessary."

"An added precaution," Kwaku said. "As I said before, it has no bearing on your skill or my trust of you, Manu. I find Kofi's presence comforting."

Manu didn't seem convinced.

"Comforting?" Manu frowned. "Is he your companion?"

"This is my decision," Kwaku said. "It would be disruptive if I have to replace you, but I will if you persist."

Manu scowled. "So be it."

He stepped up to face Omari.

"My warriors do not take orders from you," he said. "If you have any need of them, you come to me. Understand?"

Omari place his palm on Manu's chest then pushed him away.

"I take orders from Kwaku. I doubt if I'll have any use for your rabble."

"That's settled then," Kwaku said. "Kofi come with me. We must make sure everything is in order."

Omari followed Kwaku, his mood dark as they inspected the servants, wagons, and supplies for the safari. This situation was becoming more complicated every second. Once again, he considered marching into the jewel room, grabbing as much as he could carry then fleeing for the bush. But that was a rash decision that would most likely end with him dead. This safari was a perfect way for him to get what he sought. It would be easier to take the jewels while on the road and disappear. Besides, there was no need to be in a hurry despite Manu's attitude and the other men's suspicions. He was being paid and fed, which was a marked improvement from a few weeks ago.

Kwaku and Omari ended their inspection then parted ways. The next time they would see each other would be at the morning for the beginning of the safari. Omari was heading for his room when the two men from Manu's force approached him.

"Ket," one of the men called out. "A word."

Omari sighed then turned to meet them.

"Chamani, Masimba. What do you want?"

Chamani stepped close to him. The bald man gripped his belt then smirked. He was as tall as Omari but soft in places where Omari was firm. Still, he was a skilled fighter and dangerous man.

"The same thing you want," he said. "Since when did you become a constable?"

"He's not," Masimba said. Masimba sauntered to the opposite side of Omari. He was a head taller than Chamani, a lean ebony-skinned man and master grappler. Omari put distance between him and the two.

"Don't worry about why I'm here," Omari replied. "Just stay out of my way."

"I wonder what Kwaku would think if he knew you were just a common rogue like us?" Chamani replied.

"He'd toss him out of the compound no doubt," Masimba answered. "Call the real constables and have him beaten and locked up."

Omari folded his arms across his chest. "Like I asked before, what do you want?"

"An even split," Chamani said. "We figure whatever you're planning is going to be big. We keep quiet and you do the work."

"We figure you're planning to take what you can then disappear during the safari," Masimba said. "A good, simple plan."

Omari glared at them both. His right hand fell to his sword hilt, as did Chamani and Masimba. Chamani seemed unperturbed; Masimba's hand trembled.

"Agreed," Omari said.

He turned to walk away, then drew his sword and spun around, cutting Chamani's throat. Masimba scrambled backward attempting to draw his sword but Omari was too quick. He drove his sword into the man's chest then cut his throat as fell to the ground. Someone yelled and in moments Omari was surrounded by gawking servants.

Manu pushed through the crowd. He looked at Chamani and Masimba's bodies then glared at Omari.

"Why in Daarila's name did you do this?"

Kwaku appeared moments later.

"Kofi, what is the meaning of this?"

"I know these men," Omari said. "They're thieves. My guess is that they were planning to rob you once the safari was under way."

He shifted his eyes to Manu. "Did you know these men well?"

Manu swallowed before speaking.

"No, I didn't. I needed two more warriors to fill Kwaku's request and they were available."

"That was irresponsible," Omari said. "You jeopardized all of our lives."

"This comes out of you pay, Manu," Kwaku said. "I'll send for more constables to clean up this mess."

"No need," Omari said. "I'll handle this. I need a wagon and an ass."

Kwaku sent a servant for the wagon and the beast. The other servants loaded the bodies on the wagon then covered them with canvas. Omari led the beast from the compound and into the streets. Once again, he made his way to the river's edge, waiting until he was alone before dumping the bodies into the swift currents. As he made his way back to the compound, Omari decided he'd had enough of this charade. The first opportunity during the safari he would take whatever he could stuff in his bag and abscond. He'd make do with whatever he stole.

The morning came and the safari began. Omari rode at the lead with Kwaku. Manu and his warriors were scattered along the train of animals and wagons. They set a brisk pace once they were clear of the village, only stopping to eat and rest. Day after day passed but Omari could not find a perfect opportunity to execute his plan. Manu seemed determined to make up for the lack in judgement for choosing Chamani and Masimba. Security around the jewel wagon was extremely tight; Manu had his guards running twenty-four-hour shifts. They were getting closer to their destination. If Omari didn't make his move soon, he would end up with nothing.

A week away from their destination Kwaku summoned Omari to his tent to join him for dinner. The two sat opposite each other at a table that had no reason to be in the bush other than Kwaku's extravagant request. Kwaku prattled on about nothing while Omari picked at his food.

"My friend, what bothers you?" Kwaku asked. "We have almost reached our destination without incident."

"I'm aware of that," Omari replied.

"Then you should be happy," Kwaku said.

"My mood is because this journey will soon come to an end," Omari said.

Kwaku burst out laughing.

"I didn't take you for the sarcastic type," he said. "But if it will make you feel better, I have one more task for you."

Omari looked up from his plate. "What is it?"

"I need to send someone ahead to prepare for our arrival. Someone I can trust," Kwaku said. "I can think of no one better than you."

"What about Manu?" Omari asked.

"He's preoccupied with making up for his bad judgement."

Omari huffed. Another opportunity wasted. "What must I do?"

Kwaku opened a box resting by his left hand then took out a solid gold bar imprinted with adinkra hanging from a silver chain. He handed the necklace to Omari.

"You will take this into the city tomorrow. Once you arrive, go to the marketplace then put on the necklace. It identifies you as my representative. A member from the merchant guild with contact you and take you to my partners. They will arrange safe passage for us through the city."

A smile came to Omari's face as he admired the necklace. This was the moment he waited for. The necklace itself was worth enough to fill his pockets with stacks and pay his way back to the east. He gave the necklace back to Kwaku.

"When do I leave?" Omari asked.

"At first light," Kwaku said. "The journey will take two days at least. If all goes well, you and the others will reach us by nightfall on the third day."

"Everything will be fine," Omari said. "This I promise."

"I hope so," Kwaku said. "The success of this safari depends on it."

Omari's appetite returned and he ate with enthusiasm. He found it hard to sleep in anticipation of the next day. When morning came, he jumped from his bed and donned his uniform. He hurried to the animal corral and selected the best horses then made his way to Kwaku's tent. The merchant was waiting, having his breakfast outside his tent.

"You are punctual. Excellent!"

Kwaku stood with the case holding the necklace. He handed it to Omari, who put it in his waist bag.

"Remember, don't put it on until you reach the market district," Kwaku said. "Safe travels, Kofi!"

Omari bowed, climbed onto the black Sokoto, then rode away, holding the reins of the Malian warhorse. His plan was simple. He would ride to the town, but he would never meet with the merchants. Sati-Baa Lake was a few miles beyond his destination. Omari would go to the nearest port, sell the horses and the necklace then take a dhow across the sea. He was tempted to visit Sati-Baa, but he was not certain if his banishment was still being enforced. It was safer to sail to Haiset. The time to go home would come later.

Omari munched on hard bread, enjoying the peaceful ride. The Sokoto was a gentle horse, and the Malian was behaving. They climbed a steep rise then entered a section of the bush populated with trees whose canopies were tangled with vines. The undergrowth was sparse, a sight unusual for the bush of the region. Omari reached into his food pouch and frowned when he discovered it empty. He shrugged and whistled to pass the time.

The Sokoto stopped. Omari tugged at its reins, but it refused to move.

"Come on, beast!" Omari said. "Move!"

The Sokoto neighed then shifted, its large head swinging from side to side. The Malian snorted, pounding its hooves into the packed dirt.

"What the Cleave is . . ."

The Sokoto reared and Omari tumbled from its back. He hit the ground hard, the blow knocking the wind out of him. He watched the horse gallop by the Malian, running back to where it came. The Malian stood its ground, snorting and pounding its front hooves. Omari struggled to his feet. Something was coming.

Omari heard a piercing screech then was lifted off his feet by the neck. Sharp talons bit into his shoulders and he yelped in pain. He twisted his head upward and stared into a monstrous face of an asanbosam. Its primal eyes met Omari's terrified stare. The creature pulled Omari into the vines with its prehensile tail then attempted to bite his throat. Omari jerked his head away then hit the creature where its temple should be with his fist. The creature screeched again, letting him go. Omari fell then hit the ground, the air whooshing from his lungs.

The ngisimaugi sparked, his back warming as his shoulder wound healed. As he scrambled away from the beast attacking him, he heard the Malian neighing frantically. Asanbosams surrounded the beast. The horse kicked and stomped but they continued to come, running from within the woods and falling from the trees like hulking rain. Omari attempted to flee but was suddenly surrounded by a score of beasts that fell from the treetops. He decapitated the first beast to reached him then winced as another beast bit his calf. Omari stabbed it through the head then ducked as another beast jumped toward him. He rolled to a clear space, coming to his feet in time to meet the savage onslaught. Omari slashed, stabbed, kicked, and cursed his way through the vicious attack, pushing back fatigue and the fear of being eaten alive. His ngisimaugi burned, healing energy surging throughout his body attempting to seal the tears and bites destroying his flesh. Omari kept killing but the beasts kept coming. His legs gave way and he fell to his knees, refusing to succumb to the weakness spreading through him. Another chorus of sharp barks reached Omari's ears and it took everything in him not to be swallowed by despair.

The tree beast froze, then ran. Moments later a large pack of wild dogs surged by Omari in pursuit. The ansanbosams were now prey, chased by the small but voracious canines. They swarmed the beasts before they could climb to safety, dragging them down to their deaths. Omari staggered into the bush, the pain of his wounds and healing forcing him to hide. The dogs paid no attention to him, so focused they were on killing and consuming the tree beasts. Omari slumped against a tree, allowing the enchanted tattoo to do its work.

He was dozing off when a growl snapped his eyes open. A wild dog stared at him, one much larger than the others. Omari reached out for his sword, then stopped. There was something odd about the way the dog looked at him, something that told him he was not in danger. The dog inched closer, Omari's grip tightening on his sword hilt. The dog's nose flared, and Omari's chest scar itched. Its ears perked up, then it let out a sharp bark then trotted away.

Omari touched his scar, the wound he'd received long ago Wandatu.

"Eda blessed," he whispered.

Omari kept his diligence until the sounds of the feasting dogs lessened. He waited a moment longer before allowing the ngisimaugi to pull him into a dreamless sleep.

The discordant sounds of animals and people pulled Omari back into consciousness. He sat up then stood, pushing through the dull ache of his wounds. Trudging through the trees, he stepped into the road then gazed toward the commotion. It was Kwaku's group. The lead rider galloped up to him, his spear lowered. He raised it when he recognized Omari despite his ragged state.

"It's Kofi!" the man shouted.

The guards hurried to him, Manu the last to arrive. He looked at Omari in wonder.

"We saw the carcasses and assumed you were dead," Manu said. "How did you survive that slaughter?"

Omari shrugged. "I was lucky."

"Make way! Make way!"

Kwaku rode into the gathering. He clambered off his horse, ran to Omari and hugged him like a long-lost child.

"Praise to Eda!" he shouted. "I'm so happy to see you alive. I was afraid I would have to waste good gold to bury you."

Omari chuckled. "I'm happy to save you the expense."

Kwaku's expression turned serious. "Speaking of gold, do you still have the ingot?"

Omari's bag still hung from his shoulder. He reached inside then extracted the box.

"Excellent!" Kwaku said. "Manu, get Kofi to a wagon. He must rest and heal."

Omari followed Manu to a supply wagon then climbed inside. The commander looked at him skeptically.

"You're a lucky man, constable," he said. "Very lucky."

Omari laid back then grinned.

"As Kwaku said, Eda blessed."

They arrived in the city at dusk. Kwaku took the lead as they made their way to the market and met with the merchant guild. Omari was sent to their guild house where a healer tended to his wounds and provided him with fresh garments. He was sipping on a healing concoction when Kwaku entered the room.

"How do you feel?" he asked.

"Better," Omari replied. "I will be ready to return by morning."

Kwaku grinned. "Oh, you won't be returning with us. But that was never your plan, was it, Omari Ket."

Omari's eyes went wide.

"I don't know who . . ."

"Oh please, you can stop now," Kwaku said "I knew who you were the moment I saw you in my house that night. A rogue with a healing tattoo can't keep himself a secret."

Omari smirked. "I guess not." He sat up in the bed. "If you knew who I was, then why did you let this go on?"

Kwaku leaned into his chair. "To be honest, I didn't think I was going to survive the night. Your encounter with Efum was pure chance. I knew why you both were there, and I was sure one of you were going to kill me. I said all those things about you saving me praying to Eda that you would accept the ruse. And you did."

"Yes, I did," Omari replied. "I saw a chance to take more."

"As I hoped you would."

Kwaku pulled a chagga pipe from his robe. He lit it, took a puff then offered it to Omari. Omari took the pipe and took a long pull. This was good chagga.

"You discovering the other rogues was my good fortune," Kwaku continued. "The rest, I must confess, was my doing."

Omari handed the pipe back to Kwaku. "What do you mean 'your' doing?"

"I never intended to come here," he said. "I have always traded with Egbado because the road to Ile-Ife was too dangerous. The asanbosam made it so."

"You knew about them?" Omari felt his anger rising.

"Yes," Kwaku said. "When you showed up, I figured if anyone could survive an encounter with them, it would be you. So, I sent you ahead with the ingot. To be honest, I didn't expect you to return. I figured you'd either fail or clear the way and die in the process."

"The Cleave take you!" Omari said.

Kwaku raised his hands. "I understand your anger, and there's nothing I can do to keep you from killing me right now. Except this."

Kwaku clapped his hands. A servant entered the room with a large box. He placed the box on the bed then opened it. It was filled with stacks.

"Your payment," Kwaku said.

Omari's anger shriveled to the size of an ant.

"This safari made me extremely wealthy. Ile-Ife was always the more lucrative market. Now that I don't have to worry about the blood suckers, I can visit more often. I have you to thank for it."

Kwaku stood. "I have arranged for your stay with the guild until you are well enough to travel." Kwaku gave Omari another box. Inside was the ingot.

"Something to remember this safari by, although knowing you, it will all be gone by the next moon."

"I guess I should thank you, but based on what you did I won't," Omari said.

"Fair enough," Kwaku replied. "Goodbye, Omari Ket. Safe travels."

"Safe travels to you, Kwaku," Omari said.

Omari ran his fingers through the stacks as Kwaku left the room.

"This will last more than one moon," Omari said to himself. "Three at least!"

He climbed out the bed and began dressing in the clothes left for him near his bed. He was wealthy for a moment. He had much to do.

THE MARKET QUEEN

Omari hated the din of the Kuinus market. The smells, the crush, the yelling, and the laughter meshed to create a ruckus only an Asanteman merchant could love. But Kori had paid him well, so he would remain standing by the wood carver's stall until the cowries ran out or he completed the duty Kori hired him to do. As he watched the market goers walk by, he contemplated how unnecessary this job was. Kori was paying him more cowries than the person he owed. It was the principle, Kori said. He would not be intimidated to pay back a loan that he did not owe, at least not yet. It didn't matter to him that his creditor had lost thousands of stacks supporting the Asantehene's unsuccessful war with Oyo. He shouldn't have to pay for another man's mistake.

A crescendo of curses from his left caught Omari's attention. The crowd parted, revealing three men dressed in kente garb carrying clubs striding in his direction, their intent clear.

"Shit," Omari said. None of the men were carrying swords or knives, which meant he couldn't kill them lest he get in trouble with the local nyamas. Asanteman prided itself on keeping the peace, and Omari didn't want to be locked in a prison crypt. He took his war club from his shash, faced the approaching men, and waited.

It took the trio a moment to realize Omari's purpose. They ran at him, clubs raised and eyes focused. Omari stood his ground until the last moment, then sidestepped to his right. He smashed his club on the head of the man closest to him then watched him fall face first into the dirt as the others checked their rush. The men attacked in unison, Omari frantically dodging their blows. He ducked a wild swing then stomped one man's foot which made him howl. Omari punched him in his open mouth which he quickly regretted. The man's teeth cut his hand and his ngisimaugi flared to heal the wound. The other man tackled Omari, grunting when Omari brought his club down on his back. Omari hit the ground and the air rushed out of his lungs. He gasped as he turned his head to avoid the club meant for his face. The club struck the dirt, throwing grit into his eyes. Omari rolled, throwing the man from him then kicked out, hitting the man's nose, and breaking it. A club grazed the back of his head; he grimaced and rolled to avoid more blows.

Omari finally scrambled to his feet to face the man with the broken teeth. He caught the brute's club wielding hand then headbutted him, knocking him out. He then staggered to the big man who still held his nose. He hit him across the jaw, sending him into darkness.

Omari took a moment to catch his breath. When he looked up, a crowd of people stared at him, smiling and chattering. One person stood out, a richly dressed full figured attractive woman surrounded by a gaudy entourage. Gold necklaces covered her neck; golden bracelets climbed from her wrists to her elbows. A thick gold chain encircled her waist, and golden anklets complimented the golden thongs of her sandals. A man servant stood beside her, holding an umbrella to protect her from the sun. Omari grinned as he straightened up. Her smile widened and her eyes narrowed. Omari knew that look. He was about to approach her when a heavy hand fell on his shoulder. He spun around; his club ready to strike.

"No! It's me! Kori!"

"Cleave, man!" Omari said. "You startled me!"

Kori looked at the beaten men, a big smile on his face.

"Crawl back to Ekow and let him know what happens when you mess with Kori!" he shouted.

"This isn't over," Omari said.

Fear held Kori's face. "What do you mean this isn't over?"

"These fools were sent to wreck your stall," Omari said. "The next group will come for you."

"What will we do?" Kori asked.

"We won't do anything," Omari said. "You paid me to protect your merchandise. Protecting your life will cost more."

"How much more?"

"Twice what you owe me for this," Omari said.

Kori's fearful expression turned to anger.

"You're crazy!"

"Then our business is done," Omari said. He sauntered toward the woman who was still admiring him.

"Wait Omari!" Kori shouted. "We can work something out!"

Omari stopped before the woman then folded his arms across his chest.

"Impressive," she said.

"Thank you," Omari replied, ignoring his throbbing skull.

"Were you hurt?" she asked.

"No more than usual," Omari replied.

"Omari!" Kori yelled.

"I am Sintim Amba," the woman said.

Omari prostrated before Amba. "Omari Ket."

"Get up, no need for that," Amba said. "I have a feeling we have many things in common."

"I would like to find out," Omari said.

The servant holding the umbrella jumped between them.

"Watch your mouth!" he said. "Do you realize who you are speaking to?"

"Calm down, Manu," Amba said. "Omari is obviously not from Kuinus. Otherwise, he would know my status."

"And what is that?" Omari asked.

"I am market queen of Kuinus," Amba said.

Omari's eyebrows rose. This was very interesting.

"Walk with me, Omari," Amba said. "I'd like to get to know you better. I'll take you to my healer. He'll treat your wounds then you and I will go somewhere more private to discuss our . . . similarities."

"That sounds excellent," Omari replied.

"Omari! Talk to me!" Kori shouted.

"Your friend is calling you," Amba said.

"What friend?" Omari said. "We had business. It's over. Let's go see your healer."

Amba hooked her arm around Omari's.

"Let's continue," she said to the others.

They took a slow tour of the market, Amba's domain. She took time to speak to every merchant, hearing their words of good fortune and their grievances. Omari observed the merchants as they spoke with Amba. Some were friendly, others angry, and some hateful. But no matter their emotions, they all showed deep respect. No matter what they thought of her, they recognized her position.

The final merchant Amba spoke with was an elderly woman tending to a yam stand. She held a yam in her spindly hand, shaking it as she spoke.

"They're too expensive!" she said. "It's not like when you sold your baba's yams. These farmers are thieves!"

Amba shared a sympathetic smile with the woman.

"I know how you feel, Aunt Fayola," she said. "I will talk to the yam farmers soon. We must take care of our elders."

Amba bent over and kissed the old woman on the cheek.

"All will be well tomorrow," she said. "I promise you."

Amba took a ring from her finger then gave it to the woman. The old woman's eyes brightened.

"You are a true queen," the woman said. "You should be the Asantehema!"

"Don't say that too loud," Amba teased. "The Asantehene might hear!"

The woman pressed her finger to her lips and laughed. Amba ambled back to her entourage. She looked at Omari, her eyes heavy.

"Aunt Fayola always complains," Amba said. "She would fuss if the farmers gave her free yams."

Omari laughed and Amba smiled.

"You have an attractive smile," Amba said. "Has anyone ever told you that?"

"No, they haven't," Omari replied.

"Most people don't notice the little things," she said. "I do. That is why I'm market queen. I see the things people need that everyone else ignores."

"That is a talent," Omari replied.

"I can see what you need, Omari Ket," Amba said.

"I think anyone would if they looked in the right place," Omari said.

Amba laughed. "I think so, too. Come, let's see about your wounds."

They went a sonchai hut near the edge of the market. The building was covered with gris-gris; a Ndogo stood guard over the entrance. Amba nodded to one of her servants; the man hurried to the Ndogo and placed an offering of kola nuts at its feet.

"Kairu!" Amba called out. "Come out greet and me!"

The door slid aside and Kairu stepped out. He was a medium sized man with a balding head and wrinkled bearded face. Kairu checked the Ndogo totem for the offering then nodded at the basket of kola nuts.

"It is good to see you Amba," he said. "It has been some time."

'My health has been good thanks to your prayers," she replied. "This is Omari Ket. He needs your assistance."

Kairu gazed at Omari. He walked up to him then studied his head.

"You've been in a fight," he said. "Come inside. I have something for the pain and swelling."

Omari and Amba followed the sonchai into the hut. Like most sonchai huts, it was filled with shelves cluttered with gourds of various healing and medicinal concoctions. Kairu gestured to a stool.

"Sit," he said.

Omari sat then watched Kairu as he rummaged among his shelves. He finally grabbed a green container and a thin, stick-like object. He extended the stick to Omari.

"Chew this," he said.

Omari took the stick, stuck it in his mouth then chewed. A rush of pleasure spread throughout his body and the pain in his head subsided. Omari caught a whiff of the ointment Kairu applied to his wounds and grinned. He was very familiar with buku.

"What do you have for me?" Amba asked.

"It's on the third shelf," he said.

Omari watched Amba as she ambled to the shelf then picked up a small glass vial containing an amber colored liquid. She placed the vial in her pouch.

"Take this with you," Kairu said to Omari. He handed him the buku gourd. "Rub it on your wounds every few hours. It will speed the healing."

"Thank you, Kairu," Amba said. "It is always good to see you."

Omari and Amba left Kairu's hut and rejoined her entourage. They continued out of the city, walking through the surrounding farmland until they came upon a huge compound with magnificent painted walls.

"My home," Amba said.

The members of the entourage broke into song, and those within the compound answered. The gates swung open, and they were greeted by a throng of people. The people noticed Omari and surrounded him.

"Take him and prepare him," Amba said. Her eyes met his. "I will see you soon."

Omari grinned. "I hope so."

A servant led Omari to a row of small houses. She took him to the smallest of the houses then opened the door.

"Attendants will arrive soon with food, clothes and a bath for you," she said. "Welcome to our home."

Omari entered and the servant closed the door behind him. He sat at the table, leaning the chair back until his back rested against the wall. He dozed off for a moment and was awakened by the opening door. Two burly men carried a water filled tub into the house, followed by a servant with a tray of food and another carrying a kente robe.

"We will be right outside," the servant said. "Please let us know if you need assistance."

"I think I remember how to bathe," Omari said.

"You don't smell like it," the servant replied.

Omari slammed the door, almost hitting the servant. He took off his clothes, grabbed a warm yam from the serving plate then jumped into the tub, splashing water on the floor. He took his time eating before taking a proper bath and finishing the remainder of his meal. He picked up the kente robe and frowned; he had no idea how to wrap it.

"Hey," he called out. "I need help with this robe!"

The servants entered; their eyes went wide when they saw him standing naked holding the robe. A few of them smiled.

"If you stare any longer, I'm going to have to ask for payment," Omari said.

The servants set about dressing Omari. Once they were done, he slipped his feet into the gilded sandals then followed them to Amba's house. Amba waited in her greeting room, sitting on a cushioned stool surrounded by her entourage. She stood as Omari approached.

"Outstanding!" she said. "You look like an Asanteman noble."

"Some of them wished they looked like him," one of her sycophants commented.

"Now, now Thabisa. Let's not insult our own," Amba said. "Even if your right."

The others laughed. Amba extended her hand.

"Come with me, Omari."

Omari took Amba's hand then followed her into the next room. The servants closed the door behind them. In the room was a large bed. Amba took the vial she procured from Kairu and opened it. She placed a drop on her finger, then licked it. When she looked at Omari there was a sly grin on her face.

"Come here and take off my clothes," she said.

Omari obliged. As he disrobed her, he noticed her body change. Her skin became smoother, the lines about her eyes faded and her breasts lifted. By the time she was naked she seemed years younger.

"Do you approve?" she asked.

"I liked you the way you were," Omari said.

"But you're not complaining," Amba said.

Omari stripped off his robe. "Of course not."

He lifted Amba into his arms as they kissed then carried her to the bed.

* * *

Omari and Amba lay naked on the sheets, Omari twirling his finger in Amba's hair as she traced his chest scar with her fingertips. It had been a long time since Omari had slept with a woman so skilled, and he was thankful for it. From what he could tell, Amba was satisfied as well.

"Where are you from Omari?" Amba asked.

"Sati-Baa," Omari replied.

"The Jewel City," Amba said. "I've been there. It's amazing."

"Yes, it is," Omari replied.

"Why did you leave?"

"I had to," Omari said. "I offended a powerful woman. Someone a lot like you."

"There is no one like me," Amba said.

"She was rich like you, and beautiful like you," Omari said. "She came from fine lineage, like you."

Amba sat up. "Rich like me? That's possible. Beautiful like me? I doubt it. Fine lineage? That's where I know we're different."

Amba left the bed, Omari watching her hips sway as she walked to the table for a gourd of palm wine. She took a swig on her way back to the bed then handed it to Omari before climbing back into bed.

"I'm a farmer's daughter," she said. "My mama and baba raised yams on a farm not far from Kuinus. Feel my hands."

Omari put down the wine gourd then took Amba's hands. They were rough, with callouses at the base of each finger. He pulled her down and she lay on top of him.

"We worked the land every day during the growing season," she said. "At the end of the season a merchant would come from the city and buy our harvest. It was barely enough for us to get what we needed to last to the next season. When I was young, all I could do about it was be sad. When I became older, I decided to act."

"What did you do?" Omari asked.

"When the merchant came for our harvest one season, I hid a few yams for myself," she said. "After he was gone, I told my parents I was going to fetch water. Instead, I went up the road from our farm, sat on the ground and sold my yams. I made more cowries from that one basket than my parents made from the entire wagon load. I ran home to show my parents."

Omari kissed her breasts. "What happened?"

"My baba beat me," Amba said. "He told me I was going to ruin our business with the merchant, and that wasn't how things were done. We all had our place."

Omari slid his hands down Amba's back to her buttocks. Amba reached back and grabbed his wrists.

"Are you listening to me?" she asked.

"Of course, I am," Omari said. "You said your baba beat you for selling the yams."

Amba pushed her pelvis against his and grinned. "You have an interesting way of paying attention."

"I can't help it if your ass is distracting me," Omari replied.

They made love again. Afterwards Omari lay on his stomach. Amba lay on top of him, rubbing his back.

"Mama must have yelled at baba because next harvest she brought me two baskets of yams," she said, picking up where she ended. "We went up the road and sold them. When mama showed baba the cowries we made, he frowned.

"Do what you want, woman," he said. "If we lose our farm, it will be your fault!"

Amba sat up and stretched. "Some of the other farms began bringing us their produce because we paid them more than the merchant. Soon we had our own market."

"I bet the other merchants didn't like that," Omari said.

"They didn't. One day they showed up with clubs and knives, telling us if we didn't shut down our market, they would tear it down. Me and mama refused."

Omari rolled onto his back. He was interested now.

"What did they do?" he asked.

"They tried," Amba said. "That's when I learned something new about mama. She was a very good wrestler. She beat one man and two women so bad the others ran away. After that the other farmers said they would only sell their goods to our market. I realized that's why Baba didn't try to beat Mama when we returned with the money. He couldn't. I asked her to teach me how to wrestle, and she did."

"So how did you end up in Kuinus?" Omari asked.

"I wasn't a fool," Amba said. "I knew there was more cowries to make in Kuinus. So, I traveled to the city and made a deal with the market queen. I told her I could sell goods to them much cheaper than the other merchants. If she made me a member of the guild and let me set up a stall in Kuinus, I would get them produce at a good price."

"And she agreed?" Omari said.

"On one condition," Amba said. "I had to marry her. So, I did. It was a marriage of convenience. She paid a handsome bride price to my parents and I got my stall in Kuinus. As she aged, she gave more responsibility to me. When she died, I took her place as market queen."

It was Omari's turn to fetch the palm wine. Amba smacked his butt with her hand as he walked to the table and came back with the wine.

"So, do you have wives?" Omari asked.

"Many," Amba replied. "Most are marriage alliances. Only a few share my bed and my confidence."

"How many?" Omari asked.

"Twenty-three," Amba replied. "Why does this interest you? I don't take you as the jealous type. Besides, we haven't known each other long enough for that emotion."

"Just curious," Omari said. "I've never met anyone like you that was not of lineage. I'm impressed."

"See, we have much in common, Omari Ket," Amba said. "We both came from nothing, and now we are something."

"You are more something than me," Omari said as he lay back down in the bed. Amba wrapped her arms around his waist and pulled him to her.

"Give me more of whatever something you have," she whispered.

"My pleasure," he whispered back.

* * *

Omari woke alone. He yawned, stretched then threw the covers aside then climbed out of Amba's bed.

"Where are you going?"

Omari turned his head to see Amba standing before her bedroom door fully dressed.

"Away," Omari asked. "I suspect you're done with me."

"I didn't say that," Amba replied.

"You don't look as if you're staying," he said.

"I'm market queen," Amba said. "I must make sure the market opens successfully."

"Don't you have someone else to take care of that?" Omari asked.

"No," Amba replied. "I will return midday."

"Then I will return at midday as well."

Amba came to him then kissed him.

"Or you could just stay," she whispered.

"I have things to do as well," Omari said.

Amba shrugged.

"It's up to you," she said. "I can't make you. I hope to see you later. We have much more to talk about."

Amba left the room. Omari caught a glimpse of her entourage waiting for her and shook his head. He dressed then exited into the sitting room. To his relief everyone was gone. He found his way back to the guest homes. The tub was gone, and his clothes lay folded on the bed. He picked them up and sniffed them; they had been washed. He took off the robe and dressed. As much as he enjoyed Amba's company, Omari knew it was time for him to leave. He didn't need anyone to get attached, especially a person of power and wealth, which Amba definitely was.

Omari left Amba's compound and began his walk back to Kuinus. Kairu owed him the other half of his payment and he was going to collect. The stacks would be enough to purchase a good horse and enough supplies to get him to the interior to Nicran. From there he'd take a dhow across the Sati-Baa. As far as he was concerned, he was done with Asanteman.

Midday found him at a village searching for a small market to buy a meal. He was haggling with a woman selling a savory chicken and goat stew when he heard wailing coming from the main road. Moment later he saw the source of the commotion. It was Amba's entourage. The market queen was not with them.

Omari paid the woman for the stew then ambled to the entourage as he ate. One of the servants spotted him then ran toward him. He fell to Omari's feet, grabbed his ankles, and sobbed.

"What in the Cleave is going on?" Omari said.

"They took her!" the servant said. "They took Amba!"

The others ran to Omari as well.

"Who took Amba?" Omari asked.

"The Asantehene's warriors," another servant answered. "They were waiting for us at the market. "They said she was under arrest for conspiring with the enemy!"

Omari lowered his bowl. "Was she?"

The servants fell silent.

"Yes," someone said.

A slender young woman with beaded braids stepped forward.

"Who are you?" Omari asked.

"I am Efua, Aba's senior wife."

"So, what did she do?"

"Aba gave money and weapons to the Ngola of Oyo during the war," Efua said.

"Why would she do that?" Omari asked.

"Because the Ngola is one of her wives," Efua replied.

"That's too bad," Omari said. "I liked her."

He walked away eating his stew.

"Omari, wait!" Efua called out.

"This has nothing to do with me," Omari said.

"You are a fighter, are you not?" Efua asked.

"I am," Omari replied. "But I don't get involved with such things."

"Amba showed you hospitality," Efua said. "This is how you repay her?"

Omari laughed and kept walking. "We showed each other a few things."

"We will pay you," Efua said.

Omari stopped walking. "Pay me for what?"

"We will pay you if you rescue her and take her to Oyo," Efua said.

Omari scratched his chin. "Couldn't you send word to the Ngola? She could ransom her."

"To contact the Ngola would put the rest of us in danger," Efua said.

Omari handed his bowl to one of Amba's servants. "Do you know where she might be?"

"We know exactly where she is," Efua replied. "The Asantehene is holding her in his compound near Kongo. He will keep her there until a new merchant queen is selected, one more favorable to him. Then he will have her killed."

"I'm not sure I want to be . . ."

"Bring me the cowries," Efua called out.

A servant came to her side holding a large bag of cowries.

"This should be more than enough," Efua said. "I'm sure Amba will give you even more once she is free."

Omari did his best not to smile as he took the cowries.

"I'll need four horses and a guide," he said. "But I can't guarantee I'll succeed."

"That's all we can ask," Efua replied.

Omari joined the despondent entourage back to Amba's compound. He was given the horses as promised. His guide was a young boy who knew the land near Kongo. They left the compound, traveling three days before reaching the Asantehene's compound. Omari paid the boy a handful of cowries and he rode away with a happy grin. Once the boy disappeared down the road, Omari tied his horses in the bush then crept close to the compound. His plan was simple. If the compound was lightly guarded, he would wait until nightfall, slip inside, free Amba then ride for Oyo. It if was heavily guarded, he would take his cowries and head for Oyo. He liked Amba, but there was only so far he was willing to go for someone he barely knew.

Omari's reconnaissance revealed the compound to be mostly unguarded. Except for two guards at the gate, the only traffic he observed were servants. Apparently Amba was being well treated for the time being. Omari went back to his horses and found a soft spot beneath the ironwood trees. He would wait until dusk, then make his move.

When he woke up, he cursed. It was dark; he had overslept. Omari picked his way through the blackness with the horses in tow until the night torches from the compound came into view. With few guards, Omari decided to abandon stealth. He climbed onto one of the horses then rode onto the compound grounds. He was almost to the gate when the guards challenged him.

Omari unsheathed his sword and cut both guards down before they could raise their spears. He kept riding until he reached the main building. Omari stopped the horse, leapt off its back then ran into the building. Startled servants screamed and scattered as Omari searched from room to room for Amba. He finally found her bound and gagged in a servant's room. There were bruises on her face and her bottom lip bled. Omari untied her gag and her hands. Amba leaned into his arms.

"Omari? What are you doing here?"

"Efua paid me to find you," he said.

"Sweet Efua," Amba said. "She is a good wife. I'm afraid she made a mistake."

Omari lifted her to her feet. "How so?"

"This is a trap," Amba said. "The Asantehene knew someone would come for me. He hoped it would be Ngola warriors. If so, he could prove to the elders I betrayed him and confiscate my wealth and property. After he had me killed, of course."

"He told you this?" Omari said.

"No, it's obvious," Amba said. "If he wanted to get rid of me, he would have killed me moons ago."

Omari heard voices shouting orders and the sound of running feet.

"Shit," he said.

He took his jambiya from his belt and gave it to Amba. Amba frowned.

"This? This is all you give me?"

Omari frowned. "Follow me," he said.

Omari ran down the hall, Amba close behind. Just outside the compound door the Asantehene's warriors assembled, preparing to into the building. Omari swung his hand cannon round then loaded it.

"What is that?" Amba asked.

"Our only chance," he replied. "When I run, you run."

Amba nodded.

The warrior commander was still shouting orders when Omari emerged from the house with the hand cannon, the matchstick burning in his left hand. The warriors pointed at him and the commander spun about to face him.

"Who are you?"

Omari lit the hand cannon. The blast took down four warriors and sent the others scrambling for cover. Omari ran to the gate, Amba close behind. The market queen stopped long enough to take a sword from one of the fallen warriors They were almost to the bush when another rank of the Asantehene's warriors emerged from the cover.

"Give me my jambiya and get behind me!" Omari shouted.

"Here's your little knife." Amba tossed him the dagger. She raised the sword then charged the warriors.

"Amba!" Omari shouted. His heart dropped as he ran after her, knowing he would be too late. The nearest warrior threw his spear. Amba sidestepped it then drove her sword into the man's neck.

"By the Cleave!" Omari said.

He attacked the warriors before they recovered from the shock of being assaulted by Amba. Together they cut their way through and plunged into the bush.

"I was supposed to save you," Omari said.

"I told you my Mama taught me to wrestle," Amba replied. "How about we save each other?"

They ran through the bush the entire night, finally stopping as daylight spread through the trees and shrubs. Both collapsed as they caught their breath.

"Praise be to Eda," Amba said panting.

"Do you know where we are?" Omari asked.

"Yes," Amba said. "I've been to the Asantehene's southern compound many times as a guest."

Amba stood. "Come. We will stay close to the bush. The warriors will be seeking us on the road. There is a village not far from here. We can bribe a fisherman to take us to Oyo. We will be safe there."

Omari and Amba reached the fishing village that night. They rested in the bush overnight until entering the village the next day. The village chief, another one of Amba's wives, found a fisherman willing to take them to Oyo. Two weeks later they arrived in Ajalaland, Oyo. To Omari's surprise Amba's entourage waited for them.

Efua ran across the beach to meet Amba, hugging her tightly. She greeted Omari the same way.

"I knew you could do it!" she said to him.

"You knew more than I did," Omari said.

Efua turned her attention back to Amba.

"The Ngola sends her best wishes," Efua said. "She said you can remain here as long as you like."

"That won't be long," Amba said. "The Asante-hene is probably attempting to name a new market queen as we speak, but no one will vote until he can prove I am dead."

"We will prepare to depart then," Efua said. She walked away shouting orders to the others.

Amba looked at Omari. "Come with us."

Omari shook his head. "I don't want to be involved in a war, which is where you are headed."

"A war I will win," Amba said. "It's about time the person who truly rules Asanteman sat on the Gilded Stool."

"I'll pray to Eda for you," Omari said.

"Marry me," Amba replied.

"What?"

"Marry me," Amba said. "I'll make you commander of my army. You will also have access to my bed. We'll have strong children, and they will continue to rule Asanteman long after we become ancestors."

"It's a tempting offer," Omari said, "but I can't. I'm not one to stay in one place for long, and the politics of rule don't appeal to me."

"Then promise me you will return," Amba said. "There are still many things we don't know about each other."

"We'll see," he said. "There is a matter of my cowries."

Amba laughed. "Always the businessman."

She took off one of her gold necklaces and draped over Omari's shoulders.

"That should be sufficient."

"Yes, it is," Omari replied. "One more thing. Can I borrow your fisherman?"

"He will take you anywhere you wish," Amba said.

"Thank you, market queen," Omari said. "I won't forget you."

"Nor will I forget you, Omari Ket."

Omari sauntered toward the beach then stopped. He turned around and walked back.

"Amba!" he shouted.

Amba turned to face him.

"What would my bride price be?"

Amba grinned. "There's only one way to find out."

Omari grinned, turned about, then walked away.

THE SHADI KHAIN

Omari trudged through the Malian sands under a relentless sun. He reached for his water gourd then thought better of it; it was his ration for the day. When it was gone there would be no more until tomorrow. He cursed the circumstances that forced him this far north to serve in the mansa's mercenary reserves. He was too far away from the moist forests and coastlines of southern Ki Khanga, and he was in a foul mood.

That mood darkened when he spotted a group of Malian horros approaching the reserves. The muwanis normally rode at the head of the column, Malian infantry in the center, and the lowly mercenaries reserves in the rear. The horros saw harassing the mercenaries as entertainment. Sometimes the games became dangerous, and mercenaries were fatally wounded. Omari kept his eyes averted from the muwanis; he had no time for their sport.

"Mikijen!" a horro shouted.

"Shit," Omari whispered. He continued to walk without meeting the horro's eyes.

The horro invaded the mercenary ranks, blocking Omari's path with his horse. Omari looked up at the gaudy dressed man as he shielded his eyes from the sun.

"What?" he said.

"They say the Mikijen are the best mercenaries in Ki Khanga," the horro answered. "I say the best mercenary is the worst fisi!"

The other horros laughed. Omari smirked then walked around the horro's horse. The horros followed him.

"Where are you from, Mikijen?"

"Sati-Baa," Omari replied.

"Ah, the merchant city! Now I am sure you are not a muwani unless we were fighting with money purses!"

The other muwanis laughed harder than the insult deserved. Omari was losing his patience.

"They say the people of Sati-Baa cower when they hear the Frog Hag is nearby. Tell me, is she your mother?"

Omari stopped in his tracks. He turned and glared at the horro.

"No," he replied. "Your grandmother was."

The horros ceased laughing. They jumped from their horses; swords drawn. Omari turned to face them. There were five horros; he figured he could kill at least three before sprinting into the desert. He looked the other way; three horros were still on their horses, blocking his escape route. There was no place to run. He shrugged. He was tired of marching anyway.

The horro stomped up to him. "You have insulted me! I demand a Test!"

Omari began to take out his sword but a blue robed Targani mercenary grabbed his hand.

"No, my brother, this is not a duel," he said through his veil.

"Then what the Cleave is it?" Omari asked.

"There are rules to challenges," the Targani replied. "If you kneel to him and acknowledge that you are inferior to him, he will leave you be."

"That's not going to happen," Omari said.

"That's too bad. We will need all the men we can gather if we are to face the Fezzani. Your death will be unfortunate."

"What's next?" Omari said.

"You must determine who has the stronger ashé," the man said.

"How do we do that?"

"Each man is allowed shoot an arrow or throw a spear at the other. If your ashé is strong it will deflect the projectile. Whichever man is hit and falls must concede."

"That's stupid," Omari replied. "The man that goes first will win."

"Not always," the Targani said. "Malian horros are not very good archers."

Omari pulled away from the Targani.

"I am ready," he said.

The others spread out. The horro took his bow from his horse. The Targani tried to give his bow to Omari but he refused it. Omari took a wide-legged stance then stared at the horro.

"I'm in your hands, Eda," he whispered.

The horro grinned as he drew back the bow-string. He let the arrow fly. It struck Omari in the shoulder. He grimaced and stumbled backwards from the impact of the arrow, but he did not fall. The wound burned; the arrow was poisoned. The ngisimaugi on his back warmed, fighting the poison's effect. He was about to break the arrow but the Targani stayed his hand. He gripped the arrow then gently twisted it before pulling it free, Omari clenching his teeth. The Targani tossed the arrow to the ground.

"Who are you?" Omari asked.

"Amma Ag Salla," the man replied.

"Why are you helping me?"

"Because I hate horros."

"So why are you here?"

Amma grinned. "It is a long story. I will tell you if you live."

The horro handed his bow to one of his companions then smirked as he placed his hands on his hips.

"Your turn, Mikijen," he said. "Strike while you can!"

Omari's time was running out. His vision blurred; the ngisimaugi wasn't working fast enough. He snatched a jambiya from his waist sash then threw it hard. The blade struck the horro in the center of his forehead. The shocked look on the horro's face fell away as he collapsed into the sand.

"So much for your ashé," Omari said. His legs gave way and he collapsed to his knees.

"You Malians make good poison," he slurred.

The horros were rushing toward him when he blacked out.

* * *

It was dark when Omari awoke. The desert heat fled with the sun and he shivered. He lifted his head to see a thin blanket covering his body. Omari looked up expecting to see the night sky but saw canvas instead. He sat up to get a better assessment of his situation. He was inside a large tent, surrounded by items that were not his.

"What's going on?" he whispered.

"Ah, you are awake at last!"

Amma appeared over him. He removed his veil, revealing his bearded brown face and wide smile.

"Where am I?" Omari asked.

"In your tent," Amma replied.

Omari scratched his head. "I don't have a tent."

"You do now," Amma said. "The horro you killed was wealthy. The others determined that since you killed him during a formal challenge whatever was his became yours, even if you are not a horro. Such are the rules of a challenge."

This was good news, Omari thought.

"What did I inherit?" he asked.

"This tent and all that is in it," Amma said. "You also gained three Bornu stallions, one camel, and two pack donkeys."

"No servants?"

Amma shook his head. "No, but that is no issue. I will be your servant, as will the other Targani."

Omari frowned. "Why? What's in it for you?"

Omari couldn't imagine Amma's smile getting any wider, but it did.

"Better rations and better portions of the loot once the battle is done."

"If we survive," Omari said. "By the way, who's paying for these better rations?"

"You are, of course."

"And why should I do that?"

Amma's smile faded.

"I took you to be an honorable man, Mikijen. I would think you would feel some obligation toward me and my brothers since I assisted you during your duel."

"Assisted me? I seem to remember that I was the only one pierced by an arrow."

"True, but it was because you followed proper duel protocol as I instructed that we have benefitted. In addition, a true horro would have a proper entourage. It reflects your status and is a guarantee of protection from any disgruntled horros."

"What about the horro's entourage?"

"You killed a man of their bloodline and possibly a close friend to many. Do you want to trust your wellbeing to them?"

Amma made sense, but Omari didn't trust the Targani any more than the Malians. At least he understood the Malians' motives.

"How many more Targani are there?"

"Fifteen."

"Shit."

It would take a lot of stacks to feed sixteen warriors. He looked about the tent until he spotted a large wooden chest.

"Twenty stacks," Amma said.

"What?"

"There are twenty stacks in the chest," Amma said. "More than enough to feed me and my brothers."

"And I'm supposed to trust your count?"

"Yes," Amma said. "Unlike you, I am an honorable man."

"You are now that I'm still alive."

Amma grinned. "That too."

"I'll give you eight," Omari said. "Half a stack per man. That's more than the Malians are paying you."

"The Malians aren't buying our loyalty, only our swords," Amma countered.

"Neither am I. Eight stacks. Yes, or no?"

Amma rubbed his chin as if contemplating Omari's offer. Omari didn't care. If Amma said one more thing he would strangle him.

"It is not a good offer, but we will accept it," Amma said.

"Good," Omari said. He started to lay down.

"Only if you promise to share your spoils with us after we defeat the Fezzani."

Omari jumped from the bed. Amma had barely grasped his knife hilt when Omari kneed him in the groin. As Amma bent over to grabbed himself his chin met Omari fist. Amma fell onto the sand, holding his groin with his left hand and his chin with his right. Omari opened the tent flap, revealing the other Targani. He grasped Amma's shirt then dragged him out of his tent.

"Eight stacks for all of you!" Omari shouted. "And if I get killed, I want them back!"

He stormed back into the tent, shutting the flap behind him. He was sitting when the flap opened. Amma peeked inside, still holding his chin.

"What is your name, Mikijen?"

"Omari Ket," Omari answered.

"It is a good name," Amma said.

"Go away, Amma," Omari snapped.

"Sleep well, Omari Ket."

* * *

The next morning Omari found the Targani gathered outside his tent, forming a ring around a camel dung fire. The smell of sand baked targuella bread, meat sauce and tea reached him and he was suddenly famished. The Malians ate separately, a few of them cutting glancing at their gathering. The Targani nodded as he approached then made space for him. Amma sat opposite him, smiling despite his swollen chin.

"It is good to see you Omari," Amma said.

Omari grunted then accepted the bread and tea. The bread was gritty but filling; the tea excellent. Amma turned to one of the other Targani, a tall man with a narrow face.

"Badis, what do the horros say?"

"They say we will fight the Fezzani tomorrow," Badis answered. "They have marched a long way as well and are eager to rest."

"Good," another Targani said. "I'm tired of all this walking. We could be back home raiding caravans."

"We've made more stacks marching than fighting," Amma said. "And now that we are companions of the Mikijen, we will make more."

"You better earn it," Omari said. "Or I'll kill you myself. Besides, the Fezzani will attack today," Omari said. "They want the Malians to think they're resting. It is a ruse I've used many times."

"You should say something to them," Amma said. "Warn them."

"Why?" Omari poured meat sauce onto his bread then ate. It was delicious.

"Because we all will be fighting them," Amma replied. "Our lives will be in danger, too."

Omari shrugged. "All we have to do is stay to the rear. Let everyone else do the heavy fighting. If the Fezzani lose the advantage, we will join. If they begin to overwhelm the horros, we will be the first to flee."

Amma nodded. "I see why you have survived so long as a mercenary. You know when or when not to fight."

Omari's words sobered the mood which was his goal. He didn't like these Targani, but it was always good to have more muwanis around when going into battle. It increased the chances of survival.

"Mikijen!"

Omari dropped his head and sighed.

"This early?"

The Targani stood and pulled their swords from their baldrics. Omari finished his bread as he trudged back to his tent and retrieved his weapons. By the time he returned a contingent of horros confronted his group. One of the riders nudged his horse forward then lowered his face scarf, snarling through his beard.

"Mikijen! The man you killed yesterday was my friend, a horro of noble standing and strong blood. His family will mourn because of you!"

Omari shrugged. "So?"

Amma rushed to Omari's side.

"What my master meant is that he feels remorse for what occurred, but your noble friend's death occurred in an honorable manner. His family will mourn, but they will do so knowing that he died with his reputation intact. Isn't that what you meant, bwa Ket?"

"I meant what I said, Amma," Omari whispered.

"Let me handle this," Amma whispered back, "unless you want to fight this army."

"And why should our ways apply to you?" the horro asked.

Amma bowed.

"They should not, but it is known throughout Ki Khanga that the horros of Mali are the most generous and honorable of all."

The horros nodded among themselves, apparently soothed by Amma's platitude.

"I am Boubakar Fode," the horro announced. "I have come to avenge my friend Amadou Soros and reclaim what was his."

Another horro rode forward, leading a horse.

"You will fight me on horseback," the horro said. "I choose lances."

"Give me the lance. Keep the horse," Omari said.

The horro threw the lance. It stuck in the ground near Omari's sandaled feet. Omari smirked as he pulled it free.

"You should use the horse," Amma advised. "Horros are poor archers, but they are excellent lancers."

Omari rested the lance on his shoulders. "Find out what he owns."

The horros and mercenaries cleared as Omari and Boubakar took their places. Omari gripped the lance with both hands then waited. Boubakar pulled back the reins of his warhorse and the beast rose up on its hind legs before charging toward Omari at full gallop. Omari dug his feet into the sand, measuring the decreasing distance between him and the beast. When he sensed the timing was right, he lifted the lance over his shoulder with his right hand, twisted his waist and threw the lance. The lance tore through the horse's neck, almost impaling Boubakar. Rider and horse tumbled head-first into the sand. Omari was not a good horseman, but he was an excellent spearman.

He was sauntering up to the two when Boubakar stood. He was not dead or injured. The horro drew his sword and shield then advanced. Omari took out his sword and jambiya. Steel clashed and the duel began. Omari's confidence diminished with each exchange for Boubakar was an excellent swordsman. A swirl of dust and sweat rose over them as they fought, neither gaining nor losing ground.

A blaring trumpet halted their fight.

"To arms!" someone shouted. "The Fezzani are attacking!"

Boubakar broke away. He sprinted to the horse meant for Omari, mounted, then rode away with the horros.

"I hate being right," Omari said.

The Malian force formed ranks, rallying around the banner bearers. The skirmishers formed the front line, followed by the spearmen and then the horros. Omari and the other mercenaries formed the reserve. Once organized they marched to battle. Omari and the Targani walked slowly as the other mercenaries followed the army in tight formation.

"Remember what I said," Omari said. "Stay in the rear until the outcome of the battle is certain either way."

"This does not feel right," Badis said. "It isn't honorable."

"You've spent too much time in Mali," Omari replied. "Dead men can't spend stacks. Horros fight to die. Mercenaries fight to live."

"Omari is right," Amma said. "We didn't come here to die."

The Targani nodded and Omari smirked. Amma had become the unofficial second in command of their group. The others seemed used to taking commands from him; he was probably a person of rank among their kel. In the end it didn't matter. Once this battle was done, they would go their separate ways.

The army marched up a low incline then down into a depression. As the mercenaries reached the summit the Fezzani army came into view. They were a sight to see, their white robes and bright orange turbans is stark contrast to the Malians muted ivory uniforms. A raucous noise of horns and tap drums filled the space between them. Omari's experience told him the armies were about equal in size, which meant superior tactics and spirit would win the day. He had no sense of the Fezzani's disposition, but his dealings with the Malians indicated their arrogance might be the death of them.

One person stood out among the Fezzani; a dark dressed figure on a stately horse surrounded by retinue of heavily armed muwanis covered in red robes. Probably some noble who had come to observe, one who thought watching hundreds of muwanis kill each other good entertainment. As the Fezzani marched into the depression to meet the Malians, the person and its muwanis remained at the crest of the hill, as did Omari and the mercenaries.

The battle began with a collective war cry from both sides and a feeble exchange of arrows. The skirmishers crashed into each other, followed by the heavy infantry. As the foot soldiers engaged, the cavalries from both sides moved to flank the opposing armies. Camels, horses and warriors clashed on both flanks, struggling for advantage. The battle seemed a stalemate, each side taking as good as it gave. Omari spotted the weak point minutes later. The Malian infantry was making headway in the center; with the right support they could split the Fezzani front and perform a double-flanking maneuver, forcing the Fezzani to either retreat or be slaughtered.

"Let's go!" the mercenary commander shouted.

Omari grinned; the commander had seen the advantage as well.

The mercenaries marched double-time down the slope for the center. Omari and the Targani lagged, Omari assessing the battle as they advanced. His eyebrows lifted in curiosity as he watched the noble's entourage move toward the fray. Apparently, this was a person who liked to get a little bloody. Whoever it was, they had miscalculated.

His musing was interrupted by the horns and drums of the Fezzani. The army began to withdraw in an orderly fashion, their cavalry and skirmishers providing a buffer to allow the others to form ranks. The Malians displayed discipline as well, holding their positions instead of breaking ranks to press their advantage.

It was then Omari saw the noble throw back their hood. It was a woman, a stern countenance ruling her otherwise pleasant face. She raised her hands over her head and mouthed words Omari could not hear. Green luminous tendrils seeped from her fingers, coalescing into a ball of light resembling fire.

"Run!" Omari shouted. He spun on his toes, sprinting as fast as he could. The Targani needed no urging. They turned and followed him.

"What is happening?" Amma said between breaths. "Why are we fleeing?"

Omari looked over his shoulder. The woman stabbed her arms toward the Malian force and the green flames swept down the slope, expanding to a torrent twice the size of the army. Men and animals screamed as the flames overtook them. Terror gripped Omari as the fiery wave surged toward them. There was no way they could outrun it.

"Get down!" Omari yelled.

He dove face first into the sand then prayed to Eda. Omari clenched his teeth, waiting for the burning. He'd been scorched before, so he knew what was to come. Instead, he was engulfed by a coldness he'd never experienced. Frigid pain stabbed him like ice daggers, sapping the heat and spirit from him. As darkness replaced the cold, a sudden burst of heat made him cry out. The source was his ngisimaugi. The tattoo burned his back like a brand iron, driving away the green flames then spreading out to cover the hapless Targani. Just when Omari thought he couldn't stand the heat any longer it subsided, replaced by a warm afterglow.

Omari pushed himself onto his back, his heavy breath forming a cloud of mist over his face. After a few moments he sat up. The Targani writhed in the sand, moaning and cursing. Amma's eyes found his, then focused beyond him. Omari sat up then turned his head in the direction Amma stared. The Fezzani wandered among the dead Malians, searching their garments for valuables. The woman that caused the carnage and her entourage galloped through the looting muwanis directly toward Omari. He struggled to his feet then drew his sword. The Targani did their best to do the same. The sight of them standing with weapons drawn caught the attention of the other Fezzani. They stopped their looting, raised their weapons then followed the sonchai and her muwanis.

The Fezzani surrounded them, leaving a gap for the sonchai's group. They passed through the gap then stopped before Omari. The sonchai dismounted then stood before Omari. She spoke to the others without taking her eyes off Omari.

"Put down your weapons and you might live," she said. "Keep them and you will die."

Omari was the first to drop his swords. The Targani did the same, glaring at Omari as they did.

"Take off his shirt," she said.

The sonchai's muwanis converged on Omari. In moments he stood naked to the waist. The sonchai circled behind him and he felt her palms press against his back.

"Kipande," she whispered.

She strode away.

"Take him. Kill the others."

The Targani reached for their swords as the Fezzani moved in with their lances lowered.

"No!" Omari shouted. "They are my men. They are not Malian. You have no quarrel with them. We are only mercenaries. Whatever you want from me you will not get if they don't come."

The sonchai turned to face Omari, a smirk on her face.

"You talk as if you have something to negotiate."

It was Omari's turn to smile. "I'd be dead if I didn't."

The sonchai's smile faded.

"Bring the Targani as well. Take their weapons."

Omari looked at Amma and nodded. The Targani gave up their weapons then crowded around Omari.

The sonchai smiled.

"We are done here."

The muwanis tied Omari and the others together. The sonchai mounted her steed then rode
away, her muwanis and her captive trailing behind.
The Fezzani army took a few more minutes to finish
their looting then fell in line behind the sonchai.
They marched up the dune then disappeared beyond the hillcrest.

* * *

A cool night breeze slipped through the Fezzani encampment like a mischievous interloper,
stirring the victory banners and rattling loose
chords on the sturdy tents. Omari waited for the
sonchai in a small tent near her camp, sipping on
date wine and nibbling on sweet cakes. This was not
what he expected. Despite his protests the Targani
were taken elsewhere with assurances they would
be well treated. He'd been given fine Fezzani robes
for warmth and perfumes to cover his stench.

Though he was being well treated, he worried. The sonchai wanted something from him,
most likely the secret of his ngisimaugi. She probably wanted to know how it protected them from her
green fire. Such knowledge would be valuable to her
and the Fezzani. But Omari had no idea how or why
it happened. Never had he seen the tattoo respond
in such a way. It healed wounds, but it never protected him from harm, until now.

His tent flap opened and two of the sonchai's
muwanis entered. Both swept the tent with their
eyes then stood at attention on either side of the entrance. The sonchai entered, walking to Omari then
sitting opposite him. She wore a heavy cotton robe
with a hood protecting her head. She said nothing

as she stared into his eyes without blinking. Omari shifted nervously then smiled.

"My name is Omari Ket," he said.

Her eyebrows rose.

"Interesting. You are from Sati-Baa."

"Yes, I am," Omari answered. "How do you know?"

"Your accent and your name. I am familiar with the merchant city. I spent some time there."

The sonchai looked about the tent.

"Are you happy with your accommodations?"

"Yes I am. But I am curious about why you are treating me so well. If you are going torture me, I wish you would get about it."

The sonchai tilted her head, seemingly confused.

"Why would I torture you? Your ngisimaugi would heal you. Such a thing would go on forever."

"Then what do you want from me?"

The sonchai stood then began to pace.

"I need your help, Omari Ket. There is an object I must possess, and I can only obtain it with your assistance. In return I will make you one of the wealthiest men in Ki Khanga."

"And what makes you think I can or would help you?"

"You can help me because of your ngisimaugi," the sonchai replied. "It is said that the tattoo disappears when a Mikijen leaves the service of the Kiswala or dies. Yet here you are with your tattoo intact. Why is that?"

"I don't know," Omari confessed.

"It is because the gods favor you, that's why," the sonchai answered. "You have been allowed to retain your ngisimaugi for a purpose. Maybe my quest is that purpose."

Omari didn't think so, but he would let this sonchai continue to delude herself. He remembered well the day he stood face to face with Eda. If this were her reckoning, he would know.

"The reason you will help me is because you are a mercenary, and you value money above all else."

The sonchai clapped her hands. The tent flap opened again, and two more muwanis entered the tent, struggling with a large wooden chest they carried between them. They sat the chest near the table, bowed, then left the tent.

The sonchai grinned. "Open it."

Omari knelt before the chest. He opened it then gasped. A tear formed in his right eye and rolled down his cheek. Never his life had he seen so many stacks!

"There will be another one if we return," the sonchai said.

"When do we leave?" Omari asked.

"At sunrise," the sonchai answered.

"I'll be ready."

The sonchai stood then turned to leave. After a few steps she halted the turned again to face Omari.

"What about your companions?"

"What companions?" Omari asked, still gazing at the stacks.

"The Targani. What is to become of them?"

Omari had forgotten about Amma and the others. He sighed as he closed the chest.

"They will come with us. They might be useful."

"I could have them killed if you wish," the sonchai said.

"No," Omari replied. "I hear the Targani are excellent fighters. I have a feeling that wherever we're going, we will need them."

"You are correct, Mikijen," she said. "By the way, my name is Kurat ul-Ain. You may call me Kurat."

"I'll see you in the morning, Kurat."

"You most certainly will," Kurat said.

The sonchai left Omari's tent, followed by her muwanis. Omari went back to the chest, knelt then hugged it. He had no idea if he would survive this journey, so for at least this night he would enjoy being one of the richest persons in Ki Khanga.

* * *

Omari woke with the morning sun. He dressed then made his way to where the Targani were being held. Kurat had been true to her word; the desert people sat together as was their way, enjoying their sand-baked bread, meat sauce and tea. Amma was the first to see him. He clambered to his feet, greeting Omari with a bow.

"Omari! It is good to see you are well."

"Good to see you, too."

"It seems you are the reason for the change in our circumstances," Amma said.

"They haven't changed much," Badis said. "We are still among these Fezzani dogs and we are still following you."

Badis scratched his ass then farted. The others laughed.

"You ungrateful jackals," Omari said. "The sonchai asked if she should kill you and I said no. I'm sure there will be fighting wherever we go, and I trust you more than I trust them."

"Pardon my asking, but how will you pay us?" Amma said. "The Fezzani took everything."

Omari opened his pouch and took out a leather bag.

"Like this," he said.

He tossed a bag to each of them. It was more that they would have earned with the Malians plus what he would have shared with them. A large sum to them, but a small dent in the chest at his tent.

Badis jumped to his feet, took out his sword and began to dance. The others clapped in time with his steps.

"I take my fart back!" he said to Omari.

"I wish you could," Omari replied.

Amma did not join in the celebration. He tossed his bag up, caught it, then put it in his pouch.

"I assume there is much more in your tent," he said.

"You assume right. Don't get greedy," Omari replied.

"No, no. What you have paid us is more than enough. What must we do that is worth so much?"

"We must help the sonchai get something of great value to her. Like I said, I trust you more than I trust the Fezzani. When we march off with her, I want you with me."

"And most of us will follow you," Amma answered.

"Most?"

"You have given us a small fortune," Amma explained. "When we reach the city, we will buy camels, goats, cloth and gems then take them back to our kel. It will lift our status."

Omari frowned. "That sounds practical."

"It is," Amma agreed. "We are not true mercenaries like you. We have families and lineages we must support."

"Do what you want," Omari said. "Just make sure the best fighters stay."

"I'll try my best," Amma said.

It was all Omari could ask for. He shared breakfast with the Targani then returned to his tent.

The Fezzani army marched for three days before reaching the oasis city of Rakat. The city lay on the border between Fez and Targa and was the first stop for all caravans entering the country. Three large springs fed the fertile landscape and the local people thrived among the bounty of farming and trade. It was also in Rakat where the Fezzani army separated, each unit heading to its homeland. By the end of the first day the force had dwindled to a few local units, Kurat and her muwanis, and Omari and his Targani.

The Targani were anxious to get about their business and Omari did not stop them. He was anxious too, but his intentions were far different from theirs. It took him longer than he liked, but he found the bath house near the largest spring. The ornate tent was so massive it resembled a permanent structure. Two hulking guards stood on either side of the entrance; their arms folded across their well-muscled bare chests. Both men word red pantaloons with gold sashes tied around their narrow waists. Wide bladed scimitars sheathed in leather baldrics hung from their shoulders. The men gripped the golden hilts of the weapons as Omari approached. Omari reached into his shoulder bag then pulled out a pouch of stacks. The men smiled in unison then opened the tent flap for him to enter.

Omari entered paradise. The smell of frank-
incense and roasted goat filled his nose as his eyes
reveled in the parade of scantily clad men and
women before him. They all smiled at him as they
went about their duties of waiting on and pleasur-
ing the myriad of patrons. A tall, plump lovely
woman wearing a sheer silk dress approached him.

"Hello sahib," the woman said. "I am Yasmine, and this is my establishment. How can I serve
you?"

"I need a bath for starters," Omari said.
"Maybe three. We can discuss my other needs later."

"Follow me," Yasmine said.

Omari followed the matron, his eyes transfixed on her swaying hips. It had been a long time
since he'd felt a woman's touch, and he was anxious
to clean up and make up for lost time. Yasmine led
him to a room within the vast tent, a tent within the
tent. The attendants pulled back the flap, revealing
a large wooden tub, steam rising from the hot water.

"If you need anything, please ask one of your
attendants," Yasmine said.

"I definitely will," Omari replied.

Omari proceeded to immerse himself in
wonders of the pleasure tent.

* * *

Three days later Omari emerged from the
pleasure tent into the bright morning sun.

"There you are!"

Amma, Badis and the remaining Targani
waited on their camels outside the tent. There were

half as many as they were when they arrived at Rakat. Omari frowned.

"Where are the others?"

They have set out for Targa," Amma replied. "Did you enjoy yourself, Mikijen?"

"Yes," Omari replied.

Badis stepped close to him then frowned.

"You smell like debauchery."

"Whatever I smell like, it's better than your farts," Omari replied.

Badis fought back a grin.

"The sonchai sent her commander to fetch us," Amma said. "The time to depart had come."

"Let's not keep them waiting then," Omari said.

Omari followed the others on foot, refusing to ride the camel they'd bought for him. There would be plenty of days ahead rocking to and fro on the back of the beast.

The sonchai and her muwanis waited at the edge of the oasis. Omari counted forty; twenty belonging to the sonchai, the others Fezzani muwanis probably lured by the prospect of payment. They stared at Omari and the Targani with frowns on their faces.

"It seems we are not welcomed," Amma said.

"Did you expect to be?" Omari asked.

"No," Amma answered.

"Then you weren't disappointed."

Kurat acknowledged Omari and the others with a curt nod and the journey began. They traveled for three days, taking rest during the night. They veered off their route twice to take advantage of nearby oases but on the most part remained on course. On the fourth day Kurat called a meeting among her commanders. Omari and Amma were invited to represent the Targani.

The meeting began that night before a roaring fire. How Kurat's caravan managed to bring so much wood was a mystery. Omari suspected, but he was not going to say, even after the journey was over. Sorcerers were obsessed with their secrets and Omari didn't want to be on the list of Kurat's enemies. He was on too many lists as it was.

Kurat appeared flanked by two guards. Their ivory-colored garments were like the Targani, yet they carried no weapons. Tattoos covered their faces.

Omari leaned close to Amma.

"Who are the men with Kurat?"

"They are Al-Askari, warrior priests. This is not a good sign."

"Why," Omari asked.

"The Al-Askari protect all sorcerers of Fez. If Kurat has summoned them, that means this is a particularly dangerous journey."

Amma grinned at Omari. "I hope you enjoyed the bathhouse. That may have been your last opportunity. We are truly in Eda's hands now."

A tall, wide woman dressed in the turquoise robes of a mapmaker stepped between Kurat and the others, a leather map case tucked under her arm. She knelt in the sand, opened one end of the case then took out a map and unrolled it. Kurat sat beside the woman; the woman gave her a carved pointer then disappeared into the darkness.

"We are almost to our objective," Kurat said. "We journey to the Sand Cliffs, the home of the Shadi-Khain."

Kurat pointed to the bluffs on the map. The Fezzani shared nervous glances. Kurat waited until they settled down.

"Don't worry," Kurat said. "We are prepared."

One of the Fezzani raised his hand and Kurat looked at him.

"You have a question, Aziz?"

"There is no way we can surprise them," he said.

"That is not our intent," Kurat replied. "We want them to see us."

"We will lose many," another Fezzani said.

Kurat's eyes narrowed as she looked at the woman.

"As I said Faiza, we are prepared."

"With what?" the woman asked.

"Dear Faiza, always the difficult one," Kurat said. "Don't forget who I am. You of all people know what I'm capable of."

Faiza nodded then looked away. There was history between the two, Omari thought, and it wasn't pleasant.

"Our assault will be a distraction," Kurat said. "Our main attack will take place here."

Kurat pointed at another section of the cliffs bordered by forests and a river.

"That looks worse," Omari said.

"There is a path that leads to the top of the cliffs," Kurat said. "It is steep, yet climbable. The Targani will sneak into the Shadi-Khain city and obtain the object we seek."

Omari raised his hand. "How will we know what we're looking for?"

"I will be with you," Kurat said.

"Then who will lead the decoy assault?" a third Fezzani asked.

"I will."

The man who answered emerged from the darkness, his appearance a terrible memory for Omari. He wore a white robe contrasting with his blue-black skin. His eyes radiated a bluish hue. He scanned the warriors, his attention lingering on Omari. The other Fezzani didn't seem disturbed by his presence.

"I am Jat," the man said. "I assure you the object we seek is just as important to my people as it is to yours. It is why I have come to guarantee this task is successful."

"Then why aren't you coming with us to retrieve it?" Omari asked.

"The Mikijen speaks," Jat said. "You have a history with my people. I believe it was unpleasant."

"It was, for him," Omari replied.

Jat's eyes narrowed, and Omari realized he'd made a mistake. His right hand found his sword hilt. To his surprise, Jat laughed.

"It seems that it was," he said. "Maybe it was destined that you are here. It gives you a chance to redeem your past discretion."

"The Targani and I will leave at first light," Kurat said, interrupting Omari and Jat's uncomfortable exchange. "The rest of you will follow the next day. I will send a signal to Jat when we are in position. That is all. Rest well."

The commanders returned to their men.

"Omari," Kurat called out.

Omari sauntered up to the sorcerer.

"Yes?"

"Take your warriors and gather your things. We leave now."

"We haven't had time to rest," Omari complained.

"We'll rest when we reach our destination."

Omari and Amma returned to Targani camp.

"We're leaving now," he said.

"But Amenokal, we must rest!" Badis protested.

"Gather your possessions. We ride tonight."

The Targani grumbled but did as they were told. Omari finally succumbed and climbed onto his camel. He led the way to Kurat and her protectors and they proceeded into the night. By daylight they reached the forest edge. To their right the Shadi-Khain Hills rose over the treetops. Djeles sang that the cliffs were the remains of massive mountains destroyed by Daarila's blow. The land was once a forested paradise, but Daarila's vengeance robbed it of its vitality.

As they neared the woodlands a path came into view. Kurat and the Al-Askari followed, Omari and the others close behind. It took two days climbing the gradual slope for the forest to reach the highest level of the cliffs. A river separated the green forest from the tan sands.

"We'll camp here," Kurat said.

As Omari and the others set up their camp, he observed Kurat take a wooden bird figure from her robes. She held the inanimate object close to her lips then whispered. Omari jumped as the figuring came to life, fluttering its wings and hopping in Kurat's palm. She tossed the bird into the air and it flew away down the path in the direction from where they had come.

Omari and the Targani made a fire then prepared their evening meal. Kurat and the Al-Askari ate separately.

"She studies us," Amma said.

Omari munched his bread and meat paste. "Does she?"

"Yes," Amma said. "I don't think she trusts us."

"If she didn't, we wouldn't be here," Omari said. "She trusts us to do what we're here for. We're safe for now."

Badis lowered his cup from his mouth. "For now?"

Omari nodded. "She needs us to get whatever she came for. Why, I don't know. The sticky part will be what happens once she gets it."

"She will have no use for us," Amma said.

Omari nodded again.

"What will we do once she gets it? Run?" Badis asked.

Omari laughed. "None of you goats are that fast. We make sure we get it and keep it until we return to Fez."

"The Al-Askari will kill us and take it from us," Badis said. "We are dead."

"Shut up, Badis," Omari said. "Like I said, we're safe until Kurat finds what she's looking for. But just in case, we'll take turns on the watch tonight."

"The Al-Askari will be on watch too," Amma said. "It is said they never sleep."

Omari finished his bread then washed it down with a swig from his water gourd.

"We'll find out tonight, won't we?" he said. "Badis, you have first watch."

Badis grimaced. "I'm beginning to think you do not like me, Amenokal."

"I don't," Omari replied. "Let's get some rest. Wake me for second watch."

Omari slept as soon as his head touched the ground. He dreamed of Sati-Baa, its wide avenues, bustling streets, tall buildings, and vibrant people. In his dream he was the boy he barely remembered, running through the throngs, stealing food from merchants, and fighting other street children. Badis's calloused hands woke him from his nighttime revelry.

"It is your turn, Amenokal," he said.

Omari grunted as he sat up, glancing toward Kurat and the others. The sorcerer slept, but the Al-Askari remained awake. One guard stared into the surrounding forest. The other watched the Targani.

"So, they don't sleep," Omari commented. "And they don't trust us."

Omari sat on watch until daybreak. The camp awoke, and after a short meal they crossed the river into the land of the Shadi Khain.

"Keep your eyes to the sky," Amma said.

"Why?" Omari asked.

"The Shadi Khain ride the giant gora," Badis answered. "When they kill you, they let their mounts eat you."

"Is this true?" Omari asked Amma.

"It is," Amma confirmed.

"Great," Omari said.

"Be quiet," Kurat said. "We are near their city. Ket, come with me. Everyone else stay here."

Omari was about to urge his camel forward when Kurat shook her head.

"No," she said. "We will walk."

Omari motioned for his camel to kneel and he dismounted. He joined Kurat and they walked ahead of the others.

"What is so important that you trust me more than your Al-Askari?" he asked.

"They protect me, but they don't serve me," Kurat said.

"Then why are they here?"

"They were sent by Hamid Al-Hamza, Sultan of Fez."

"What does he have to do with this?"

Kurat frowned. "Al-Hamza is the most powerful sorcerer of Fez, which is why he is sultan. He suspects I'm gathering talisman to challenge his rule."

"Are you?" Omari asked.

Kurat grinned. "Al-Hamza is short-sighted. He has rested his fat ass on the Fez throne for so long he thinks ruling our land is all there is. He has no idea of what's to come."

"And what is that?" Omari asked.

"If you survive this journey, you will see," Kurat answered. "In the meantime, I require you to perform a task."

"What is it?"

"At the moment we begin our attack on the Shadi Khain, I need you and your warriors to kill the Al-Askari."

"I thought we were to attack with you," Omari said.

"That was the plan, until the Al-Askari arrived. I need them dead so Al-Hamza eyes will be blinded to what I claim."

"Are they powerful sorcerers?"

"How do you know they are sorcerers?"

"They are bodyguards, yet they carry no weapons."

"They have some skills," Kurat admitted. "But they are not immortal. They die like everyone else."

"This will require more payment," Omari said. "Another chest of stacks."

"You shall have it," Kurat replied.

Omari smiled. "Then consider the Al-Askari dead."

Kurat smiled. "Good. Let's return to the others."

The Al-Askari eyed both with suspicion when they returned. The Targani gathered around Omari.

"What did she say?" Amma asked.

Omari scanned them all before speaking.

"Follow my lead," he said.

They gathered at the edge of the cliff; their eyes fixed on the east. As they waited, the wooden bird Kurat sent away days ago returned, alighting on her shoulder. She grabbed the bird, opened it then read the script that had been written inside.

"They will be here soon," she said. "We must be ready."

Kurat nodded at Omari and Omari turned to the Targani.

"Follow me."

Omari ran to Kurat the placed himself between the Al-Askari.

"Go!" he shouted to Kurat. "Targani, surround . . ."

He was silenced by a blow to the mouth from one of the Al Askari. Before the man could strike him again Badis tackled him. They rolled across the ground then the Askari threw Badis aside. The Targani remained on the ground, his head twisted at an odd angle.

"Shit!" Omari said.

He drew his sword and jambiya and attacked. To Omari's amazement the Askari blocked his blades with his hands and forearms without any damage. The other Askari was surrounded by the Targani who despite their numbers could not kill the man. Omari's distraction cost him; the Askari drove his fist into Omari's gut, knocking the wind out of him and sending him to the ground on his back. Omari expected the Askari to attack him, but instead the man ran after Kurat.

Omari rolled onto his back then struggled to his hands and knees. The Askari was gaining on the sorcerer. Omari stood then stumbled after them. Though his breath slowly returned, there was no way he would reach the Askari in time. There was only one way he could stop him.

Omari reached for his hand cannon and began loading it. He was almost done when an ear-piercing screech shattered his concentration. There was a blur before him and the Askari was gone. Omari looked up and saw a terrible sight. A huge gora clutched the man in its claws. It climbed into the sky, guided by the Shadi Kain warrior riding its back. Screeching filled the air as the Targani ran for cover, leaving the other Askari alone. The warrior ran toward Omari then joined his companion, swept away in the claws of a giant gora.

Omari completed loading the hand cannon then ran after Kurat. The sorcerer had to survive or they wouldn't get paid. Another loud screech grabbed Omari's attention. He took a matchstick from his bag and lit the cannon fuse before turning his head toward the sound. A swarm of gora bore down on him, their riders grinning through their helmets. Omari grinned back as he swung the hand cannon toward them. The charge exploded, riddling both birds and riders with lead shot. The force of the blast knocked him to the ground. He rolled then clambered back to his feet. The blast had the desired effect. Some goras wriggled in the dirt, their wings shattered, their riders dead. The other goras scattered in every direction, startled by the sound. Omari caught up with Kurat just as she was entering a cave entrance ringed with carvings. He reached out and touched her shoulder. Kurat spun and sliced the air with a short sword, barely missing Omari.

"What are you doing here?" she shouted. "You should be dealing with the Al Askari."

"They're dead," Omari said. "I came to help you."

"I don't need your help," she said.

"You can't go in there alone," Omari said.

"You forget who I am," Kurat said.

Omari turned and began walking away.

"Wait!" Kurat called out.

Omari turned around and returned to Kurat.

"Lead the way," she said.

Omari entered the cave. The damp granite under their feet was grooved to improve traction. Torches burned on the damp walls lighting the way.

"Where are we going?" Omari asked.

"I don't know yet," Kurat replied. "I will know when I feel it."

Urgent shouts and curses reached them as they advanced. The passageway widened until they stood just outside of a large cavern. Sunlight lit the space filled with Shadi-Khain and their grotesque mounts. Half-eaten bodies of fallen Fezzani lay scattered the cave floor. Kurat's decoy attack was working, but at a great cost. Kurat glanced at the bodies with no emotion.

"This way," she said.

Omari followed the sorcerer to the rear of the cave. They entered another torch lit passageway, following it until it ended before a crudely carved door. Though the seams between the door and the cave wall were visible, there was no knob, latch, or handle to open it.

"This is it," Kurat said.

She closed her eyes then whispered in a language Omari didn't recognize. Kurat's hands glowed; her pressed her palms against the stone door then pushed it open. Bright blue light poured from the room and filled the passageway. The light source was the largest piece of kipande Omari had ever seen. Omari was fascinated and horrified. That much kipande radiated enough energy to kill them both if they ventured too close.

"How do you expect to claim that?" Omari said. "We should leave now before the Shani Khain discover us."

Someone shoved Omari aside. His head struck the wall, dazing him. When his vision returned, he saw Jat, the strange sorcerer, standing before the kipande.

"You've done well, Kurat," he said.

Kurat went to Jat.

"Is it enough?" she asked.

"More than enough," Jat replied. "Take my hand."

Kurat took Jat's right hand. With his left hand Jat touched the kipande. Omari expected the sonchai to burst into ashes. Instead, a bright flash blinded Omari and triggered his ngisimaugi. A shield of heat engulfed him, causing Omari to cry out. When the light and the heat dissipated Omari found himself sprawled on the cave floor. His eyes cleared to Jat and Kurat standing over him. Kurat had transformed, her skin and eyes the same as Jat.

A wide smile filled her face. Jat's expression looked at Omari with curiosity.

"Interesting," he said. He raised his hand, the appendage glowing blue. Omari's ngisimaugi responded, the heat almost unbearable.

"No," Kurat said. "I told you he was special. That's why I chose him."

Jat looked disappointed. He lowered his hand then glared at Omari.

"Another time, Mikijen," he said. "This is your second time. There won't be a third. The sonchai never forget."

Jat and Kurat's features blurred then they dissipated like ashes blown away by gentle wind. Omari lay there for a moment longer, struggling to comprehend what just happened.

"By the Cleave," he whispered.

He scrambled to his feet and ran back the way he came. He entered the main chamber and stumbled to a stop. The stench of burned gora and Shani Khain bodies was terrible. He covered his nose and dashed through the passageway leading out of the cave.

Omari emerged into the glaring sunlight. The sand outside the cave had been melted into glass. Ahead of him the river dividing the forest from the cliff was a trickle, the water vaporized. The forest didn't fare much better. Burned trees stood like spent matchsticks and the smell of charred fleshed wafted through them. The damage was less the further he traveled. He stopped when he reached the place where he left the Targani.

"Amma!" Omari called out.

"Amenokal!" Amma replied.

The Targani emerged from the bush. There was a smile on his smudged face and his garments displayed signs of damage.

"We thought you were dead," Amma said.

"Then why did you linger?" Omari asked.

"There was the matter of the extra pay," Amma said with a smile.

Omari counted four Targani and frowned.

"This is all that are left?"

Amma nodded. "The fire caught them before they could find cover. How did you survive the explosion?"

"I don't know," Omari replied.

Amma looked behind Omari as if expecting someone else.

"Where is the Fezzani sorcerer? Is she dead?"

"She's gone," Omari said. "At least for now."

Amma's face fell. "So how do we get our stacks?"

Omari laughed. Amma was a kindred spirit. The man had survived something neither had ever witnessed but could only think about his pay. He walked up to Amma and patted his shoulder.

"Be glad Eda spared us," he said. "Our life is payment enough this time."

Omari walked through the Targani, following the trail deeper into the bush.

"It's a long walk back to Targa," he said. "The sooner we get started the better."

The Targani fell in line behind him. As he tramped down the trail, he thought of Jat's parting words.

Another time, Mikijen.

"Not if I can help it," Omari whispered.

RESPITE

Omari sat on the steps of his bungalow, watching the sun creep over the horizon as the breeze from the ocean cooled his skin. He took a sip of his Uchi Gwensi tea and closed his eyes as the warm brew caressed his throat on the way to his empty stomach. He bit a large chunk from the flat bread in his left hand, chewing slowly to enjoy the savory herbs baked inside.

Clamorous voices reached his ears, and he turned his head toward their source. Fishermen strolled toward the waves with their nets hanging from their shoulders. Omari finished his tea and bread then went into his hut to get his net. He hesitated as he looked at his armor and weapons piled in the corner opposite of his bed, then grabbed his net and went back outside wearing only his loincloth. He sauntered across the sandy beach, feeling more relaxed than he had in years. As he waded into the warm waters, someone called his name.

"Ket! You out here beating the waves again?"

Omari turned to see Jabali's grizzled face split with a snaggle-toothed grin.

"The sea won't be the only thing I'm beating if you keep talking," Omari shot back.

Jabali dropped his net then lifted his fists. "I'll send you to Daarila with a sweet cake on your head!"

Omari laughed with the others. He made his way over to Jabali.

"I'm ready for another lesson," he said. "What are we catching today?"

"You won't be catching anything," Jabali chided. "The rest of us are catching devilhorns."

"I've never heard of them," Omari said.

"No one has outside of Bwejaa," Jabali replied. "They come from the deep twice a year to spawn. The best time to catch them is when the great moon appears. The high tide pushes them close enough for us to net a few."

Adia, Jabali's daughter, waded close to them. A dingy tunic covered her from shoulders to knees, her short-beaded braids dangling about her ears. The lithe woman took her net from her shoulders before nodding to Omari.

"They are a fragile fish," she said, "because they come from the deep. We take them to market and sell them as soon as we catch a net full. Most people eat them raw. They are a delicacy."

Omari frowned. In his experience delicacy meant they tasted terrible, but people acted as if they were delicious because of the rarity. Still, he would try his hand at it. He had more than enough cowries but adding to his pile never hurt.

"How do we know where they are?" he asked.

"We look for the graywings," Jabali said. "When you see graywings, you find devilhorns."

"Ya haa!" a fisherman shouted.

Omari, Jabali and Adia turned to see Reth gesturing toward the sea. A flock of birds, graywings, formed a writhing cloud of feathers and wings as they dove into the surf. The avian swarm followed the tide to the shore. The fishermen hurried through the water, positioning themselves for the approaching school. Minutes later the devilhorns were within casting distance, their dorsal fins slicing the surface. Omari gripped the net with his teeth then casted with his hands, letting the net go as it flared out into a circle. The net crashed into the waves, sending devilhorns skittering over the surface, some of them leaping into the air. A few of the airborne fish never returned to the waters; they were caught by the swarming graywings.

Omari pulled in an empty net. He watched in frustration as Jabali and Adia tossed their nets then pulled them back in packed with devilhorns. Omari gathered his net, tossing it out again, and again and again with no results. The others were wading back to shore with full nets when Omari threw his net again. This time when he went to retrieve it, it didn't budge.

"Daarila's breath!" he yelled. Jabali warned him about catching his net on a rock. It would be torn and need repairs once he freed it if he freed it. Omari gathered the slack in his net, bent his knees then jerked with all his might. The net moved toward him, then to his surprised surged the other way. This was not a rock. He dug his feet into the submerged sand to prevent whatever was in his net from pulling him out to sea. Omari moved back one step at a time, struggling with the thrashing net. As he dragged his catch into shallower water, he saw a large tail flicking about. He heard splashing behind him; moments later Jabali appeared beside him, his eyes wide with excitement.

"Keep pulling!" Jabali said. "You have a big one!"

"A big one what?" Omari asked.

"We'll soon see!"

The other fishermen flocked around him, each grabbing a portion of the net and helping him pull the thrashing behemoth onto the shore. Adia ran to the net with a club, whacking the fish until it lay still. She looked at everyone with wonder.

"It's a bunafish! A bunafish!"

The fishermen began dancing. Omari dropped the net then rubbed his sore thighs.

"What in the Cleave is a bunafish?" he asked.

"It is a wonderfully expensive fish," Jabali answered. He grabbed Omari's hands and began dancing with him.

"It must have followed the devilhorns in to eat them," Adia said as she joined their dance. "We will make enough money to keep us fed for months!"

Omari stopped dancing. "We?" His hands gripped his waist. "I seem to remember this bunafish being caught by my net."

Jabali ceased his prancing and approached Omari. "Our lives are hard, Omari. There are times when all of us catch fish and times none of us do. To keep from starving we always share our bounty."

"I'm not one of you," Omari replied.

Jabali's shoulders slumped. "That is true. You are not. We will do what you wish. We understand you not wanting to share with us, even after we gave you a bungalow and taught you how to throw the net."

"And we will honor your choice, even though you will need our help cleaning the bunafish, taking it to market and smoking what you do not sell so it will not spoil," Adia added.

"Okay, enough!" Omari said. "I get eighty percent, you get twenty."

Jabali smirked. "That is acceptable. For that we will do twenty percent of the work."

"To the Cleave with all of you!"

Omari didn't know why he was angry. He didn't need the cowries. He could give the entire fish to them and be content.

"So, what do you wish to do?" Jabali asked.

"Even split," Omari said. "But I get to keep the teeth."

"Agreed!" Adia said. She and Jabali danced.

They dragged the bunafish to the dunes then went to work. Omari watched the fisherman butcher the fish then carve it into thick filets. Adia cut a sliver of meat from the fish then took it to Omari.

"Taste it," she said.

Omari popped the meat into his mouth. The flesh possessed a blend of sweet and savory flavor, unlike any fish he'd tasted before.

"This is delicious! I see why it is so expensive."

Adia ate a slice as well. "They say when eaten raw, bunafish is an aphrodisiac." A sly smile formed on her face and she winked. "I guess we will soon see."

Omari frowned. "They say a lot of things."

"Stop flirting you two," Jabali said. "We need to get this fish to market!"

"I'm not flirting," Omari replied. "It's your daughter."

"Leave Omari alone, Adia," Jabili said. "You have enough husbands."

"Don't tell me what to do, baba!" Adia snapped. "Mama had eight."

"And look where it got her, Eda keep her soul."

Omari walked away to assist the others. One of the fishermen, Jimoh, pulled a rickety wagon to them and they loaded it with the bunafish and the devilhorns then covered them with heavy canvas. They hitched a donkey to the wagon then proceeded to the market. The fishermen's families gathered around with drums, pipes, sticks and whatever they could make noise with, forming a raucous band announcing their arrival to the market. Market patrons left the vendors and came to them, curiosity in their eyes.

"What is this?" a curious woman asked.

Jabili pulled back the canvas.

"Devilhorns . . . and bunafish!"

A collective gasp filled air then became a verbal melee as patrons and merchants swarmed the wagon. Omari and the others had to bat away stealthy hands attempting to steal a fish or two from the cart. They continued the procession until they reached the market center. After they secured the wagon behind a stall, the fishermen placed their money gourds on the counters and the wild bidding began. Omari did not join in the fracas; he had no talent for bartering. He would have to trust that the fishermen would be more honorable than he would be when it came time to divide the cowries.

"What's all this?"

Omari turned to see a woman with dark brown skin wearing leather breast armor and pants standing next to him. A sword and dagger hung from her waist belt. Like Omari, she was not from the village, most likely a traveling merchant or the bodyguard of a local headman.

"I caught a big fish," Omari said. "My friends are selling it."

The woman studied Omari, her eyes lingering on his ngisimaugi.

"Since when did Mikijen learn to fish?" she asked with mirth in her voice.

"Since two week ago," Omari replied. "And I am no longer a Mikijen. Haven't been one for a long time."

"I was mistaken," the woman said. She extended her arm. "I am Thandiwe."

Omari took the woman's arm. Her grip was firm, that of a fighter.

"Omari," he said.

"Tell me, Omari, why would a former mercenary give up the sword for a fishing net?"

"One has nothing to do with the other," Omari replied. "I gave up serving the Kiswala long ago. Fishing suits me for now. What brings you here?"

"Just passing through," Thandiwe said. "Our dhows needed supplies, and this seemed to be as good a place as any to stop for them. It's a good thing. Looks like we'll have bunafish in our bellies tonight."

"Eda smiles on you," Omari said.

"I think I'll go put in my bid," Thandiwe said. "I hear bunafish is an aphrodisiac. It would be interesting to find out if that's true."

Thandiwe's eyes swept Omari again before she ambled away.

"Good to meet you, Omari. Keep your sword sharp."

"And your eyes open," Omari replied.

A grin came to his face. Whoever this Thandiwe was, she had much experience with the

Mikijen if she knew one of their sayings. It was then Omari became suspicious. He watched her as she made her way to the fishermen's stall, how she studied each person as they passed her by. As she neared the booth, two others joined her; a tall, dark man that reminded Omari of the Nuba warriors from the north and a woman with the girth and musculature common among the warriors of Oyo. They examined the crowd as Thandiwe focused on buying fish.

"Slavers," Omari muttered.

He sprinted back to his bungalow, then donned his clothes and weapons. By the time he returned to the market Thandiwe and the others were gone. He hurried back to the beach. If they were truly slavers, their dhows would not be far. He walked the beach for spans, searching for the vessels with no luck. He relaxed; maybe Thandiwe was being truthful. They may be merchants passing through, seeking a respite just as he was. He recalled the woman; she was pleasant looking and full framed. A smile came to his face. He sheathed his sword and returned to the market.

By the time Omari returned the fishermen had sold most of bunafish and devilhorns. Everyone squatted in a circle behind the stall as Jabili counted out the cowries, dropping them one at a time in gourds. He spied Omari approaching and frowned.

"Where did you go?" he asked.

"For a walk," Omari replied. "I'm sure you counted out my portion while I was gone?"

Jabili frowned.

"Let's start over."

The other groaned as they poured their cowries back into the collection basket. Omari squatted with them and Jabili began counting again.

It was almost dark when the tallying was done and the remaining bunafish smoked and shared between the fishermen. The additional cowries meant Omari could extend his rest, but he wasn't sure it would be in Bwejaa. He'd had his fill of quiet; he was ready for a bit of gambling and debauchery.

"Omari, wait!"

Omari turned to see Adia jogging toward him, a big smile on her dimpled face. He thought of running, but instead continued his laconic pace.

"Omari, did you eat more bunafish?" Adia asked.

"Yes, I did," Omari replied. "It was delicious, especially the smoked meat."

"How do you feel?" she asked.

"I feel full," Omari replied.

"Full where?" Adia asked while reaching for his crotch. Omari caught her wrist and guided her hand to his stomach.

"Full here."

Adia's smile faded. "That's disappointing."

"I guess bunafish doesn't work for everyone."

"Maybe you should eat more," Adia said.

"I'm tired, Adia," Omari said. "You should look for Jimoh. He told me the back of your thighs make him sweat."

Adia's face glowed. "Really?"

"Yes."

"Rest well, Omari!" Adia scampered away to find Jimoh.

Omari reached his bungalow. He latched his door just in case Adia decided to be persistent, took off his clothes then fell into his cot and immediately to sleep.

His slumber was shattered by the breaking down of his door. Bodies fell on him, fists striking his face while hands grabbed at his arms and legs.

"Hold him tight so we can tie him!" a gruff voice said.

"Hurry up!" another voice said. "The dhow is ready to leave."

"Thandiwe won't leave without him," a third man said. "He's the prize."

Omari felt a rope slide over his ankle. He drew his left leg in hard, kneeing one of the men on top of him. The man howled and his grip loosened; Omari slipped his right arm free then punched another man in the face. He wriggled free and a fist fight took place in the darkness with Omari giving more than he received.

"Let's go!" one of the men shouted. "He's not worth it!"

The men fled Omari's bungalow. Omari grabbed his sword and dagger and chased them. He stumbled when he saw Bwejaa burning and heard the wailing of the villagers. The men sprinted toward the shore where two canoes waited.

"Where is he?" he heard Thandiwe shout.

"He fought back," one of the men said. "If you want him so bad, you go get him. We have enough."

The men climbed into the canoes. Thandiwe smiled then blew Omari a kiss.

"Another time, Omari!" she shouted.

Thandiwe climbed into the canoe with the others. Omari watched them row to their dhow, climb aboard then sail away.

Omari ran to the village. The shabby buildings were fully aflame; no effort would stop the destruction. In a matter of moments, the town ceased to exist.

The cries from behind him took him by surprise. He turned to see Jabili and the other fishermen running toward him. He held his arms wide.

"Stop," he said. "There is nothing you can do."

The fishermen ignored him. They ran to the edge of the fire, a few of them attempting to enter the flaming wreckage. Eventually they fell to their knees, crying as the fire continued its rampage. Omari walked up to Jabili then sat beside him.

"How can this be?" Jabili asked. "Who would do this?"

"Slavers," Omari answered.

Jabili's head jerked toward Omari.

"Slavers?"

"I met a woman when we were at the market. I suspected she and her friends were slavers, but I wasn't sure. Now I am."

Jabili jumped to his feet trembling with anger.

"You knew this, and you did not warn us?"

Omari stood. "As I said, I wasn't sure. I'm sorry."

Jabili collapsed to the ground and continued to cry. The others huddled around him and joined him in mourning.

Omari trudged back to his bungalow. There was no reason for him to delay his departure. He gathered his possessions, stuffing them into his pack. When he opened the door Jabili and the others were waiting.

"You must help us, Omari," Jabili said.

"There is nothing I can do," Omari replied. "There's nothing any of us can do."

Omari climbed down his stairs and walked through the survivors.

"You are a warrior," Jabili said. "You can get our families back."

"I'm a mercenary," Omari replied. "I fight for pay and when the odds are in my favor."

"We will pay you," Jabili said.

"With what?" Omari asked.

"The cowries from the bunafish," Adia said.

"And anything we can salvage from the fire," Jimoh added.

Omari stopped. He knew he didn't need the money, and even if he decided to take the offer, he wasn't sure if he could find the slavers, let alone rescue the villagers.

"The cowries from the bunafish are a good start," Omari said. "I will stay until morning to see what you can reclaim from the fire."

Omari returned to his bungalow. He was sure they wouldn't be able to find enough valuables in the ashes to get him to risk his life to free a village of enslaved people. He would give them a chance only because of how generous they had been when he first arrived.

Jabili and the others greeted him the next morning. They carried a large gourd filled with cowries and baskets of whatever they could retrieve from the fire. Omari inspected it all and was pleasantly surprised. He might be able to make this work.

"I'll take the cowries with me," he said. "The rest will remain here. If I don't return, you know I failed, and you should get on with your lives."

"You will not fail," Jabili said. "We have given offerings to Eda."

Omari shrugged. "Best make sacrifices to Daarila as well."

Omari ambled toward the beach where the fishing canoes were secured, the others behind him carrying the cowries. He climbed into one of the boats and helped the fishermen load the gourds. Adia gave him a wooden box.

"Smoked bunafish," she said. "For your journey."

Omari took the box then sat it next to the cowrie gourd. He rowed away, the village survivors waving and praying as he headed north along the shore. The slavers had a head start, but they would have to seek the nearest harbor to either sell their captives or buy supplies to sail north to Haiset. That dark land possessed the most lucrative slave markets and was far enough away that the captives would have little chance of finding their way home if they managed to escape. Omari knew the ways of the market well, despite detesting it. It was that knowledge that gave him a chance to retrieve the Bwejaans.

It took him weeks to reach Peba. Each day diminished his chances of catching the slavers, but he owed it to Jabili to make the effort. He ran his canoe aground a few strides from the merchant city, secured his cowrie gourd to his back then walked the rest of the way. Being in a busy city whetted his appetites, but he focused on the job at hand. Work first, pleasure later.

Omari went to the docks. He studied the moored dhows as was quickly rewarded. The slavers' dhow was moored separate from the others because of its stench. Omari thought of approaching then changed his mind. He would go to the trading house. The slavers were most likely looking to get rid of their human cargo quickly, and the trading house would be the place to begin. A dock worker pointed him in the right direction and minutes later he entered a large stone building similar to the stone houses that peppered the Kiswala coastline. Merchants crowded inside, talking, shouting, and gesturing to acquire what they had come to buy. Omari stood by the door, scanning the faces until he saw who he was looking for. He pushed his way through the crowd to the woman sitting at a short table flanked by two men whose faces still bore the bruises from his fists. The woman noticed him approaching and slid her beer gourd aside as she stood.

"Omari," Thandiwe said.

"Thandiwe," Omari replied.

The men recognized him then jumped to their feet, their hands on their sword hilts.

"Sit down," Omari said. "We are in a trading house. Draw your swords and we'll all be killed."

The men looked to Thandiwe.

"He's right," she said. "Sit down."

The men eased back onto their stools; their eyes locked on Omari. Omari pulled up a stool then sat. Thandiwe sat as well.

"It seems we parted on less-than-ideal circumstances," Thandiwe said.

"We did," Omari replied. "You attempted to enslave me."

Thandiwe reached out and touched his forearm.

"No hard feelings, Mikijen?"

"I'm not here to make up," Omari said. "I'm here to buy your cargo. I have cowries."

Thandiwe's eyes brightened. "Do you now? And why should I sell them to you?"

"Come now," Omari said. "You don't care who buys them, as long as you get paid."

"The Haisetti pay well for slaves," Thandiwe said.

"Yet you're still here," Omari answered. "I'm assuming no one is eager to buy a group of malnourished fisherfolk."

"What are you proposing?" Thandiwe asked.

"I'd like to see them first," Omari replied.

"You've seen them before."

"Three weeks ago."

Thandiwe drummed her fingers on the table before answering.

"Okay. But let me finish my beer."

Omari waited as Thandiwe drank, her cohorts glaring at him the entire time. She winked at Omari as she stood then they made their way from the trading house to the dhow. Omari counted the baharia manning the dhow as they went below to the hold. It was a disgusting scene, dozens of men, women, and children sitting among their own filth. They barely acknowledged their presence.

"Not the best cargo," Thandiwe said. "But they are worth something."

"Let's go to your cabin and negotiate," Omari said, his intent clear. Thandiwe's eyes widened.

"Yes, let's do that."

Her face became stern.

"Make sure we're not disturbed," she said to her men.

"Yes, nahoda," they replied.

Omari followed Thandiwe to her cabin. She opened the door and entered.

"I'm looking forward to our negotiations," she said. "You impressed me the first day we met."

"So, you decided to make me your slave?" Omari said.

"You can't fault a woman from trying," she replied.

Thandiwe turned to face Omari. Omari punched her across the jaw, knocking her unconscious. He searched her until he found the keys to the slave shackles. Omari placed her on the bed then tied her hands and feet together. After making sure his knots were secure, he put the keys into his pouch then took out his sword and jambiya.

"Now for the rest of them."

Omari pounced from Thandiwe's cabin, killing the guards outside her door. He rushed down the narrow hallway then onto the deck, attacking any baharia he found. In the beginning the baharia rallied to confront him, but they soon realized they were no match for him. They fled the dhow in terror.

Omari turned about to make his way back down into the hold. More baharia emerged, armed with spears and swords. These were the fighters, the ones who raided the towns for cargo. The two he trounced in his bungalow seemed to be the leaders. They would not be so easily frightened.

"Time to die," one of the said.

Omari charged into them. It was a vicious melee, with Omari slashing, stabbing, and hacking his way toward the hold. Blades sliced his skin, sparking the ngisimaugi to heal the wounds as they appeared. He left dead and wounded in his wake as he fought closer to the hold. The last baharia standing dropped his weapons.

"Please, do not kill me!" he pleaded.

Omari hit the man on top of the head with his sword hilt, then stepped over his body. He entered the hold and the Bwejaans groaned.

"I'm not here to buy you," Omari said.

He went to the closest Bwejaan, a girl with fear in her eyes. He unlocked her shackles. He moved quickly, freeing the others in minutes.

"Come to the deck when you're able," he said.

Omari dragged the baharia bodies to the edge of the deck. Once he was done, he tossed them over the side of the vessel. As the freed Bwejaans emerged from below, some of them helped, shouting curses as they did so. A crowd had gathered by the time their grim work was complete. Omari went to the bow then placed his hands on his hips.

"If any of you know how to sail a dhow, this one is yours once we reach our destination," he yelled.

A horde of baharia rushed onto the ship with their hands raised. Omari selected the ones that seemed the most capable the shooed the others away. As the new crew prepared for departure, Omari went back to Thandiwe's cabin. The nahoda was awake and furious.

"Damn you to the Cleave, Omari!"

Omari lifted Thandiwe onto his shoulders then carried her off the ship and onto the docks. He dropped her.

"Be glad you're still alive," he said.

"You're stealing from me, you fisi!" she said. "You won't get away with this!"

"Yes, I will," Omari replied. "Be blessed, Thandiwe."

"Daarila split you!" Thandiwe shouted.

Omari boarded the ship. One of the new crew, a stout man with a grim expression, was giving orders to the others.

"What's your name?" Omari asked.

The man bowed. "Odoyo."

"Odoyo, you are nahoda. Do you know the way to Bwejaa?"

Odoyo nodded. "I do."

"That's our destination."

They set sail immediately, leaving Peba before the local authorities could intervene. They made landfall at the nearest port, Omari using a portion of the cowries to buy supplies and clothing for the crew and the Bwejaans. One week later they arrived at Bwejaa. The people cheered as their home came into view. Jabili and the others could not wait for them to anchor. They rowed out to meet the dhow, their faces bright with smiles and tears.

Omari made landfall with the last Bwejaans. Jabili met him with a hug.

"You did it!" he said.

"Yes, I did. Now where's the rest of my pay?"

"Jimoh! Adia! Bring the baskets!"

Omari and Jabili walked together to the village ruins.

"We found more valuables after you left," Jabili said. "I hope it is enough."

"It will be," Omari replied.

Jimoh, Adia and the other fisherfolk emerged from the village with a wagon full of baskets. Omari inspected them and was pleased.

"Thank you, Jabili," Omari said. "I'll be leaving now."

"No!" Jabili said. "You must celebrate with us! We have smoked bunafish and more devil-horns."

Omari shook his head. "My time in Bwejaa is over."

The Bwejaans followed him back to the boats, thanking him along the way. Adia planted a wet kiss on his lips that made him reconsider leaving so soon, but he shook his head clear and climbed into his boat filled with the baskets. The baharia lifted him and the bounty onto the dhow.

"This is for you," Omari said to Odoyo. The nahoda hugged Omari.

"You are a blessing from Eda!" he said.

"If only that was true," Omari replied.

"Where do we go now, bwa?" Odoyo asked.

"South," Omari replied. "I'll leave you at the first port."

"You don't wish to stay with us?" Odoyo asked.

"No," Omari replied. "I've rested long enough. It's time I spent some stacks."

Odoyo nodded. "So be it."

The baharia lifted the anchors and they set sail. Omari watched the waving Bwejaans fade into the distance from the stern then ambled to the bow and gazed out onto the open sea. He had no idea what lay ahead for him, but at least he was well fed and well paid. That was all he could ask.

RAIDERS OF

KIWA ISLAND

The drinking began at dusk and continued deep into the night. When it was over, people, beer bowls and drinking straws lay strewn on the dirt floor of Baba's Hut, a well-known gathering spot for mercenaries after a successful, or unsuccessful, adventure. Omari Ket lay among the pile, a pleasant smile on his face. It was always good to be alive with a pouch full of stacks, even though much of it would be gone before the end of the week. Such was the life of a hired sword.

Reality hit Omari's face at daybreak in the form of the hard-pack street. He grimaced as he opened his eyes then checked his mouth to see if he'd lost any teeth. His ngisimaugi, his healing tattoo, warmed his back, indicating something was injured. He discovered what when he examined his right hand. His little finger was bent at an odd angle.

"Cleave!" he said. "Who did this?"

"I did," someone answered.

Omari turned his head to see Gituku sitting beside him. The big man massaged a knot rising over his left eye.

"Why did you do that?" Omari asked.

Gituku stopped rubbing the tender bump for a moment then shrugged.

"Either I headbutted your fist, or you punched my head. I don't remember," he said. "Doesn't matter. Your squid will have you right in a few hours.

"That's not the point," Omari replied. "My damn finger is broken!"

Gituku found his pouch, opened it then reached inside. He pulled out a hand full of cowries then tossed him at Omari.

"That should be what a pinky finger is worth," he said.

Omari glared at Gituku. If it wasn't for the fact that the hulking Kikuyu kept him working, he'd cut off his head. Instead, he picked up the shells with his left hand as his finger slowly healed. He stuffed them in his pouch, stood then walked away.

"Where are you going?" Gituku asked.

"To find a place I can sleep for a day, maybe two," Omari replied.

"And after that?"

"I don't know. Another village where I can find work."

"You should stay longer. I might have something for us," Gituku said.

Omari thought about Gituku words. He'd come through on a few lucrative and easy jobs, and a few more stacks in his pouch couldn't hurt.

"I'll send you a message when I find lodging," Omari said.

"Good deal," Gituku replied. "See you soon, Mikijen."

Omari shook his head as Gituku strolled away. He kept calling Omari Mikijen even though it had been years since he fit the description. His life as a Kiswala mercenary ended many years ago in a burning fort. As far as the real Mikijen knew, Omari Ket was one of many muwanis lost that day. He'd been on his own since, selling his skills to the highest bidder. His life wasn't better, but it certainly was different.

Omari made his way to one of the boarding houses on the docks that catered to merchants and their crews. He paid the proprietor extra for a private room, a washbowl and whatever food they served. The proprietor led him to a space at the rear of the establishment. It was cramped, but sufficient. A servant arrived a few minutes later with his meal, a spicy chicken stew, hard loaf, and a gourd of beer. Omari's stomach growled at the sight of it; he hadn't eaten since yesterday afternoon. He slurped down the stew, wiped the bowl clean with the bread then washed it down with the beer. The food was good for such a small establishment. He became drowsy as the meal settled in his stomach. Moments later he lay snoring on the small bed.

An insistent knock woke him. He stood then opened the door to see Gituku.

"You were supposed to send a messenger," Gituku said. "You know how long it took me to find you?"

"I forgot," Omari said. "Besides, I just saw you. You have something for us already?"

"Just saw me? It's been three days. Have you been asleep that long?"

Omari scratched between his legs. "I guess so. No wonder I'm so hungry."

"That explains why the proprietor didn't want to open your door. He probably thought you were dead," Gituku said.

"What's the job?" Omari asked as he dressed. "How much does it pay?"

"It pays two stacks," Gituku said. "As for the details, you'll find out when we get there. For two stacks you shouldn't need to know the particulars."

Gituku had a point, but Omari was more wary.

"I'm not committing until we get the facts," Omari said.

Gituku frowned. "I already told them you'd be on board. As a matter of fact, this job needs you."

"Then my price has gone up to three stacks, if I decide to do it."

"Shit, Omari, don't be that way," Gituku griped.

Omari secured his weapons then smiled like a fisi finding a fresh corpse.

"Let's go get my money," he said.

Omari paid the proprietor then followed Gituku out into the hot bright day. A breeze blew in from the ocean, carrying the smell of brine and fish with it. Luckily their destination was nearby.

"There," Gituku said, pointing at a fine dhow bobbing with the waves. Whoever owned it was a person with means.

They approached the gangplank flanked by two tall, lean, and muscular guards, most likely Nuba warriors. The owner was probably from the north, most likely Aux. If Omari was still a Mikijen, meeting with a person from Aux would have meant a death sentence.

The guards allowed them on board. A man dressed in a multicolored robe waited for them.

"You found him!" the man said.

"Yes, I did," Gituku replied.

"Excellent! The master will be very pleased."

Omari folded his arms over his chest. "Before we meet your master, we have a few things to discuss."

"Four stacks," the man said. "That is what my master is willing to pay you for this job."

"What are we waiting for?" Omari replied. "Let's meet your master!"

Omari and Gituku followed the servant to the stern. A group of mercenaries gathered under the canopy, some sitting, others leaning against the bulwark. Standing before the wheel was a lean man dressed in traditional Kiswala finery. A broad grin creased his face when his eyes fell on Omari, revealing a collection of jeweled teeth. This man was not Kiswala, Omari thought. No bwa would ruin their teeth like that.

"Ah, our special guest has arrived!" the man announced.

All heads turned to Gituku and Omari. Some of the faces Omari recognized, most he didn't.

"Ket," one of the mercenaries spat. "What make that jackal so special?"

"He is the man who will lead us to a treasure beyond all our dreams," the man replied. "Cabdi, bring him forward."

Cabdi led them to the merchant. He took Omari's wrist, and they shook.

"Your arm grasp and clothing say you are Kiswala, but your smile says otherwise," Omari commented.

"You have found me out," the man replied. "I've always been captivated with the Kiswala style, even as a boy. I am Warsame Nuur. Welcome to my beautiful dhow."

"Don't welcome me yet," Omari replied. "If this job is dependent upon me, I'm going to need a bit more encouragement to sign on."

"Are four stacks sufficient?" Warsame asked.

Omari grinned. "It'll do. And another stack for my friend." He gestured toward Gituku.

"Done," Warsame said.

"Now that that's out of the way, where is it you wish me to guide you?"

"Kiwa Island," Warsame said.

Omari's eyes went wide. He felt dizzy and his stomach churned. Omari turned on his heels then stumbled away.

"No," he stammered.

"Omari! Wait!" Warsame shouted.

Gituku chased after him.

"Omari! What are you doing? You can't walk away from four stacks!"

"Five stacks!" Warsame shouted.

Omari was down the gangplank and swaying down the docks when Gituku finally caught up to him.

"Omari, stop," Gituku said. "What's going on?"

"Can't . . . go . . . to . . . Kiwa Island. It is . . . forbidden," Omari said.

He fell to his knees then threw up. Gituku knelt beside him.

"Why?" Gituku asked.

"I don't know," Omari replied.

"Do you know how to get there?" Gituku asked.

"I might, but that doesn't matter. Kiwa Island is forbidden."

Omari struggled to his feet and continued to walk away.

"Omari, wait! Let us talk about this!"

Omari turned to see Warsame running toward him, Cabdi close behind.

"There's . . . nothing to talk about," Omari said.

"What if I were to tell you that your fear of Kiwa Island was not your own?" Warsame asked.

"Who said I was afraid?" Omari replied.

"Are you?" Warsame asked.

Omari began to reply but stopped. He was afraid; why he did not know. He'd never experienced anything that should make him sick with worry, but the thought of going to Kiwa filled him with dread. When he finally looked at Warsame, the merchant returned his gaze with a knowing smile.

"If you can give me a few moments of your time, I'm sure I can change your mind. There is someone you should meet that can explain everything."

Omari looked at Gituku, who nodded his head.

"It's worth a listen," Gituku said. "You have nothing to lose."

Omari shrugged. "Okay."

Omari leaned against Gituku and the duo followed Warsame back to his dhow. The other mercenaries had dispersed, leaving the deck almost empty. Warsame walked to the steps leading below deck and gestured.

"Come."

He led them below then through the narrow hallway to a cabin at the stern. Cabdi slipped by Warsame and opened the door. Both men fell to their knees, prostrating before entering.

"Honored elder," Warsame said. "I bring you guests."

"There is a Mikijen among you," the person replied.

"Yes, there is, honored elder."

"Only he can enter."

Cabdi and Warsame quickly cleared the way. Omari gripped his sword hilt as he entered.

"You have nothing to fear from me," the voice said. "All I offer you is freedom."

Omari stepped into the cabin. The normal accoutrements of a nahoda's lair were gone. In their place was a mud cloth blanket and a large cushion on which the woman who Warsame referred to as 'elder' sat. She wore an ivory robe decorated with mud prints of tembos. The robe sagged around her thin frame; her face wrinkled like an ancient valley cut by rivers. Despite her aged appearance, her eyes shone with vigor and her smile radiated quiet energy.

"Come, Mikijen," she said. "Please sit."

Omari tipped forward then sat cross-legged before her.

"Who are you, aunt?" he asked. "And how is it that you knew I was a Mikijen?"

"I am Nalah," the woman said. "And I know what you are because I can feel your ashé."

"I used to be a Mikijen, but not anymore," Omari commented.

"You still bear the ngisimaugi," she said. "You are still bound, yet you serve another."

Omari was puzzled. "Who?"

Nalah chuckled. "You will learn soon enough."

Omari cleared his throat and tasted bile.

"Warsame says that you will free me. Free me from what?"

"The Kiswala did many things to you during your training. Some were obvious, others weren't. You cannot go to Kiwa Island because they have imbedded the fear in your mind."

"How could they do such a thing?" Omari said.

"The same way they created a tattoo that heals your wounds," Nalah answered. "Nyama. Kiswala sonchai are powerful, but they are not all powerful."

Nalah extended her hands. "Come closer."

Omari shifted to his knees then moved closer. Nalah took his head between her frail hands then placed her forehead against his.

"Close your eyes and think of nothing," she whispered.

Omari did as told. In an instant he was tumbling back in time, every moment of his life playing back in reverse. The journey stopped at a moment of his life he had no recollection; the night his ngisimaugi was tattooed on his back. He lay on his stomach unconscious while the tattooist did his work. There was another person present that didn't participate in the process. She hovered over him, chanting as the tattooist worked. Nalah took up the chant, repeating the words trapped in his mind for a moment, then changing them. The sonchai in his memory changed her words to match Nalah's, then suddenly looked at Omari. She snarled and a piercing pain blinded him.

"Argh!" Nalah shouted. The woman fell back onto her pillows as Omari collapsed onto his side.

"Bring the elixir, quickly," Warsame shout from the other side of the door.

Hands grasped Omari's arms, pulling him upright. A water gourd touched his lips and he sipped instinctively. The pain in his head subsided as the liquid flowed into his mouth and down his throat. His eyes cleared and he saw Nalah sitting before him, her eyes less vibrant than before.

"It is done," she said. "Now Mikijen, is there any reason why you wouldn't travel to Kiwa Island?"

"I . . . no," Omari said.

Nalah looked at Warsame and Warsame clapped his hands.

"Omari, do you feel strong enough to walk?"

"Yes, I do."

"Good! We will leave you to your healing, Nalah," he said. "I will post a guard at your door. When you are ready to talk to us again, please send him."

"I will, Warsame," Nalah said.

Omari bowed before leaving.

"Thank you," he said.

Nalah waved him off. "Go eat something. It will help you recover."

Gituku helped Omari out of the door then back to the deck.

"We are about to have our evening repast," Warsame said. "Will you join us?"

Omari looked at Gituku and Gituku shrugged.

"Why not? It can't be worse than the swill they served at my lodging."

Warsame and Cabdi flittered away to handle the details of the evening meal. Gituku eased Omari down to sit against the bulwark. He became a bit dizzy when seated and his stomach churned, but otherwise he felt much better.

"I feel like a veil has been lifted from over me," Omari said. "I remember everything now."

He slammed his fist against the bulwark.

"By the Cleave!"

He stood and paced.

"There is a very good reason the Kiswala don't want anyone to visit Kiwa Island."

"What is it?" Gituku said.

"Because the foundation of their wealth is there."

"Which is why Warsame wants you to lead us to it," Gituku added.

Omari stopped pacing. "The question is, how did Warsame find out?"

"I will tell you how."

Warsame approached with his hands clasped behind his back. Cabdi stood beside him holding a tray with two steaming bowls of pilau rice and chapati bread. Omari stomach growled as Gituku handed him the food.

"As you observed, I am not Kiswala," Warsame said, 'but my father was. His name was Jumaane Simba. You may have heard of him."

"I've heard of his lineage," Omari said. "It's one of the Twelve Clans. But your mother was not Kiswala."

"No," Warsame replied. "She belongs to the Omomo people."

"The landlocked merchants," Gituku commented.

"Yes," Warsame confirmed. "Her name is Caali Ayenew."

"The Ayenew are an influential clan," Omari said.

"Yes, they are, but they are not Kiswala," Warsame replied. "My mother and father met as children. Their parents spent much time together because of their business dealings. When they became adults, friendship blossomed into love. They knew their clans would not consent to marriage, so they did so in secret. When it was discovered, they were both disowned. My parents moved to another village and started their own trade house. They became successful despite the others. My mother's family eventually forgave her. My father's family did not."

"I'm sorry to hear that," Omari said.

Warsame dismissed his sympathy with a hand wave.

"They lived a happy life, as did I," he said. "My father told me stories of his life before marrying mama. That is how I learned of Kiwa Island."

Omari felt much better after eating. He stood and stretched.

"You seem to be doing well, Bwa Warsame," he said. "Why would you risk going?"

"As you said, the island is the foundation of Kiswala wealth. According to my baba, it was the treasure of the Old Ones that sustained the Kiswala when they were driven from Aux. If I take that away from them, not only do I hurt their pride, but I also hurt their pockets."

"They won't let you get away with that," Omari said. "They will send the Mikijen for you."

"They would, if they know who did it," Warsame replied. "I'm paying every person on this mission a fortune for their skills and their silence. I hope since Nalah freed you of their nyama I can trust you to be silent, too."

"I owe nothing to the Kiswala," Omari said. "But if we are successful, I'll take my stacks and get as far away from here as possible. I suggest you do the same. There are two things that will loosen any tongue; pain or pleasure. The Kiswala are masters of both."

"Only Eda knows," Warsame said. "When you are rested, I would like for you to look at our map. It's time we began this adventure."

Dusk had come before Omari met with Warsame. The nahoda set up a table under the stern canopy, with torches held on each corner by his baharia. Cabdi stood by his side as always, the rolled map tucked under his arm. Omari was surprised to see Nalah at the table, the woman leaning on a plain wooded staff. Beside her was another woman with a hard countenance and piercing hazel eyes. She nodded at Omari, then turned her attention to Warsame.

"I'm glad everyone was able to make it," Warsame said. "Cabdi?"

Cabdi spread the map on the table, and everyone moved closer.

"As you know, we are here," Warsame said, pointing at Peba. "The winds are against us, so it will take at least two weeks to sail to the Kiswala Islands."

"It will take longer," Omari said. "Kiwa is further out. Plan on at least another week."

The woman with the stern expression spoke.

"Where exactly is it?" she said.

Omari studied the map. A throbbing sensation formed in his head, increasing to a sharp pain.

He clinched his eyes and reached for his forehead. Nalah shuffled toward him.

"Move aside," she said.

The others stepped away from the table.

"Look at me, Omari," she said.

Omari faced Nalah. She grasped his head as she did before. The slight touch of her forehead dissipated the pain. Just as before, the woman looked weakened. Omari steadied her on her staff.

"You shouldn't do this, aunt," he said. "What you take from me hurts you."

"I'm fine," she replied. "I have my own reasons for helping Warsame. Besides, I'm old. If I die, I have no regrets. My family awaits me, and I am anxious to see them again."

Nalah waved at the woman to help her. She gripped Nalah's arm and led her to the other side of the table.

"Your daughter?" Omari asked.

Nalah nodded. "Her name is Hadiya. She's not very talkative."

"She is also the best navigator in the eastern sea," Warsame added.

"You exaggerate," Hadiya said.

"What do you think of our plan, Hadiya?" Warsame said.

"We can't sail through the Kiswala Islands," she said. "It is forbidden. We'll have to sail either north or south around the islands and pray that we do not encounter Mikijen or pirates along the way."

"What about here?" Omari said. "We can sail between Kiswala and Barke. The waters are not heavily patrolled, and no pirates dare come this close to the islands."

"The winds are strong there," Hadiya replied. "It could be touchy."

"True, but it will save us at least a week," Omari said.

Warsame studied the map as he weighed Hadiya and Omari's words.

"We will sail through the gap and pray for Eda's protection," he finally said. "The more time we save, the more time we have at Kiwa."

"This is a risk," Hadiya commented.

"This entire expedition is," Warsame replied.

Omari surveyed the group. Everyone seemed to agree. He still felt nervous about the safari but gone was the fear the Kiswala had planted inside him. This journey was dangerous, but no more than any he'd taken on before.

"Everyone rest well tonight," Warsame said. "If it is your way to celebrate before embarking on an adventure, make sure you return by first light. We won't wait for anyone, except Omari."

Warsame nodded to Cabdi. The servant placed a bag of cowries on the map for each of them. Gituku and Omari were the first to grab a bag, the others laughing at their enthusiasm. Cabdi rolled up the map and tucked it under his arm.

"See you at first light," Warsame said.

The duo walked away. Hadiya guided Nalah away, the two of them heading for their quarters. They left their cowries on the table. Omari and Gituku looked at each other, wide grins on their faces.

"No need to let good pay go to waste," Omari said.

They grabbed the extra bags then hurried off the dhow and into Peba.

* * *

The sun crested the eastern horizon with its usual dry season brilliance. Omari and Gituku helped each other up the gangplank to Warsame's dhow, struggling to shake off the effects of the previous night's celebration. The baharia preparing the dhow for launch looked at them with amused expressions. Omari spotted Hadiya striding across the deck. Hadiya looked back; a disapproving look on her face.

"Don't mess with her," Gituku said. "We don't need an angry navigator."

"I have no intentions of doing so," Omari replied. "Not that it would matter. I get the feeling I've been judged and found unworthy."

"You say that like you had a chance," Gituku said.

"Look at me," Omari replied. "I always have a chance. I'm beautiful."

Gituku laughed then let Omari go. Omari fell onto the deck.

"Shit!" he exclaimed. "What did you do that for?"

"Because you get on my nerves sometimes, conceited bastard," Gituku shot back.

"You're only angry because you know it's true," Omari replied.

He stood then extended his arms to steady himself. Warsame and Cabdi approached them.

"I see you're on time," Warsame said. "There is food below deck if you require it."

Omari shook his head. "I have no intentions of eating anything I might see again in a few minutes."

"A wise decision," Warsame said. "Cabdi will take you to your quarters to store your gear."

They followed Cabdi to their cabin. It was more spacious that most, a reward for Omari's contribution to the expedition. Gituku fell into his hammock. Omari stripped down to his loincloth then walked toward the cabin door.

"Where are you going?" Gituku asked.

"To lend a hand," Omari replied.

"What do you know about working a dhow?"

"I used to be a Mikijen, remember? I know a thing or two. Besides, it's either work on deck or stay here and smell you all day."

Gituku sniffed himself. "It's not that bad."

"You wouldn't think so."

Omari exited the cabin.

Omari emerged onto the deck and walked directly to the baharia. The first mate, a gruff looking man with a wiry body and leathery skin, looked him up and down.

"What do you want?" he asked.

"I'm here to help," Omari said.

"We have a crew," the man replied.

"I've been on enough dhows to know that there's always a need for more. What nahoda has ever spent enough stacks for a full crew?"

The first mate smirked then extended his arm.

"I'm Tukufu."

Omari grasped his forearm, and they shook. "Omari," he said.

"Find somewhere to be useful, Omari," Tukufu said. "And watch out for this crew. They are a lazy lot. You might find yourself doing all the work."

The crew jeered Tukufu as they laughed.

"Okay, let's get to work!" Tukufu said.

The mooring ropes were untied, the anchor lifted, and the safari began. Omari settled into the routine quickly. It took the other mercenaries time to get used to the rolling waves and monotony of the sea, but they eventually adjusted. Warsame was a calm nahoda compared to most Omari had experienced and his crew respected him. Omari split his time between working with the baharia, training with the mercenaries and gambling with both. The weather remained docile as it was prone to do during the dry season, gentle breezes pushing the dhow east at a leisurely pace.

On the second week at sea Omari spied Hadiya observing him. He interrupted his chores and sauntered to her, a smile on his face.

"It's been an easy safari so far," he said to her.

"It has," she replied.

"By my estimate we should reach the gap in another week."

Hadiya nodded. "Your guess is correct. I must admit, you're not what I expected."

Omari hands fell to his waist and he pushed his chest out.

"You're not the first person to say that."

Hadiya face shriveled like an old date.

"I didn't mean that," she said. "I meant your skills. You're actually a decent baharia."

Omari's smile faded as he pulled his chest in.

"I was a Mikijen for a long time," he said. "You pick up a few things over the years."

"Have you ever considered becoming a nahoda?" Hadiya asked.

"By the Cleave no!" Omari replied. "It's the last thing I would ever do."

Hadiya looked shocked. "Why? You know the sea, you know dhows, and people seem to respect you. And the work is a lot steadier and less dangerous than being a mercenary."

"Just because I'm good at something doesn't mean I like doing it," Omari said. "I enjoy my freedom. Being a nahoda locks me down and I never want to be that way again."

"Who locked you down?" Hadiya asked.

"It's a long story that I don't want to tell," Omari replied. "Let's just say becoming a Mikijen wasn't a choice."

Hadiya's eyes widened and she took a step back. Omari chuckled.

"What about you?" he asked. "A navigator is one step away from a nahoda."

"Warsame promised me my own dhow when we return from this safari. It's the reason I'm here," she replied. "That and assisting my mama."

"Well, I hope you get your wish," Omari said. "If there is nothing else you want from me, I'll be off."

"There is nothing at all I want from you, Omari Ket."

Omari shrugged then went about his chores. This safari would be longer than he anticipated.

Warsame's dhow finally reached the gap. All sails were raised, and the crew took out the oars to increase their speed. The sooner they were through the strait, the less chance they would be seen. The baharia in the observation nest peered at the horizon in every direction, looking for signs of an approaching vessel. The mercenaries were on deck as well, armed and armored. If there was to be a fight, they would be ready.

Warsame paced from one end of the dhow to the other, Cabdi right on his heals. Omari and Gituku stood watch at the stern with Hadiya, who steered the dhow. Omari took his time loading his hand cannon and placing the fuse. It would be ready if there was trouble.

"How much longer?" Warsame asked Hadiya.

Hadiya looked at the sky.

"A few more hours at least," she said.

"A few more hours," Warsame repeated. "Good. Good."

He marched away. Gituku laughed at the nervous nahoda.

"He looks like a goat before the slaughter," he said.

"Don't make fun of him," Omari replied. "If we're spotted by Mikijen, we're done. There's no way this dhow will outrun a patroller, and the mercenaries on this dhow are no match for a Mikijen regiment."

"How can you say that?" Gituku replied. "These men are fighters, every one of them."

"That's true, but they don't have ngisimaugis tattooed on their backs. It takes a lot to put a Mikijen down for good. I should know."

"There! There!"

All eyes went to the baharia in the observation post. He pointed beyond the bow.

"What do you see?" Warsame shouted.

"I see two!" the baharia shouted back.

"Dhows?" Omari asked.

"No," the baharia answered. "Mtepes!"

"Shit," Omari said. "Pirates."

"Pirates? How do you know?" Warsame said.

"Pirates always use mtepes. They leak like sieves, but they're faster than dhows," Omari replied.

He turned to Gituku. "Get the mercenaries ready."

Gituku nodded then ran across the deck shouting orders. Omari stood beside Hadiya.

"We can sail between them," she said.

"No," Omari replied. "We won't make it. We'll be attacked on both sides. Steer the dhow toward one of them. We'll take them on one at a time."

"Which one?" she asked.

"Doesn't matter," Omari replied.

Hadiya turned the rudder and the dhow angled to the left. Omari hurried to Gituku and the mercenaries.

"Split them up," he said. "Half on the right, the others on the right."

"Who put you in charge?" Gituku said.

"We don't have time for this," Omari said. "How many sea battles have you fought?"

"I just wanted to make sure you knew who's in command," Gituku said.

"Warsame is," Omari said. "And if you want to be alive to get paid, don't interrupt me again."

Omari didn't wait for Gituku's reply. He trotted to Tukufu. The mate met him, holding a short sword.

"What do you need, Omari?" he said.

"I need a cargo net," he said. "And two baharia to handle it."

Tukufu nodded then hurried away. Omari went portside then squatted so he could not be seen. The other mercenaries did the same.

"What are we to do?" one of them asked.

"Stay low until the pirates appear on the bulwark then keep them from boarding the ship," Omari answered.

"We should take the fight to them," another person said.

"No," Omari answered. "We have the advantage. Besides, we will be taking the fight to them."

The dhow fell silent as they neared the first mtepe. Omari grinned as he listened to the curses the pirates hurled at them. If they meant to scare the mercenaries, they fell short. He looked at their faces and was assured that Gituku chose well. He had a good eye for experienced people.

The dhow jerked as it hit the mtepe.

"Now!" Omari shouted.

The baharia tossed the cargo net over the side. Omari lit the fuse of the hand cannon. He climbed over the bulwark then jumped, landing on his feet in the middle of the mtepe. The pirates looked stunned; before they could attack Omari pointed the hand cannon at the bottom of the mtepe and it fired, blasting a wide hole. Omari jumped onto the cargo net and clambered to the top, the pirates following in anger and desperation. As the pirates reached the bulwark the mercenaries attacked, cutting them down like a grim harvest. The pirates remaining in the mtepe jumped overboard as the vessel sank.

"Pull up the net!" Omari shouted. "Hadiya, you know what to do!"

The dhow veered right, heading for the second mtepe.

"Follow me!" Omari said.

The mercenaries trailed Omari.

"Let's show them what they're up against," he said.

Omari stood on the bow, raised his sword and shouted. The other mercenaries joined him. The baharia who were not working the sails joined as well. The mtepe's sails turned; soon after the vessel veered away, heading in the direction it came.

Cheers and ululations swept the dhow. As Omari climbed down from the bulwark, Warsame ran up to him and hugged him.

"Magnificent!" he exclaimed. "Simply magnificent!"

Omari pulled himself free.

"It worked this time," he said. "Now with your permission, I'm going to my bunk."

"You may do whatever you like," Warsame said.

The mercenaries nodded and patted Omari on his shoulders. Last to congratulate his was Gituku.

"Show off," he said.

"Pure luck," Omari said. "I'm happy not to be on the bottom on the sea with that first mtepe."

"Now that you mention it, that was stupid." Gituku said.

"I agree," Omari confessed. "Never let me do anything like that again."

"I tried to stop you," Gituku said.

"You did. Next time try harder."

Omari ambled across the deck. He glanced at Hadiya and nodded. She nodded back, a smirk on her face that caused Omari to grin. Maybe this safari wouldn't be so long after all.

* * *

When Omari awoke Gituku was snoring in his bunk. He rubbed his eyes then left the cabin, his destination the deck. He emerged into the illumination of a full moon. The deck was still, the baharia asleep on or below deck. Omari decided to go to stern, taking out his dagga pipe on the way. He'd kept his stash of the narcotic grass hidden for a moment just like this. He climbed the stairs and was surprised to see Hadiya still at the wheel.

"What are doing here?" he said.

"Waiting for you," Hadiya said.

Omari laughed. "I doubt that."

She secured the wheel with rope then amble to him. She pointed at his pipe.

"What's that?" she asked.

Omari took his dagga bag from his pouch.

"Dagga."

Hadiya reached into her pouch and took out a similar bag.

"I have something better."

She handed the bag to Omari. He opened the bag then poured the purple-colored leaves into his palm.

"What is this?" he asked. "I've never seen anything like it."

"And you won't," Hadiya said.

Omari continued to study the shredded leaves.

"Fascinating."

"Are you going to spend the night in wonder or are we going to smoke?" Hadiya asked.

Omari filled his pipe then lit Hadiya's grass. The aroma was pleasant, unlike dagga. The two of them went to the bulwark and sat. Omari extended the pipe to her.

"It's your leaves," he said.

Hadiya took a long drag then let out the smoke from her nostrils.

"Your turn," she said.

Omari took the pipe and pulled. The effect was immediate. His shoulders slumped and he closed his eyes.

"This is amazing," he said.

"Yes, it is," Hadiya said.

They smoked in silence for a moment, watching the stars through the drifting smoke. Hadiya finally broke the pleasant silence.

"Once again, you surprised me," she said.

"How?" Omari asked.

"I expected Gituku to command the mercenaries during the attack. Not you."

"Gituku is a great leader, but he knows nothing about sea-fighting."

"It was more than that. You've done this before. More than once, I suspect."

Omari shrugged. "I earned some rank as a Mikijen, only because those higher than me kept getting killed. That was damned inconsiderate of them."

Hadiya laughed. "I thought so. The others took your commands easily," she said. "It's like I said before. You should be a nahoda."

"And like I said before, no."

Hadiya stretched and Omari smiled. Hadiya noticed his attention, but this time she didn't frown.

"What awaits us when we reach Kiwa?" she asked.

"I don't know," Omari confessed. "I can't remember any details. There may be wealth, there may be nothing. Doesn't matter to me either way. I've been paid."

"It could destroy Warsame," Hadiya said. "He's spent everything on this safari. If we don't find anything, he'll be ruined."

"I doubt that," Omari replied. "Warsame has Kiswala blood. He's spending a fortune, but I'm sure he has another waiting for him when he returns to Peba."

"Perhaps," Hadiya said. "Still, I hope he's successful."

Omari tried to take another pull from the pipe but the leaves were spent.

"Well, this isn't good," Omari said. "We're out. What do we do now?"

Hadiya scooted close to Omari then straddled his lap as she draped her arms around his neck.

"I can think of a few things," she said.

"I was thinking we could smoke my dagga," Omari answered with a smirk.

"Shut up," Hadiya said right before she kissed him.

* * *

Omari managed to make it back to his bunk before daybreak. Hadiya didn't want anyone to know they'd enjoyed each other's company and Omari reluctantly agreed. Gituku broke his sound sleep with his insistent shaking. Omari finally sat up then shoved his hands away.

"What?" he barked.

"We're here," Gituku said.

Omari shook the dregs of Hadiya's herb from his head as he dressed. The sight that greeted him as he emerged from below deck cleared the rest away. The dhow bobbed before an archipelago unlike any he recollected. Warsame, Hadiya and Nalah stood at the stern near the wheel, their faces bunched with concern. The others expressions caught his eye, but it was Nalah's that troubled him most. Omari had not seen her for a few days, but it was obvious the light that shone bright in her eyes when they first met had diminished. She turned to him as he neared and managed to smile.

"Our mapmaker had arrived," she said.

Omari walked up to her, ignoring everyone else.

"Aunt, you shouldn't be here" he said.

"Warsame will not find what he seeks if I'm not," she replied.

"Maybe he shouldn't," Omari said.

Everyone on the ship glared at him.

Nalah grasped his hand. Despite her frailness her grip was strong.

"Did I ever tell you where I'm from?" she asked.

"No," Omari replied.

Nalah nodded toward the collection of islands.

"This is my home," she said. "I was a young girl when my family and our people were driven away by the Kiswala. The Mikijen defeated our warriors, destroyed our homes and forced use to flee to the mainland. Many did not make it. Those who did wished they hadn't. My parents were never the same. They managed to make enough of a living to feed and clothe us, but nothing more. And the sadness they carried eventually killed them."

"I'm sorry, aunt," Omari said.

"Why are you sorry?" Nalah said. "You did not do it."

Nalah coughed, a loud hacking cough that made Omari wince.

"I became a sonchai for one reason," Nalah continued. "To find my way home. And now here I am."

"What you did for me weakened you," Omari said. Nalah waved her hand.

"Don't feel guilty," she said. "I knew the consequences; you did not. Now I will ask you one last favor, although your answer will bring about my death."

"Then I will not answer," Omari replied.

"Look around you, Omari," Nalah said. "Everyone on this dhow is here on their own free will and for their own reasons. If you deny them the chance to make this safari worth it, their lives will never be as they were. Do you wish to be responsible for such a disappointment?"

"Yes, if it means that you must die in the process."

"You would disappoint me as well," Nalah said.

Omari fell silent. The connection created between them to remove the Kiswala spell bonded them almost like mother and son. Omari did not want to see Nalah die, but he knew he could not stop her from doing what she wished. He looked toward Hadiya for support.

"I tried," Hadiya said. "She is determined."

"So, it is settled," Nalah said. "Give me your hands. You waste precious time."

Omari extended his hands. Once again, he felt Nalah's firm grip, and once again he shuddered as Nalah took hold of his mind. Omari was no longer on the dhow. He hovered over the ocean waves staring at the archipelago. Omari looked at himself and was terrified. He was translucent, his body resembling that of a ghost, or at least how he heard ghosts described.

He twisted his head to see the dhow resting behind him. He and Nalah sat cross-legged, their eyes closed.

"Don't be afraid," Nalah said.

Omari jerked his head to the left. Nalah hovered beside him, her body translucent as well.

"This is only temporary. You will return to your body as soon as I've had my rest. Let's find Kiwa.

Omari and Nalah accelerated forward, weaving between hundreds of islands. The isles became a continuous blur that seemed to last forever. When they finally stopped, Kiwa Island loomed before them. Nalah reached out and touched Omari's head.

"When you return you will remember our journey here," Nalah said. "I also implanted your promise to me. Tell Hadiya not to mourn long for me. I go where I want to be. Don't fail me, Omari Ket. The ancestors will be watching."

Omari sat on the deck again. He fell backwards, striking his head on the hard wood. He lay still for a moment, then sat up, rubbing the back of his head. Nalah sprawled on the deck opposite him, surrounded by everyone. Hadiya knelt beside her, crying. Warsame noticed him then came to his side.

"At least you are still alive," he said.

"What happened?" Omari asked.

"That's what I was going to ask you."

"This archipelago was Nalah's home," Omari said. "Did you know this?"

"No," Warsame replied. "But I suspected. Did she show you the way to Kiwa Island?"

"Yes," Omari said. His attention shifted to Hayida's tear stained face. "But she showed me something else first. She showed me her home. We are taking her there. This is what she wanted all along. It's why she helped you . . . and me."

Omari stood as Cabdi cradled Nalah in his arms and lifted her lifeless frame. He carried her away. Hadiya trailed behind him, sobbing into her hands.

"You will give me directions while I steer," Warsame said. "Together we will find the island."

"No," Omari replied. "First we take Nalah home, then we will find Kiwa Island."

"We have no time for sentiment!" Warsame exclaimed. "We are too close!"

"You will make time!" Omari snapped back. "Nalah is dead. I am the only one who knows the way. We can spend the next year searching this archipelago or we can bury Nalah where she belongs then find your island."

"Very well," Warsame said. "The wealth of Kiwa Island has waited this long to be plundered. It can wait a few days longer."

Warsame took the helm and the baharia went to their stations. Omari went to the bow and looked into the distance. An odd sensation overtook him as he visualized the path through the numerous islands. Part of his mind was confounded, while the other part viewed the archipelago as if he sailed its waters all his life. He carefully guided the dhow through dangerous shallows and rocky shoals, staying within the deep trenches that could handle the dhow's bulk. As they rounded a small atoll, a medium sized forested island came into view. A calming rush entered Omari's mind.

"This is it," he said. "This is Nalah's home."

"Drop anchor!" Warsame shouted.

Omari left the bow and ambled to Nalah's cabin. Cabdi and Hadiya stood over Nalah's wrapped body as Hadiya prayed for the ancestors' acceptance of Nalah among them.

"We are here," he said.

Hadiya looked at him with tears in her eyes.

"She is ready," she said.

Omari lifted Nalah from the bed, clasping her small frame like a child. Once they reached the deck, he carried her to the bulwark where a boat waited. He placed Nalah into the boat and it was lowered into the calm waters. Omari and Hadiya climbed down the cargo net into the boat then rowed to the island.

When they reached the beach, Omari lifted Nalah again then strode for the bush.

"How do you know where to go?" Hadiya asked.

"Nalah showed me," Omari replied.

They pushed through the tangled vegetation until they found the faint sign of a path. As they walked the trail it grew wider until it became a dilapidated stone road. Ruin homes built from coral infused stone lined the route. Nalah's home had once been a great city, its domiciles, streets and markets filled with vibrant umber people that thrived off the bounty of the islands, until that fateful day the Kiswala arrived and destroyed their world.

Nalah's spiritual guidance led them to a large area that by its looks had once been a clearing.

"Here," Omari said. He placed Nalah down then took the spade from Hadiya. For the next two hours he dug into the sandy soil until he reached the proper depth. Omari stretched out from the hole, took Nalah and lowered her inside. He climbed out then stood beside Hadiya.

"Goodbye mama," she whispered. "Take your place among the ancestors. Continue to guide me with your wisdom."

Together they filled the grave then stacked loose stone on top. Once done they trudged back to the dhow, Hadiya's gentle weeping melding with the sounds of the creatures of the bush. As they rowed back to the dhow, Hadiya spoke.

"Thank you for doing this," she said.

"Your mama freed me from a cage I did not know I was in," Omari said. "I could never do enough for her."

"Warsame will be ready to sail to Kiwa Island as soon as we return. Will you take him there?"

"Yes," Omari said. "I'm a man of my word."

"I have a bad feeling about this," Hadiya said.

"Me, too," Omari replied. "Stay on the dhow and be ready to sail. Something tells me that if we do return from the temple, we will be in a hurry."

They reached the dhow and climbed aboard. Warsame was waiting, an anxious look on his face.

"Do we go now?" he asked.

"Yes," Omari replied.

Omari took his place at the bow once again. He guided the dhow around Nalah's island and deeper into the archipelago. As they entered the center of the islands, Kiwa rose from the horizon. Their destination, a towering white temple, stood in stark contrast to the bush surrounding its base, its surface marred by vines creeping up its walls like thieves. The warmth Omari felt in his chest upon seeing the structure confirmed they had arrived. The baharia cheered; they had finally reached their destination.

Omari held up his hand for the dhow to stop. The anchor was dropped and the sails furled. Warsame, Gituku and Cabdi were at his side moments later.

"Why are we stopping so far away?" Warsame asked.

"The waters are too shallow," Omari replied. "It was part of the Kiswala defense strategy. Heavy dhows with manogels and catapults could not draw near, only boats of warriors. The harbor is filled with jagged stones, the same stones from which the temple was built."

"How do you know all this?" Cabdi asked.

"It was part of our Mikijen training," Omari replied. "Knowledge locked away in my memory until Nalah released it."

"Gituku, prepare your warriors for landfall," Warsame said. "We leave as soon as they are ready."

Warsame marched away, Cabdi scurrying behind him. Gituku dropped a heavy hand on Omari's shoulder.

"Well, this is it," he said. "You did it. You've earned your stacks."

"Nalah did it," Omari said. "I hope we live to see the rest," Omari replied.

"It's an abandoned temple," Gituku said. "We go in, we get whatever Warsame is seeking and we get out. The most difficult part has been the safari."

"It's the whatever that worries me," Omari said. "Too much ashé involved in this."

"Come," Gituku said. "Let's get to the boats. The sooner this is over, the better."

The mercenaries gathered at the starboard bow where the landing boats were lowered. Warsame, Cabdi and their supplies were loaded first; the mercenaries second. Once everyone was accounted for, they rowed across the calm waters to the gray sand beaches of Kiwa. The mercenaries disembarked first, jumping onto the sand then spreading out. A few penetrated into the bush then returned, giving an all-clear signal to Gituku. Gituku waved to Warsame's boats. They pulled onto the beach and unloaded.

Omari returned to his place as second commander. They were on land now and no longer needed his experience or spiritual guidance. That was good, for Nalah's ashé faded the moment he found the island. They were on their own, but Omari had all the confidence in Gituku's skills. He'd served with him enough to trust his judgement.

Warsame made the transition of command as well. He walked up to Gituku and studied the thick bush before them.

"We'll set up base on the beach," Warsame said. "Have your men run a reconnaissance into the interior to see if there are any paths or roads leading to the temple."

"Yes, nahoda," Gituku said. He turned to Omari.

"Can you lead the reconnaissance?"

Omari nodded.

"Penda, Astaria, Jengo, Nuru!" Omari shouted. "Follow me. We're going for a walk."

The mercenaries gathered around Omari then followed him into the bush.

"Spread out," Omari ordered. We're searching for anything that looks like a path or a road."

Omari took out his sword, using it to cut vines and move branches aside. The sounds of the bush animals were familiar, their calls and chatter relaxing him. Islands usually contained unique fauna because of their isolation; Omari had encountered a few that chilled his blood. However, this was a Kiswala controlled island. If anything was exotic it had value. The hapless creatures had probably been hunted or captured and sold.

"Over here!" Astaria called out.

Omari and the others converged on Astaria's voice. The woman crouched over a ruined road.

"It's not much," she said. "But it's better than fighting the bush."

"I agree," Omari said. "Let's follow it a way before reporting back. Need to make sure it's not a dead end."

The squad ambled down the ancient road until they were certain it led directly to the temple. They turned back, following the thoroughfare back toward the beach where it ended at a harbor possessing a dock constructed of wood and coral stone.

"We're east of our landing," Omari said.

"We might be able to bring the dhow in here," Nuru observed.

"We'd have to find a way through the coral, and we don't have time," Omari answered. "Let's get back to camp."

Omari and the others trekked across the sands to the camp and reported their findings to Warsame and Gituku. Warsame's smile answered for him.

"Let's leave immediately," he said. "Cabdi! Gather our supplies!"

Cabdi and the other servants packed provisions they secured to their backs and balanced on their heads. The mercenaries formed ranks then led the march to the road. Gituku and his warriors formed the rear guard and Omari and his squad led the way. Warsame and the others walked protected in between.

The journey to the temple took most of the day, the road smoothing out as they came closer. By the time they reached the temple grounds the road appeared as if it had never been used. As they came closer, they spied a stone wall surrounding the temple, the pristine gate opened as if their arrival was expected. Gituku worked his way to the front of the column, joining Omari.

"We'll halt just outside the gate," he said. "Your squad will go inside to inspect."

Omari gave Gituku a sideways glance.

"We already scouted the road, and now you want us to take lead into the temple?"

"Yes," Gituku replied.

Omari sighed then marched toward the gate, sword in one hand, jambiya in the other. His cohorts drew their weapons as well, although they walked more cautiously than their commander.

Omari stepped through the gates into a massive courtyard. What had once been a well-maintained garden had degenerated into an overgrown tangle of trees, shrubs and flowering plants. Fragrant and pungent aromas fought with each other for attention while the trees buzzed with insects, birds and monkeys. Omari had seen worse. He continued walking, seeking a path through the morass which led to the temples entrance. He finally found it, a green and black checkered track that disappeared into the foliage. He turned to his comrades.

"Penda, come with me," Omari ordered. "The rest of you wait. If we're not back in ten minutes, don't follow us. Go back to the gate."

This time Omari and the others were mindful enough to bring machetes. Penda and Omari hacked their way forward, startling the animals and drawing angry howls from the monkeys. Their efforts were quickly rewarded. The door to the temple stood twice as high as an average person, the wood detailed with carving whose paint had faded long ago. The hinges holding the door in place were rusted, yet the door handles gleamed as if installed hours ago. Omari reached out and grabbed one of the handles. A tingle passed through his fingers and up his arm, causing his ngisimaugi to warm.

"Ashé" he whispered. Doubt entered his mind. An enchantment that still existed after untold years meant this temple had once been occupied by powerful sonchai.

"Let's go," Omari said.

They returned to the others then trotted back to the gate.

"Well?" Warsame asked.

"The courtyard is secure," Omari said. "We cleared a path to the temple's entrance. The door is protected by ashé."

"So?" Warsame said.

"We should reconsider," Omari replied.

"Nonsense," Warsame snapped. "You're not the only person Nalah shared secrets with. We are prepared."

Warsame pushed by Omari then strode into the courtyard, Cabdi and his other servants close behind. Omari looked at Gituku then raised his eyebrows. Gituku shrugged.

"He's our employer," Gituku said. "We're here to do what we were paid to do."

"You and I didn't get this old in this business by making stupid decisions," Omari replied.

"You can stay outside if you like," Gituku said. "You got us here. You've earned your pay and some. No one would think less of you for it."

Omari scanned the other mercenaries. Their expressions reflected Gituku's words. He seriously considered not going inside, but his Mikijen training got the better of him.

"Shit," he finally said. "Let's do it."

The mercenaries followed Warsame and his servants to the temple door. Warsame reached for the handle then jerked his hand back, his eyes wide. He turned to look at Omari, and Omari shrugged.

"Last warning," he whispered.

"Cabdi, bring me the bag," Warsame said.

Cabdi trotted up to Warsame then extended a worn leather bag decorated with glyphs. He held it steady while Warsame opened the bag then pulled out a small pouch. The nahoda opened the pouch then whispered as he poured the contents onto the handle. Seconds later a chill wind brushed through them. Omari closed his eyes then shook his head.

"I should go back to the dhow," he muttered. "I really should go back to the dhow."

"Then go," Gituku replied, "and stop scaring the others."

Omari turned to see Gituku glaring at him.

"No, I'll stay," he said.

The door hinges squealed as Warsame swung the doors open. The courtyard forest fell silent then exploded in sound as the creatures fled. The canopy shook from birds launching into flight and monkeys jumping from branch to branch. Grasses and bush

quivered as unseen creatures scurried away. Warsame didn't seem to notice. He pushed the doors
wider then entered the temple.

Omari and the others followed. They entered
a wide hall with a stone floor similar to the path
bordered by walls decorated with faded paintings.
Omari had traveled most of Ki Khanga, but these
symbols were alien to him.

"Omari," Gituku said. "Take your squad and
join Warsame. We'll protect the rear."

Omari glared at Gituku. Though his friend
boasted of doing their duty, Omari could tell the
man was afraid, as was everyone else. He huffed
then stomped away.

"Come with me," he said. "You know who
you are."

The others joined him. When he reached
Warsame the nahoda grinned.

"I was wondering when you cowards were
going to do what I paid you to do."

Omari didn't answer. He took out his sword
and jambiya. The others did the same.

They proceeded down the hallway until they
reached a wide atrium. The space was lit by sunlight
that shone through its crystal canopy. Unkempt
plants spilled from large vases, branches and vines
splayed across the stone. On the opposite side of the
atrium were six tunnels, their entrances guarded by
tall statues on each side. The lean figures resembled
oversized string puppets made of bronze. The inanimate guardians held long curved swords in each
hand. Strange patches rested where eyes should be,
and a crown capped their narrow heads.

"We'll split up and follow each tunnel," Warsame said. "Once you reach the end of your tunnel,
return here. Do not touch anything."

Warsame selected a servant to lead a group of mercenaries into the tunnels.

"Omari, you and your warriors will come with me," he said.

"As you wish," Omari replied.

They entered the central passage. The way was narrower, forcing them to proceed two abreast. Omari and Warsame led the way.

"What exactly do you expect to find here?" Omari asked.

"I have no idea," Warsame replied. "All I know is that whatever it is, it is the key to Kiswala wealth."

"I always assumed it was their trade," Omari said.

"Most do," Warsame replied. "But if you know the value of things, and you look at the buildings and trappings of the Kiswala and their islands, you realize that the profits they generate from their monopoly isn't nearly enough to pay for what they possess. There is something here that affords them their status. I plan to find it and take it from them."

"As I said before, they won't let whatever it is go without a fight," Omari warned.

"They have to be able to afford the fight," Warsame said. "If they cannot pay the Mikijen, the Mikijen will not fight. You know that as well as I do."

"That's true. But you forget the Shuru," Omari said.

"I do not forget them," Warsame said. "Kiswala dogs, every one of them."

"Well trained dogs," Omari said.

"Their skills are renowned, but there are only so many of them. The Kiswala will howl, but they will not bite. My father assured me of this."

The passageway opened into a room similar to the tunnel atrium but smaller. Rotted benches filled the center of the room. At the end of the room was a raised platform holding a wide dais. Atop the dias was an elaborately carved chest.

"I believe we have found what we seek," Warsame said, the sound of victory in his voice.

Omari and the other warriors followed Warsame and his servants to the dais. Warsame walked up to the chest and ran his hand across the surface. He looked at the others with a light in his eyes.

"It's warm," he said.

"Don't open it!" Omari blurted. "If it's warm it can be only one thing."

"Kipande," Warsame said. "We'll take it with us. I know sonchai who can properly open it."

Warsame stepped away and his servants went to work. They wrapped the chest with leather straps and ropes then attached them to the long poles they'd brought with them. They positioned the poles on their shoulders.

"Lift!" Cabdi shouted.

The servants replied with a collective grunt and raised the chest from the dais. The strain was evident in their faces as they maneuvered it to the floor.

"We should help them," Jengo said.

"No," Omari replied. "We're not labor; we're mercenaries. I guarantee not one of them would pick up a weapon and fight beside us if we're attacked. What we will do is clear a path for them. That damned thing looks heavy."

The mercenaries did as Omari ordered, shoving aside the benches and making a path for Warsame and the burdened servants to follow. They made their way back into the tunnel and out into the central atrium.

"Bwa," Cabdi said. "We need to rest. The chest is very heavy."

"Do so," Warsame said. "We must wait for the others."

The other parties returned, each with a similar story. Unfortunately, they did not have enough servants to bring the chests out of their chambers.

"We will send teams in to bring them out, then we will take them one by one to our dhow."

"Can the dhow handle the weight?" Gituku asked.

Warsame and Omari answered at the same time.

"Yes."

It took another hour to retrieve all the chests. Warsame looked on at the bounty before him emitted a laugh that echoed throughout the atrium.

"The Kiswala will pay," he said. "They will pay dearly."

He gathered Cabdi and the others.

"Let's get moving!"

The servants gathered around the first chest. As they lifted it to their shoulders Warsame approached Gituku.

"I'll pay your men an extra stack each if they will help us carry the chests to the dhow."

Gituku scanned his cohorts.

"What say you?" he asked.

All the mercenaries nodded except Omari. Gituku frowned then turned back to Warsame.

"Agreed," he said.

Gituku and Cabdi directed the mercenaries and laborers to the chests. Omari leaned against the wall near one of the statues, picking at his fingernails. He had no intentions of lifting anything. As he cleaned his thumbnail with his jambiya, he noticed a blue light from the corner of his eye. One of the chests was beginning to glow. He jumped from the wall; his eyes wide.

"Stop!" he yelled. Gituku looked to him, visibly annoyed.

"Stay out of this, Omari," he said. "Just because you decided not to . . ."

"Ahh!" one of the laborers shouted.

The man stumbled away from one of the chests as it became bright blue. The other chests began to glow.

"Let's go!" Omari shouted. "Now!"

Warsame held up his hand.

"No! We can't abandon the kipande!"

"Like the Cleave we can't!" Omari replied. He turned to run from the chamber when two bronze swords clashed together, blocking his escape.

"What in Daarila's Axe?"

The once inanimate bronze guards stepped out of their recesses, blue light emitting from their perforated eye plates. Omari eyes swept the chamber and saw the same thing repeated at every entrance. The trunks of kipande pulsed in unison, their brightness illuminating the chamber. An eerie howl filled the space, and the bronze guards attacked.

Omari ducked a swipe at his neck then spun from another blade aimed at his heart. He cut at the nearest guard but his sword bounced on the dusty metal.

"Shit!" he exclaimed.

The guards pressed their attack, Omari blocking, spinning and dodging their bronze blades. The kipande had activated them. The chamber transformed into what it had been designed to be; a killing space for those attempting to loot the temple. The Kiswala were nothing if not thorough. They'd set a trap for anyone trying to steal their wealth. Warsame had been foolish. They would all die in this place.

Omari ducked another swipe at his neck. As he ran, he spied what looked like cords behind the automaton's knee joint. Omari charged, praying to Eda that his suspicions were true. The guardian swung down at Omari; he slipped the blow then dodged behind it. He cut the cord with his blade. Black liquid sprayed onto the stone floor and the guard's leg went limp. It stumbled sideways then fell onto its side.

"Attack the joints!" Omari cried out.

Omari hacked the guard before him at the elbow joint. Black liquid jetted from the joint and the guard's arm drooped. He swirled around the ancient automaton like a lumbering dancer, cutting every joint. The guard finally collapsed into a pool of dark ichor, writhing as it attempted to continue its duty.

The other mercenaries heard Omari's command and responded. The chamber echoed with the sound of clattering metal, the floor slick with the dark liquid from the guards. Omari finally had time to look to the others. The results were grim. Half the mercenaries lay dead on the floor. A heavy weight settled on Omari's heart when he saw Gituku among them, his empty eyes staring at the crystal ceiling.

Warsame and his servants cowered among the glowing chests. Omari stomped to them, holding back his frustration.

"Go now!" he said.

Warsame gazed at the carnage and the jittering guards on the stone.

"We must gather the chests," he said.

Omari spat then walked away.

"Do what you have to do," he said. "I'm leaving."

He ran into the chamber that led out of the temple. The other mercenaries followed. They hurried back to the dhow where Hadiya and the others waited. The navigator ran up to Omari, her face filled with worry.

"Where are the others?" she asked.

"They may or may not be coming," Omari said. "I don't care."

Hadiya punched his chest.

"You were supposed to protect them!"

Omari grabbed her wrist before she could punch him again.

"We did, and we paid a heavy price for it."

"That is your job," she said. "That is your risk."

Omari didn't reply. He let go of her hand then walked to the boats. The other mercenaries followed.

Warsame and the others burst from the bush moments later, carrying a chest of kipande.

"To the boats now!" he shouted.

A lone automaton emerged behind them, its swords raised. It sliced the servant closest to it in half.

"Shit!" Omari said. He ran toward the thing.

"Get the others in the boat!" he said to the other mercenaries.

Omari jumped between a servant and the metallic guard, blocking its swing with his sword and dagger. He tried to get around it to the joints, but this automaton was much faster than the others. They traded blows, but there was no way Omari could stop it. The guardian lifted its head, looking over Omari. He knew then what had to be done.

"Drop the chest!" he shouted.

"No!" Warsame shouted back.

Omari ducked a swing at his head then ran to Warsame.

"Drop the damn thing or we all die!"

"I won't!" Warsame said. "We leave this and our safari was for nothing!"

A screeching sound interrupted their argument. More automatons emerged from the bush.

"What's worth more?" Omari asked. "Your treasure or your life?"

Warsame looked at the approaching guardians then to the chest. He grimaced.

"Leave the chest!" he shouted. "Get to the boats!"

Everyone fled to the boats. The automatons continued to come until they reached the chest. Omari watched them from his boat as one of them lifted the chest as if it was nothing then tucked it under its arm. The automatons turned in unison then marched back into the bush.

Warsame grimaced as he watched the automatons march away

"We've failed," Warsame said.

"No," Omari replied. "We learned the truth. The Kiswala may tell others they possess this wealth, but they don't. The guardians keep it protected. I believe this is Nala's doing."

"Nala?" Warsame looked confused. "Why would she do this? She said she wanted to go home!"

"And she did." Omari looked at the nahoda with a grin. "Do you think she would let you steal from her people like the Kiswala?"

Warsame slumped as he sat. His stunned expression was replaced by a grin.

"At least I'm not ruined," he said. "There are many islands here, there must be other things of value to discover."

Omari sat beside him.

"Do we still get paid?" he asked.

"I am a man of my word," Warsame said.

"Then let's get about it," Omari said. "We still have the greatest treasure of all."

"What is that?" Warsame asked.

Omari smiled. "Our lives."

ROAD TO KAMIT

Omari dropped the seeds into the pods of the oware board, then scooped out those of his opponent. The man sitting across from him grimaced in frustration as he lost for the third time. The spectators' emotions ranged from ridicule to anger. Whoever this stranger was, he was unbeatable.

Omari lifted his right arm and opened his hand. His opponent reached into the pocket of his tobe, took out a handful of cowries then dropped them into Omari's palm. Omari grinned.

"When you actually learn how to play, come find me," Omari said. "Then you won't lose as much money."

"Damn you to the Cleave, mercenary!" the man said. He stalked away; his supporters close behind. Another man, the oware board owner, reached down and closed the board.

"Hey!" Omari said. "What are you doing? I'm just getting started!"

"I'm going home, that's what I'm doing," the man said.

Omari offered the man half of the cowries he'd just won.

"One more hour?"

The man shook his head.

"No one else is going to play you," he said. "The man you just defeated, Fakeba Banja, is the best oware player in town. Anyone else would be foolish to play you. Go away."

Omari shrugged the put the cowries in his pocket. The smell of grilled goat teased his nostrils and he stood up to find his way to the market stall. As he searched, he spotted two figures clad in familiar black uniforms talking to a woman balancing a basket of kola nuts on her head. The woman turned to look and point at Omari.

"Shuru! Shit!"

Omari turned and ran, not caring to see if he was being pursued. He dodged his way through the crowded streets, making his way to the stables. The stable owner looked at him with wide eyes as he streaked to his horse. Omari threw the saddle on the Sokoto, fastened the straps as fast as his fumbling fingers could manage then mounted.

"Ha!" he shouted.

The horse burst from the stable, the stable owner running behind them.

"My pay!" he shouted as he shook his fist.

Omari tore the cowry bag from his belt then threw it at the stable owner. The bag bounced off his head.

"Tembo dung!" the stable owner shouted and he shook his fist.

"Make way! Make way!" Omari shouted.

Most of the villagers avoided him, but a few were knocked over by his reckless ride. Omari hoped he had a good head start. His confidence grew once they reached the town outskirts and the mostly empty road. The Sokoto stretched out to a full gallop, urged on by Omari striking its backside. There was no faster horse breed in all of Ki Khanga, nor one with more endurance. He continued to push the stallion even when the road emptied. He was determined to put as much distance possible between himself and the town before nightfall.

The Sokoto finally protested the pace and its treatment, stopping so abruptly Omari almost pitched over its head. He climbed off the horse, keeping hold of the reins as he led it into the bush. Once he was far enough from the road, he removed the saddle and reins, allowing the horse to roam free for forage. Omari found a secluded clump of bushes then laid his blanket under them. He lay his sword and jambiya on the blanket then unholstered his hand cannon. As he loaded the weapon, the questions he avoided formed fully in his mind. What were Shuru doing in the town, and why were they looking for him?

He lay the hand cannon on his blanket then rested. Mali was too far inland for any Kiswala merchant. They had to be seeking him, but why? He'd done nothing to spark their ire, and whatever he'd done in the past didn't warrant him being tracked this far west. Well, at least not to him. If he was lucky, he'd never find out.

"Ket!"

Omari jumped to his feet, the cannon gripped tight and pointed toward the source of the voice. Something slammed into his back, knocking the weapon free. An arm wrapped around his neck and attempted to put pressure on his throat but Omari rolled forward, throwing his assailant over him. He continued rolling, landing on top of the person then slamming his elbow into their gut and the back of his head into the attacker's face.

The Shuru that distracted him fell on top of him. The arms of the Shuru under him gripped tight around his waist, holding him down. Omari struggled, attempting to break free of them both. As his strength waned, his only consolation was that at least they weren't trying to kill him . . . yet.

The Shuru under him forced his arms back then tied his hands together. The other Shuru managed to dodge his desperate kicks and tie his ankles together. They rolled him onto his stomach then worked their way around and squatted before him. One of the Shuru was a woman, tall with a muscular build, the sleeves of her black shirt cut short to reveal her thick arms and nyoka tattoo. The other was a man of average height but similarly muscled, a scar running from his left eye to the corner of his mouth. The healed wound caught Omari's attention. The ashé contained in the Shuru's nyoka tattoo was rumored to be much more powerful than the Mikijen's ngisimaugi. Some said they were immortal because of it. Whatever made such a wound that a nyoka could not heal must have been terrible.

"This was not necessary," the woman said to Omari.

"I guess I'm just supposed to let you kill me," Omari replied.

"We are not here to kill you," the man said. "You have been summoned by Bwa Jumaane Simba. He has a task for you."

"A bwa sent you thousands of strides for me?" Omari said. "Do the Mikijen no longer serve you?"

"Bwa Simba requested you," the woman replied. "Besides, you still bear the ngisimaugi. You are a Mikijen as long as the tattoo marks your skin. Consider your time away from us as an extended break. You have been called back to duty."

The Shuru stood.

"I am Nalla," the woman said. "This is Jabali. If you promise you will not try to escape or fight us, we'll untie you. We don't want to chase you, and we certainly don't want to cripple you."

"Is there pay involved in this summons?" Omari asked.

"It is your duty to serve the Kiswala," Jabali replied.

"If I remember correctly, the Mikijen do nothing for free," Omari said.

"Yes, there is pay involved," Nalla said.

"You can free me," Omari said.

Nalla nodded at Jabali. Jabili unsheathed his jambiya then cut Omari free.

"Follow us," Nalla said.

The trio walked back to the road. The Shuru had found his Sokoto before ambushing him and secured it to one of their war steeds. The Sokoto looked like a pony next to the Malians. There was no way Omari would have outrun them, even with the Sokoto's famed speed and endurance. Bwa Jumaane sent his best Shuru to find Omari and return him to Kiswala. The question in Omari's mind was why.

They rode through the night and into the next morning. Omari attempted to spark conversation with his captors, hoping to discover more details about his task. The Shuru were reticent, giving only short answers or none at all. After three days Omari gave up.

They traveled south to Zaria then east to Ansanga, a port city located where the mighty Sikuhani River emptied into Lake Sati-Baa. In Ansanga Nalla hired a merchant dhow to transport them across the massive lake. Omari felt a twinge of homesickness as they sailed by the lake's namesake,

Ki Khanga's largest city shimmering like a jewel in the distance. He had yet to work up the nerve to return. He wasn't sure he was ready to deal with the consequences, or if his banishment was still being enforced.

The dhow landed at Binda, the northernmost port city of Kenja. From there they traversed through Market Town, then to their final destination on the mainland, Bashaba. As they neared Bashaba, Omari's confidence in the Shuru's word became uncertain. Bashaba was a Kiswala port; once he entered, he was fully in their realm. Not only would he have to deal with the Shuru, they would be backed up by the Mikijen garrison. He glanced at his silent and serious companions and contemplated his chances of escape. They were slim. He shrugged; his fate was in Eda's hands.

Bashaba was as busy as he remembered, with people arriving from all parts of Kenja with the fruits of farming. The goods would be distributed to the islands as well as other Kiswala ports. Unlike most Kiswala towns, the Mikijen barracks was near the shoreline. Attacks from the interior were rare; it was raids from the sea that threatened the port city. Fortifications lined the shoreline and beaches, with war dhows anchored just beyond the docks. Bashaba was not one of his favorite outposts when he was a Mikijen; it was well run and its commanders were usually sticklers for detail which left little time for interesting distractions.

They traveled through the city to the Mikijen fort. The gates opened and they were greeted by ranks of Mikijen, their left palms pressed against their chests. The fort commander waited near his command building, flanked by his subordinates. His salute was brief.

"Welcome to Bashaba citadel, Shuru," the commander said. "I am Kamada Mwenye Fuli. To what do we deserve the honor of your visit?"

Nalla, Jabili and Omari dismounted. Nalla approached the commander and they grasped arms.

"I am Nalla," she said. "And this is Jabili. We serve Bwa Jumaane Simba. We are escorting this man to Kiswala. A dhow will arrive in a few days to take us there. We need food and lodging. We are willing to pay."

Commander Fuli raised his hand as he shook his head.

"That won't be necessary. Our fort is at your disposal."

"Thank you," Nalla replied. "We also need a uniform for this man."

Fuli's eyes narrowed as he scrutinized Omari.

"This is highly irregular," Fuli said. "Is he a Mikijen?"

"I used to be," Omari replied.

"He still is," Nalla said. "He still bears the ngisimaugi."

Fuli's eyebrows rose. "What is your name?"

Omari straightened, a reflex from his former days.

"Omari Ket," he said.

"How long have you been away from the ranks?"

Omari looked up as he added up the time.

"Ten years."

Fuli's eyes widened. "And you still bear the mark? Fascinating."

He turned to his subordinate on his right.

"Russom, take Omari to the tailor and have him fitted."

Russom nodded. "Yes, kamada."

"Nalla, Jabili, if you could follow me, I will take you to your accommodations."

The commander walked away; Nalla and Jabili followed. Russom motioned with her head.

"Come with me, Ket," she said.

Omari walked with Russom to the tailor's shop.

"What did you do wrong to have two Shuru hunt you down?" she asked.

"Nothing," Omari replied. "At least nothing I can remember. They claim I was summoned by the bwa. I'm still not sure I believe that. I've been gone ten years."

"I've heard of you," Russom said. "You had quite a reputation while you served."

"Good or bad?" Omari asked.

Russom smirked. "It depends on who you talk to."

"That's fair," Omari replied.

"Those who remember you will be surprised to find out you're still alive."

"I'm surprised by that, too," Omari replied.

Russom laughed. Omari noticed her smile and was encouraged.

They entered the tailor's hut. The clacking of a working loom filled the cramp space.

"Taka!" Russom shouted. "I have a fitting for you!"

The clacking stopped and Taka emerged from the back of the shop. The stooped elderly man looked at Russom and Omari then frowned.

"I know you," he said to Omari. "I thought you were dead."

"Well, I'm not," Omari replied.

Taka shuffled from behind his counter. He took the knotted rope from his shoulder then measured Omari.

"I have something that will fit," he said. "It will be a little tight around the shoulders, but you'll stretch it out eventually. If you live long enough."

Omari scowled at the old tailor. The man went to the back then returned with the uniform.

"Come on," Russom said. "I'll show you to the barracks."

Omari followed Russom to the barracks then led him to a small room with a cot and a desk.

"This will be yours while you're here," she said. "You should be familiar with it."

"I can feel my back aching already."

Russom chuckled. "You should get changed."

Omari dropped the uniform on the bed and began taking off his clothes. Russom sat at the desk.

"You need any help?" she asked.

Omari smiled. "No."

"Then I'll just sit here and watch," she said.

"You could leave and give a fellow muwani some privacy," Omari said.

"No, I think I'll stay," Russom said.

Omari shrugged then stripped down to his loincloth then slowly redressed. When he was done, Russom clapped.

"You live up to your reputation," she said.

"I never disappoint," Omari replied.

Russom winked. "We'll see."

Omari spent the next few days reacquainting himself with the routine of barracks life. He remembered what little he enjoyed about it, and how much of it he hated, although spending time with Russom made it all bearable. They were in the mid-

dle of one of their sessions when Nalla entered the
room.

"Our dhow has arrived," Nalla said, un-
phased by the sight of their tangled bodies. "Finish
up then meet us at the docks."

Omari and Russom followed orders. Omari
dressed as Russom lounged on the cot. He bent over
to kiss her and she turned away.

"Let's not get sentimental," she said. "We're
Mikijen. We live for the moment, remember?"

"True," Omari said. "Until next time."

"Don't die," Russom said.

Omari hurried from the fort to the docks.
The Shuru dhow stood out among the Kiswala merchant and warships, a small, sleek vessel with a
black hull and black sails. Omari boarded with
Nalla and Jabili. The baharia stares made him uncomfortable.

The nahoda on the vessel met them on deck.
The elderly Shuru sported a bald head and a grey
beard that grazed his chest when he moved his
head. His eyes lingered on Omari before meeting
Nalla's.

"You found him," the man said.

"Yes," Nalla replied.

"Bwa Jumaane will be pleased," the nahoda
replied.

"How soon do we depart?" Jabili asked.

"Immediately," the nahoda answered.

"Good," Nalla said.

"Your cabin is ready," the nahoda said. "We
will send someone for you when we reach Kiswala."

"Thank you, Elewisa," Nalla said.

Omari followed Nalla and Jabili below deck.
Their cabin was a large space with three hammocks

and small chests for storage, similar to the accommodations for a Mikijen warship.

Omari missed Bashaba almost immediately after they set sail. Spending time with two Shuru was stressful; a ship full of the mysterious warriors was stifling. Few words were exchanged between them beyond giving orders and sharing information, and none of those words were shared with Omari. He was relieved when the Kiswala Islands finally came into view. However, minutes after, apprehension set in. It occurred to him that he never set foot on Kiswala. As a matter of fact, very few Mikijen were granted the privilege to visit the islands, and most of them never returned. As they sailed closer and closer, his doubts grew.

Omari stood at the bow in thought when Nalla and Jabili joined him.

"It is good to be home," Nalla said.

"How long were you searching for me?" Omari asked.

"Two years," Jabili replied.

Omari's mouth dropped open.

"Two years? I would have given up, took the stacks and gone my own way."

"You are not Shuru," Nalla said. "You know nothing of service or loyalty. Besides, there is nothing beyond Kiswala that interests us."

"We live to fight and to serve," Jabili added.

"And how long have you lived?" Omari asked.

"What?" Nalla said. "Why would you ask that?"

"It is believed among the Mikijen that your nyokas contain powerful ashé that renders you immortal," Omari said. "They say your wounds heal as soon as they appear and that not even decapitating you will kill you. Is this true?"

"Our destination is Shamsa," Nalla said. "Have you been there?"

Omari laughed at Nalla ignoring his question.

"No," he said. "I've never been to any of the islands."

"You will love it as we do," Jabili said. "It is the most beautiful of all the islands, as is its people."

"You will find Bwa Jumaane a gracious host," Nalla continued.

"And you will finally have someone to talk to," Jabili said with a bitter look on his face.

"I suggest you gather your things," Nalla said. "We are almost there."

Nalla and Jabili walked away. Omari returned to the cabin for his belongings. When he came back to the deck, the dhow was sailing into Shamsa's harbor. At first glance the port looked no different than any Kiswala port, but closer scrutiny revealed different. The docks were built from dense ironwood, wood so strong swords created from it cut like the finest steel. The dockworkers pants and kilts were woven from the best Kiswala cotton, and the ropes were wound from the Zambululand hemp. Their dhow moored and the trio disembarked. They were met by the dockmaster, who held her hand out. Nalla reached into her pouch and took out a parchment yellowed from time. The dockmaster read the paper and her eyebrows rose; she looked up from the paper with a rare smile.

"Welcome home," she said. She glanced at Omari and her smile faded.

"Follow me," she said.

The dockmaster led them to the stables where they were given the massive horses the Shuru rode. Omari mounted his nervously, being one that never was comfortable on any of the beasts. To his surprise the horse did not fidget despite sensing his uneasiness. It stood still like a statue. Even the beasts were disciplined here, Omari thought.

They rode from the docks to their destination. Omari took in the amazing sights along the way. Shamsa was beautiful as Nalla has said, each road, building, tree, bush, and blade of grass a perfect example of its kind. It was like riding through a painting. Yet there was something beyond normal vision, an energy Omari could feel but could not describe. A lot of ashé was at work here, adding to the sense of perfection he experienced. Omari imagined how living under the influence of such power for decades could give someone the impression that this place was perfect and that there was no rival to its splendor. It was like living in a chagga cloud.

They reached the residential district, an area of paved roads and perfectly built compounds. The compound walls were decorated with painted symbols of the family totems and images of noted ancestors. The alleyways between the compounds blossomed with fruit trees that jostled from the birds and monkeys partaking in their bounty.

Steep hills loomed over the residential district, casting their shadows onto the closest compounds. Nestled between two of the mounds was a compound whose high walls were visible even from a distance.

"Whose compound is that?" Omari asked his cohorts.

"Bwa Jumaane's" Nalla replied.

"He must be wealthy," Omari said.

"Shamsa belongs to his lineage," Jabili said. "They were the first to land here after The Purge and they defeated the other clans for claim to the island. All the other clans answer to the Simba Clan."

They stopped at a central market for food and rest. The variety of goods was a reflection of Kiswala's trade dominance. Omari identified things from the farthest ends of Ki Khanga and saw a few items he didn't recognize. The food was more familiar, and Omari ate it with relish.

They continued their trek to Bwa Jumaane's compound. What Omari thought were hills from a distance revealed themselves as mountains as they came closer. As they reached the foothills, the peaks were too high to see. The trio guided their horses up a narrow road that zig-zagged up the slopes before finally reaching a wide flat gap between summits. Bwa Jumaane's compound occupied the expanse. Omari had never seen a compound of this size, with walls that rivaled the palaces of Oyo, Asanteman and Mali. Farms circled the compound with sweeping spaces for grazing cattle and goats. The farmers and shepherds barely acknowledged their passing.

Two Shuru flanked the compound's immense gate. They lowered their spears as the trio approached. Nalla pulled back on the reins of her horse, stopping the beast a few strides from the gate. Omari and Jabili did the same. One of the guards approached Nalla, the other kept his distance, his spear at the ready. The Shuru trusted no one, not even their own.

Nalla handed the guard the same parchment she gave the dockmaster. The man inspected it then cut his eyes at Omari. After moment he handed the parchment back.

"The Bwa will be happy to see you," the guard said. "He had almost given up hope. Come with me."

They followed the guard to the gates then waited as the massive metal doors swung open. The bwa's courtyard was as extravagant as the surrounding farmland, filled with well-manicured plants and exotic animals that paid no attention to the humans riding by. Omari strained his eyes to look ahead and saw people gathering at the large veranda. Seven chairs were set by servants behind a long table. Platters of various types of food were visible on the table, causing Omari's stomach to rumble.

"How did they know we were coming?" Omari asked.

Nalla looked at him, grinned, then looked away.

A few moments later a procession of finely dressed people emerged from the house then sat before the table. Omari suspected this was the bwa and his family. His suspicions were confirmed as they came closer.

Jumaane Simba was a tall powerfully built man. He dwarfed his wife, a petite woman with the delicate features common among Kiswala nobles. Jumaane's three sons resembled their father in height and disposition. His daughters were a contrast; one looked exactly as the mother, yet younger. It was the second daughter that caught Omari's attention. She was tall like her brothers but with a feminine stature that was unique to her. Her large brown eyes sparkled with interest and intelligence as they finally reached the veranda, her full attention on Omari.

Bwa Jumaane stood and the Shuru bowed. Omari repeated their gesture while keeping his eyes on the daughter.

"At last, you have returned!" Jumaane said. He spoke with a deep voice used to authority.

"We apologize, bwa," Nalla said. "Omari Ket was in the west."

Jumaane waved his hand then sat.

"You found him, and that's all that matters," he said. "Alika, however, is probably upset."

The woman who had caught Omari's eye shrugged.

"I'm not angry with you, Nalla," she said, her voice similar to her father's yet softer. "I'm in no hurry to travel to Kamit. Now that the time has come, I am content."

One of Jumaane's sons stood then approached Omari, inspecting him.

"So, this is the one the Kamites chose," he said. "Tell me, Mikijen, how to you plan to protect our sister during this journey?

"I can't say," Omari replied. "I have no idea where we are going or why."

The man glared at Nalla. "You didn't inform him?"

"It was not my place, bwa Baraka," Nalla said. "We were only to find him and bring him to you."

Baraka rolled his eyes then stomped his way back to his seat.

"Damn Shuru," he said.

"Calm down, Baraka," Alika said. She stood then approached Omari.

"Before I share the information with you, I need to know if you are who you say you are. Take off your shirt."

"What?" Omari said.

"Take off your shirt," Alika replied.

Nalla and Jabili started toward Omari. He held up his hand.

"I don't need your help," he said.

Omari place his baldric, hand cannon and other items on the tiled veranda surface then took off his sash and shirt. Everyone's eyes went wide when they saw the jagged scar in the center of his chest. Even Nalla and Jabili looked in awe. The only person not moved was Alika. She touched the wound with her hand and Omari's face flushed with warmth.

"That is a killing wound," Jabili said. "Even for a Shuru."

"Tell me Omari, how did you get this wound?" Alika asked.

"I . . . I don't know," Omari replied.

"What do you mean you don't know?" Bwa Jumaane said.

"I was on a safari with a sorcerer from Menu-Kash. We sought a talisman of great importance to him. We finally found it, but when we attempted to acquire it, we were thwarted."

"How were you 'thwarted?" Alika asked.

"Like I said, bwa Alika, I don't know," Omari said. "When I awoke, she was standing over me."

Alika's eyes narrowed. "She?"

"Eda," Omari said.

Alika smiled then turned to her astonished family.

"Now you know why the Kamites chose him," she said.

"How could they know this?" Alika's mother asked.

"I don't know mama," Alika said. "Which is why I'm going to study with them."

"He must be tested," Bwa Jumaane said. His sons nodded.

"Tested?" Alika approached the bwa. "What good will that do, baba? The Kamites made it clear. Omari Ket is to be my escort. If I arrive without him, they will not let me set foot in Kamit."

"I don't care what those damn sonchai said! I will not send my child on a journey with a Mikijen or Shuru unless they have been tested."

The bwa motioned to Nalla and Jabili. The Shuru drew their swords. Omari scrambled to get his weapons then took a defensive stance. He glanced toward Alika, hoping she would intervene. Instead, she shook her head then took her seat.

"This is unnecessary," she said. "They could kill him!"

"Then he was not worthy to be your escort," Jumaane said.

Nalla and Jabili pounced simultaneously at Omari. He dropped to the ground the rolled to his right, avoiding them. He was barely on his feet when they came for him again. If Omari thought his time with the Shuru had built a bond between them, he was wrong. Jabili attempted to distract him with a thrust to his body while Nalla swung her sword to decapitate him. Omari let Jabili stab him as he ducked Nalla's swing then cut her hamstrings with his jambiya. The woman yelped as she fell to the ground.

The ngisimaugi flashed to heal his wound as he twisted free from Jabili's blade. The Shuru attacked with more fury that skill, apparently angered by Omari crippling his companion. Omari parried his blades while keeping an eye on Nalla. He didn't know how long he had before her nyoka healed her wounds.

Jabili attempted a double thrust, aiming his sword at Omari's throat and his jambiya at Omari's heart. Omari bent backwards avoiding the blades. He shifted forward, driving his jambiya into Jabili's groin. The man howled, dropping his blades then reaching for Omari's dagger. Omari slit his throat with his sword.

A slash across his back sent him stumbling over Jabili. He turned to see Nalla limping after him, his blood on her blade. She jabbed at Omari's face; Omari blocked the blow then realized too late what she'd done. Her dagger entered his abdomen then traveled for his heart.

"STOP!"

Alika's voice locked Omari and Nalla's bodies. Nalla's arm lowered and Omari slid off her blade then onto the ground, his chest and back burning.

"Enough of this," Alika said. She turned to glare at her baba. "Omari has survived five minutes in battle with two Shuru. Your best Shuru. That is proof enough."

The family looked and nodded to each other. Bwa Jumaane stood.

"So be it," he said. "Nalla, take Jabili to the sangoma to tend to his wounds. Send for one to see to the Mikijen."

"I'll tend to the Mikijen myself," Alika said to Nala. "Go."

Bwa Jumaane stood. "It's not your place to wait on a . . . "

Alika glared at Jumaane. "I said I'll tend to him myself!"

Omari saw the bwa's face tremble a bit before nodding his head then leading the others back into their home. Although they maintained a stoic demeanor, Omari realized they were afraid of her.

Nalla lifted Jabili from the ground, then hesitated, her eyes transfixed on Alika. Alika smiled at her.

"I'll be okay," she said. "Get Jabili to the sangoma. We don't want him to have another scar, do we?"

"Nalla smiled back. "No, we don't."

Nalla lifted Jabili on her shoulders then carried him away. Alika knelt beside Omari then pressed around the area where he'd been stabbed.

"Be gentle, bwa," he said. "I bruise easily."

Alika laughed. "How can you joke at a time like this? Nalla almost killed you."

"Almost," Omari replied. "You saved my life. I thought I was supposed to be protecting you."

"We are not on safari yet," Alika said. "And I don't need your protection or anyone else's. If it was up to me, I'd travel to Kamit alone. An escort was the Kamites' demand and my baba's desire."

Alika grasped Omari's arm.

"Stand up. Let's get you somewhere where I can treat you."

"Just let me lie here," Omari replied. "My ngisimaugi will heal me."

"We don't have that much time," Alika said. "I have herbs that will speed the healing."

Omari stood. "Why the hurry? You've waited two years for them to find me."

"Two years too long," Alika said. "I wish to be gone from this place as soon as possible. You don't know what it's like when your family hates you."

Alika led Omari to a small structure at the
rear of the main house overlooking a wide lake surrounded by a ring of low hills. Alika opened the
door and Omari followed her inside. There was a
bed and a small table with two sturdy chairs near a
stone fireplace. Shelves filled with bottles of various
herbs, elixirs and creams lined the walls. A pestle
and mortar sat on the table near a stone plate.

"Sit," Alika said. Omari sat at the table while
Alika rummaged through her shelves. She returned
with a gourd filled with a brownish cream. Alika
scooped out the cream with her fingers then rubbed
it on Omari's wound. The pain ebbed, replaced by a
cooling sensation.

"Thank you," Omari said.

"I can't have my escort die before our safari
begins," Alika replied.

"You say your family hates you," Omari said.
"That's not what I sensed."

"We are Kiswala," Alika said. "Putting on appearances is our talent."

"You're a beautiful woman and obviously
very intelligent," Omari said. "Any parent would be
proud of you."

Alika shoulders sagged as if a sack of sorghum had been dropped on them. She sat at the table, resting her forehead in the palm of her hand.

"In Kiswala, everything has value," she said.
"Everyone is judged by their worth. In my family, it
is tenfold."

"Your baba showed much concern for you,"
Omari said. "I don't think that was because of your
worth. You are his daughter."

"My baba's worry for me is no more or less
than his worry for a bushel of yams or a wagon of
ivory," Alika said. "He hopes that I am not damaged

so I will make a proper wife for another bwa's empty-headed son. The Kamites value me beyond my bride price. My baba does not."

Alika looked into Omari's eyes and smiled.

"My baba had plans for me," she said. "I was his most valuable child. I was bright, strong, inquisitive, and as you say, beautiful. He imagined me married to a merchant son of high lineage, one with property and dhows. My union would bring more recognition and prestige, improving his power here on the island and the mainland. But I was ruined long before he realized it."

"Ruined?" Omari said. "How so?"

Alika stood then browsed her shelves.

"I was not trained to be a sonchai," Alika said. "The knowledge was not passed down to me, nor was it taught to me by a servant or a wandering healer. I was born this way."

Natural sonchai were the most powerful, Omari thought. On Ki Khanga, people would travel strides for her healing and wisdom.

"I know what you're thinking," Alika said. "Why doesn't my family embrace my gift?"

"Do you read minds, too?" Omari asked.

"No," Alika replied. "It is a question others have asked. A sonchai is essential to us all, but it is a common trait, one beneath those of the Kiswala. To my people, being a sonchai means there is inferior blood in our lineage. That is a stain to our purity and a blotch on my baba's esteem.

"And what does your mama think?" Omari asked.

Alika smirked. "My mama is Kiswala, too."

She stood. "I've done all that I can do for you. I'm assuming you can find your way back to the barracks?"

"I'll manage," Omari replied.

"Good. Meet me at the compound gates at first light. I wish to leave as soon as possible."

"No sentimental goodbyes?"

"My time in Shamsa is done," Alika said. "And I am glad of it."

Omari made his way back to the Shuru compound. He still encountered stares, but the demeanor of those staring had changed. If he didn't know any better, it seemed more respectful. His suspicions were confirmed when he reached the barracks. The Shuru nodded and made way for him. A servant met him a few moments after he arrived, leading him to a room for him to rest. Soon after he settled another servant arrived with food. Omari was guzzling down a gourd of palm wine when Nalla entered his room. He dropped the gourd and lunged for his sword.

"Sit down, fool," she said. "I'm not here to harm you."

Omari eased back into his seat, keeping a wary eye on Nalla.

"I've fought Mikijen before" she said. "You are better than most."

"Did you kill them?" Omari asked.

"A few," Nalla replied.

Omari tried not to show his nervousness as he ate his stew.

"I'm sorry I tried to kill you," she said. "But my bwa commanded it."

"I understand," Omari said. "I mean I do, but I don't."

Nalla laughed and Omari almost choked on his food. He'd never seen a Shuru smile before, let alone laugh.

"It was more than that," Nalla said. "Alika is special to me. Very special. I asked if I could accompany her, but the Kamites were very specific. Only you."

"I'm sorry to hear that," Omari said. Actually, he wasn't. He wanted to finish his meal and rest. He had no time for sad stories.

"I now know why they chose you," Nalla continued. "You could wear the black."

Omari nodded again. He finished the stew then wiped the bowl with his bread.

"The Kamites paid the bride price to Bwa Jumaane for her," Nalla said. "She is bonded to them now. She will never come back."

Nalla's eyes glistened, and Omari understood.

"You know this may be the last time you see her," he said.

Nalla lowered her head. "Yes."

"Then what are you doing here with me?" Omari said. "Go to her."

Nalla raised her head, her eyes bright. "Yes, I should. I will."

She stood then offered her arm. Omari sighed as he stood then took it.

"Safe travels, Omari Ket," Nalla said. "Do not die."

Nalla hurried from his room.

"At last," Omari said. He finished his stew, bread, and wine then laid in his bed. He'd be happy to leave Shamsa and this Kiswala drama behind.

* * *

Alika was waiting outside when Omari arrived at the compound. She sat on a Shuru horse with two smaller pack horses for her items. Her family stood in the veranda, her mama, sister and two of her brothers with tear-filled eyes. Bwa Jumaane and the other brothers shared no emotions. Nalla and Jabili horses were on either side of Alika. Jabili glared at Omari; Nalla's full attention was on Alika.

"You are late," Alika said to Omari.

"I apologize," Omari said. "Shall we go?"

Alika glanced at her family then gave them a half-hearted wave.

"Take care of my daughter, Mikijen!" Bwa Jumaane shouted. "Make sure she arrives safe!"

"I will," Omari shouted back.

"Don't let the merchandise get damaged," Alika said under her breath.

"You really don't like your baba, do you?" Omari asked.

Alika didn't reply.

Nalla and Jabili accompanied them to the docks where a merchant dhow waited. Servants met them at the gangplank, taking their horses then leading them on the dhow. Alika faced the Shuru, her eyes locked on Nalla.

"Thank you for the escort," she said. "Your service will not be forgotten."

Omari rolled his eyes.

"You're about to leave this island, never to return," he said. "I think you can drop your charade just this once."

Alika looked at him with wide eyes, then looked at Nalla.

"He's right," Nalla said.

Alika wrapped her arms around Nalla's waist then pulled her close. They kissed as though they had never kissed before. Omari smiled despite himself. He thought of Aisha. He should have kissed her that way the last time he saw her, but he didn't know that would be their last time together.

When it was over, Alika wiped the tears from Nalla's cheeks.

"You are the only person I'll miss," she said.

"Goodbye, sweet flower," Nalla said.

"Goodbye, my sunbird."

Alika turn to Omari. "Let's go."

The two of them boarded the dhow. Alika went immediately to her cabin. Omari remained on deck until the dhow was under way. A servant showed him to his cabin, which was beside Alika's. He stowed his gear then proceeded back to the deck.

"Ket," Alika said.

Omari turned to see Alika, her eyes red.

"Thank you for what you did," she said.

"What did I do?" he asked.

"You encouraged Nalla to come to me," she replied. "Neither of us had the courage to do it on our own."

Omari shrugged. "She was whining about you while I was trying to eat. It seemed the best way to get rid of her."

Alika laughed. "I'm glad there was wisdom in your annoyance."

Omari nodded then turned to go to the deck.

"Wait," Alika said. "I'll go with you."

"As you wish," Omari replied.

He leaned against the wall as Alika went back into her cabin. She emerged moment later, wearing a simple dress and headwrap, her feet bare. Together they went to the deck.

"I've never been out to sea," she said.

"Be wary of the sickness," Omari said. "It can be bad."

"I'm prepared," she replied. "I'm a sonchai, remember?"

"I wish I knew you my first time out," Omari said. "I vomited so bad I expected to see my insides floating in the ocean."

"Nalla said she would rather be at sea than anywhere else," Alika said. "She said she felt at peace here."

Omari closed his eyes and silently cursed. It seems he would spend the entire safari listening to Alika lament over her Shuru.

"It makes me angry that something as simple as rank kept us apart," Alika said. "Away from Kiswala things would have been different."

"Don't be so sure," Omari said. "Unless you come from common stock, lineage matters, more so in some places that others. Kiswala and Menu-Kash are extreme cases. In Sati-Baa lineage means very little. There, wealth is all that matters."

"I take it you have seen much of Ki Khanga," Alika said.

Omari nodded. "More than I've wanted."

"Where are you from?" she asked.

"Sati-Baa," Omari replied. An image of the grand city appeared in his mind and he grinned. "My life was hard there, but it was home. There is nowhere else in Ki Khanga like it."

"What do you miss about it most?" she asked.

"Spinfish," Omari replied. "Sweetest flesh you ever tasted, and slightly narcotic, too."

"I've eaten it," Alika said. "Baba has it brought in for special occasions. It is quite tasty."

Omari frowned as he waved his hand. "That's the smoked or dried version. When you taste it fresh from the lake, it's a spiritual experience."

Omari and Alika spent the remainder of the day walking the deck, speaking to the Shuru on the ship and exchanging stories with each other. The more Omari learned about the bwa's daughter, the more he understood why she was anxious to leave Kiswala. He only hoped she would find what she was looking for on Kamit.

After a few days at sea, the safari settled into its usual monotony. Omari donned bahari clothes and pitched in with the daily chores as he usually did on long journeys. Alika would watch them, her interest never waning no matter how many times she observed them. On the second week at sea the routine was shattered by an ominous object on the horizon. The baharia in the lookout mast blew his shell horn, warning the crew before scrambling down the mast and rushing to the nahoda. Omari and Alika emerged from their cabins at the same time. Omari was armed with his sword, jambiya and hand cannon; Alika wore a Shuru sword and dagger belt.

"You should probably stay inside, bwa," he said.

"You mistake me for a child," Alika said. "I can take care of myself."

"That may be true," Omari replied. "But you protecting yourself should be the last resort. I was hired to guard you, and I'm good at it. Let me do my job."

Alika's eyes narrowed. "And if you fail?"

Omari smirked. "I won't."

Alika returned to her cabin. Omari hurried to the deck and found the nahoda.

"What is it?" he asked.

The nahoda gave him a sideways glance before turning his attention back to the approaching dhow.

"We don't know," he said. "I've never seen a dhow like this. It has no sail, yet it is approaching us rapidly. They are not coming to talk to us, of that, I am sure."

"Evasive maneuvers?" Omari said.

"Useless," the nahoda replied. "No matter what we do, we won't outrun them. There will be a fight, and I want my Shuru well rested before it begins. Once we kill them all, we can discover what makes this ship run. The engineers back in Kiswala will be interested."

"Remember the daughter of Bwa Jumaane is aboard this dhow," Omari said.

The nahoda rubbed his chin before responding.

"Take a boat and leave the dhow," he said. "Once the fighting is over you can return. Stay on the blind side of our dhow so they cannot see you."

Omari rushed back to Alika's cabin and knocked on her door. She opened it; her face filled with curiosity.

"What is it?"

"Come with me. We're leaving the dhow."

"Leaving the dhow? Why? Where are we going? We're in the middle of the sea!"

Omari grabbed her arm and she snatched it free. Omari sighed.

"The dhow approaching us is like nothing anyone has seen," Omari said. "They will surely attack us."

"How do you know this? It could be a Kamite dhow coming to greet us."

"That might be true, but if that was the case, they would have signaled us," Omari said.

"That doesn't explain why we're leaving the dhow."

"As a precaution," Omari said. "If they attack the nahoda wants you off the dhow to avoid the fighting. We'll return after it's over."

"How is this protecting me?"

Omari slammed his fist again the wall and Alika jumped.

"Protecting you mean removing you from harm! Now will you stop arguing with me and do as I ask?"

"Watch your tone, Mikijen!" Alika snapped back. "Remember who you serve."

Omari spun around and stomped away. Alika followed him to the deck. The Shuru had prepared the boat. Omari climbed in first. There were two chests of provisions. Omari looked at the nahoda.

"Just in case," he said. "Row due west. You will eventually reach land."

Omari nodded then helped Alika into the boat. The baharia lowered it to the sea; Omari grabbed the oars and began rowing.

"He did not seem sure of the Shuru defeating these strangers," Alika said.

"I know," Omari replied. "And that bothers me."

There were two oars inside the boat. Omari took one and began paddling. Alika picked up the other oar.

"I want to help," she said.

"I can manage," Omari replied.

"We will go quicker with both of us rowing," Alika said.

"Have you ever rowed a boat before?" Omari asked.

"No," Alika replied. "But I'm a quick learner."

"Watch me," Omari said. "When you feel comfortable, you can row on the right side. Stay in time with me."

Alika nodded. Her eyes focused on Omari's movements as he switched sides. They were making good progress when Omari heard a roaring sound behind him. Alika's eyes went wide with fear as she pointed over Omari's shoulder. Omari twisted around. What he saw sent terror through his frame.

"By the Cleave!" he said.

A stream of fire arced through the air then splashed onto the dhow. Omari saw baharia jumping off the vessel, some of them in flames. As they hit the water, the flames did not abate. They continued to burn as they sank beneath the waves.

Omari turned away from the frightful carnage.

"Row!" he shouted.

Alika grabbed the oar and they both rowed hard, their strokes synced. Omari kept looking back at the terrible scene. Never in his life had he seen such a sight. Whoever this enemy was, they were more formidable than any the Kiswala had encountered.

The strange dhow appeared, a vessel without sails spewing the fire stream from its aft. Everything was different about it, even its hull shape was unfamiliar.

"Stop rowing and get down!" Omari said.

Alika obeyed. Together they ducked into the boat.

"Shouldn't we keep rowing?" she said.

"They might spot our movement," Omari replied. "If the see the boat they might believe we're debris."

"Might," Alika replied.

"We can't outrun that thing," Omari said. "Our best chance is not to be seen."

Omari and Alika continued to watch as the vessel spewed its flaming stream onto the hapless Shuru. After circling the burning dhow twice, the fire stream ceased. Omari spotted boats with people inside lowered into the water. The boats worked their way through the debris.

"What are they doing?" Alika said.

"Searching for survivors and killing them," Omari said.

The grim hunt went on for what seemed forever. The boats then rowed up to the fire dhow and were lifted up the sides. The dhow lingered as the flames died; once there was no more fire the dhow moved away, returning toward the direction from where it came.

Omari sat up with his oar. Alika did the same. They rowed with less urgency; their energy sapped by what they had just witnessed.

"Someone wants me dead," Alika said.

Omari didn't reply. He wasn't one to confirm the obvious.

"Whoever it is, they must have spies in Shamsa," she continued. "Otherwise, they would not have known of our departure."

"It's not as if your safari was kept secret," Omari said. "It doesn't matter now. Whoever it was

thinks you're dead now. And since you won't be returning to the islands, your family is safe."

"That doesn't make me feel better," Alika
said.

"You'll be safe once we reach Kamit," Omari
said.

"Will I?" Alika asked. "What if those same
people have spies there?"

"You don't know and you can't know," Omari
said. "Right now, we have to focus on our current
situation. We need to reach the shore before nightfall. Once we land, we'll get our bearings then continue to Kamit. We can only consider what we can
control. Everything else is in Eda's hands."

They continued on their way. Alika tired, her
strokes ragged and out of sync. A shrill cry overhead
caught Omari's attention. He looked up to see a
lone seabird drifting overhead and let out a breath
of relief.

"Put down your oar and rest," Omari said.

"But you need my help," she replied.

"You're not helping when you're exhausted,"
he said. "Besides, we're close."

"How do you know this?" Alika asked.

"The birds," he replied. He gestured up with
his head and Alika shielded her eyes before looking.

"They don't stray far from land," Omari said.
"At least not this kind. Put down your oar and rest."

As Omari predicted, the sight of land rose
slowly over the western horizon as the sun dipped
beneath it. Their blessing was better than imagined;
they rowed toward a small port, its landing beach
busy with merchant dhows and cargo boats. Omari
worked their boat through the others, a few loaders
giving them a curious eye. He paddled the boat onto
the shore and was immediately approached by a

dockmaster. The woman held a tablet and stylus ready to record.

"Hello," she said. "From what dhow do you hail?"

"We have no dhow," Omari replied. "It was attacked far from shore. We managed to escape."

A grim look came to the woman's face. "Any more survivors?"

"No," Omari said.

The woman's arms fell to her side. "What happened?"

Omari could tell by the tone in the woman's voice that she knew.

"It was burned," he said.

"By the Cleave," the woman said. "Another one."

Alika eyes widened. "There have been others?"

"Too many others," the woman said. "Merchants are afraid to sail between cities. Our goods are piling up in our warehouses and the farmers and craftspeople supplying them are angry."

The woman noticed Omari's uniform.

"Where are the Mikijen?" she asked. "Are the Kiswala aware of this piracy?"

"No, they're not," Alika said. "And this is not piracy. Nothing is being taken; it's being destroyed."

"Who are you?" the woman asked."

"I am Alika Simba, daughter of Bwa Jumaane Simba of Shamsa."

The woman's eyes went wide and she bowed.

"We are honored," she said.

"Do you have a Mikijen outpost?"

"No, we don't bwa," the woman replied. "The nearest is in the next port city."

"Are they aware of what is happening?" Alika asked.

The woman scowled. "Yes, they are, but they refuse to do anything."

Omari and Alika shared a glance.

"We shall see if we can change their minds," Alika said.

Omari's eyes narrowed.

"Bwa, a word," he said.

Alika and Omari walked away from the woman.

"My duty is to get you to Kamit, not discipline a wayward kamada," Omari said.

"And my duty as daughter of a bwa is to make sure the trade flows," Alika replied.

"I thought you hated your family," Omari said.

"I do, but I'm Kiswala. I can't walk away from this. And these fisis tried to kill me."

"It doesn't look personal anymore," Omari said.

"Yet it still could be," Alika replied. "Maybe they knew we were sailing Kamit, but they didn't know when. They decided to destroy every dhow leaving the islands hoping to get the right one."

"Then you can end this with a simple message," Omari replied. "Have word sent that your dhow was destroyed and you are dead."

Alika stroked her chin. "That may work. We still have to travel to this outpost to send the message. And they would have to send my message by a sonchai; a dhow may not reach the island."

Alika turned to the dockmaster. "Where can we get horses?"

"There is a stable near the warehouse district," she said. "They have good horses."

"Thank you." Alika reached into her bag and gave the dockmaster a handful of cowries. The woman's mouth gaped.

"Thank you, bwa!"

Omari and Alika hurried away from the landing beach, Omari leading the way.

"We should go to the market first," he said. "We need food and provisions. We don't know how long this journey will take."

"Lead the way," Alika replied.

They stopped a merchant woman heading to the dock and asked for directions to the market. Once they arrived, they purchased provisions then headed to the stables. Alika selected two fine Sokotos and they were on their way.

They rode hard but the strain of the day caught up with them quickly. Neither Omari or Alika relished spending the night in the bush, so when they came across the remains of a port town a few lengths south of their destination they rode to it. The closer they came to the town, the more ancient it appeared. The town had apparently been abandoned long ago; its stone road covered with vegetation sprouting between gaps, the building in various stages of decay. Despite the ruins, it was once a grand city.

Omari took the lead, working through the streets until he found the building less ruined. They dismounted, tied their mounts to the nearest tree, then broke into their provisions.

Omari stood, munching on a piece of bread. Alika sat nearby, her eyes darting back and forth.

"You picked a fortunate spot," Alika said.

"Why do you say that?" Omari asked.

"There are many medicinal herbs growing around us," Alika replied. "This was probably the house of a sonchai."

Omari studied the ruins. "A very successful one, by the looks of their house."

"Indeed," Alika said. She stood and wandered the area.

"Lots of healing plants," she said. She squatted before a small bush.

"This is buka," she said. "It's used to treat internal complications, but is also used to heal and disinfect wounds."

Her eyes shifted to another plant.

"Giracha. It relieves pain."

Alika stood then ambled to a collection of leavy plants.

"And this is hadedaan. It's also used on wounds, but is especially effective for burns."

Omari watched Alika as she inspected a few more plants then returned to stand beside him.

"I think I know why this city was abandoned," she said.

Omari stopped chewing his bread. "Why?"

"There was much violence here," Alika replied. "Wars with neighbors, pirate attacks, or maybe internal power struggles. Whatever it was, it kept the sonchai very busy."

The sound of sandals slapping against stones caught their attention. Omari and Alika unsheathed their blades, their heads jerking toward the direction of the sounds. A large fisi running a full speed appeared, its laugh-like voice echoing off the ragged stone walls. An armed man appeared moments later, wearing brown leather shirt and pants festooned with protective talisman and gris-gris. He wore a conical metal helmet, a patch covering his left eye.

"Behind me!" Omari shouted.

"I can fight!" Alika shouted back.

But Omari could not answer. The fisi leaped at him and he kicked it away. The man hesitated as the beast struck a wall and howled. Seeing the beast hurt seemed to spur him more. He attacked Omari and sparks flew their swords met. As they fought, Omari realized this was no random encounter. The fighter before him was skilled, testing every ounce of Omari's martial talent. The information from the dockmaster was a set up. This man had come to kill Alika.

The fisi returned, biting at Omari's legs. Alika jumped to his aid, driving the beast back with her sword. But her skills were not good enough. The fisi sank its teeth into Omari's leg and he felt pain like he'd never experienced before. He dropped his sword and jambiya, falling hard to the ground. Before the fisi or the man could finish him, Alika drove her sword into the fisi's torso. The creature howled and shuffled away. The warrior cried out then rushed to the beast, scooping it into his arms then fleeing.

Omari jerked in spasms. The pain burned a path up his leg to his torso. He waited for his ngisimaugi to respond, but it didn't. His back was cold.

"What . . . what is happening?" he stuttered.

Alika came to his side, examining his wound. She leaned close to it and sniffed. She jerked her head back with a look of horror on her face.

"Cleave!" she said. She hurried to the plants she'd found, tearing at the leaves and branches.

"Fight Omari!" she said. "Fight!"

Omari opened his mouth but nothing came out. The spasms decreased; his arms flopped to his side. The numbness swept over him and the world went black.

* * *

Omari woke to a foul smell. He raised his head to see Alika squatting beside a fire which heated the small pot hovering above it. The dancing flames illuminated the area surrounding them. Alika looked up, a melancholy smile on her face.

"You survived. I prayed that you would," she said.

Omari attempted to sit up, but he couldn't. His body was paralyzed.

"What's wrong with me?" he asked.

Alika dipped a ceramic cup into the pot then brought it to Omari.

"Drink this. It will help purge the fisi's poison from your system."

Omari forced his way through the terrible aroma and drank. Luckily the concoction didn't taste as bad as it smelled. He could feel the brew work its way down into his stomach and through every part of his body. He was about to speak when he felt the drink reverse its path. He twisted quickly then spewed the elixir out of his mouth and nose.

"Daarila's ass!" he shouted. "Was that supposed to happen?"

"Yes," Alika replied. "We have to get the poison out of your system for your ngisimaugi to work."

Omari felt a slight tingle across his back and down his torso to his feet.

"I think it's working," he said.

"Of course, it is," Alika replied.

Omari settled back. "I must admit, I'm surprised to see you still alive."

Alika shrugged. "Whoever they were, they're not here to kill me. They are here to kill you."

"Me? Why?"

"I don't know," Alika said. "They were not attacking me, only you. I think it has something to do with the Kamites requesting you. They never meant for you to protect me. I think they meant for us to protect each other."

Omari was confused. "I don't understand."

"I don't either," Alika said. "The only ones that can explain it are the Kamites."

Alika went back to the pot and scooped out another cup of the potion.

"But we have more immediate concerns," she said. "Those two will be back to finish their task, as soon as the fisi heals. We must be ready."

Omari drank the potion and threw up again. This time the reaction wasn't as intense. The tingle in his back increased to a warm sensation and the feeling increased in his legs.

"If they return before I'm healed, we're both doomed," he said.

"No, we're not," Alika said. "As I told you before, I can handle myself."

"That hasn't been proven," Omari said.

"Because you wouldn't let me fight," Alika replied. "Nalla and I did more than make love during the time we spent together. She taught me how to fight like a Shuru."

"We'll find out soon enough," Omari said. "At least bring me my weapons."

Alika went to Omari's gear and brought him his sword, jambiya and hand cannon.

"What is your plan?" he asked.

"There seems to be some connection between the fisi and its companion," Alika said. "I think if we kill it, the rest will be easy."

"And how do you plan on killing it?"

Alika grinned. "I won't. You will."

* * *

Omari lay still near the fire, his nervous eyes probing the surrounding darkness. The night air vibrated with the sound of night creatures, most of them familiar, some not. He cursed himself for agreeing to Alika's plan. At the time it seemed reasonable, but the more he considered it the more he realized they would both die.

He was about to call out for Alika when the night fell silent. Beyond the fire a pair of eyes glowed in the firelight, moving slowly toward him until the fisi's head was revealed. Behind it stood the assassin, his sword gripped in its right hand.

Alika charged from the darkness, her slicing sword aimed for the assassin's neck. The man stumbled away, her sword just nicking his throat. He regained his balance and retaliated. Alika fought furiously with much more skill than Omari expected, but it was obvious that she was outmatched. He would have to end this quickly for both of them to survive.

The fisi leapt at Omari. Omari raised his hand cannon then lit the fuse. The cannon did not fire.

"Cleave!" he cursed as the fisi descended upon him. Omari gripped the cannon like a club and swung, striking the fisi on the side of the head. The fisi struck the ground then flopped about like a landed fish, seriously wounded but not yet dead.

"Omari! Finish it!" Alika shouted.

The assassin's eyes were locked on the wounded fisi. He absently drove his sword into Alika's stomach then sprinted toward the fisi. Omari tried to stand but his legs failed him. Instead, he grabbed his jambiya then threw it hard at the fisi. The blade streaked across the distance and found its mark in the fisi's eye socket, tearing through the orb then piercing its brain. The fisi let out a human-like shriek then fell still. The assassin stumbled then fell to his knees. His arms dropped to his side; he stared at the dead fisi like a statue.

Omari looked for Alika. The woman staggered to a clump of one of the plants she'd talked about days ago, grabbing a handful of leaves and pressing them against her wound.

Omari crawled to her. His eyes went wide when he saw the blood seeping from the leaves.

"I'm okay," she said before he could speak. "The buna leaves will help seal the wound. I'll need to rest though. I am no Mikijen."

Omari tried his legs again. He stood still as he regained his balance.

"Excuse me," he said.

He wobbled to his sword, picked it up, then trudged to the assassin who was still hovering over the dead fisi. Omari lifted his sword and cut off the assassin's head. The body hesitated then fell on the fisi. He staggered to Alika, who had closed her eyes.

"Is it over?" she asked.

"Yes," Omari said. "Can you ride?"

"I probably shouldn't, but I will," she said. "I want to get out of this place."

Omari found their horses then loaded their supplies, his legs gaining strength with each step.

His ngisimaugi was at full strength, the heat emitting from his back a welcomed feeling.

Omari returned to Alika. She reached out to him.

"Give me your hand," she said.

Omari extended his hand. Alika grabbed his wrist, moved the buna leaves aside then pressed his palm against her wound.

"What are you . . ."

"Be quiet," Alika said. "I need to concentrate."

Omari fell silent. Alika closed her eyes and her forehead wrinkled. Omari felt the heat of his ngisimaugi increase then flow from his back, through his arm and into the palm of his hand. The warmth trickled from his skin onto Alika's stomach. For a few seconds his body when cold, and then it warmed again. Alika took his hand away and her wound was gone.

"How did you do that?" Omari asked.

Alika grinned at him like a child that had just learned s new skill.

"I don't know," she said. "I just felt it would work."

She touched where her wound hand been and flinched.

"It's still sore, but I'm well enough to ride. Let's go."

They climbed onto to their horses and left the ruined city behind.

* * *

Omari thought he'd never be happy to see a Mikijen outpost, but in fact he was. It took two days to ride from the ruins to the coastal station, two days which he and Alika healed as much as they could along the way. Alika found more herbs to brew that helped with the process, plants that thankfully didn't cause Omari to vomit. Their provisions ran out along the route; as they entered the station their stomachs rumbled at the smell of cooked food. The kamada met them at the gate entrance with a gruff demeanor that quickly transformed once Alika displayed the symbol of her family. They were taken to the best accommodations available, which for this outpost was a tiny room with a bed and mattress. Omari slept a full day before he was awakened by a junior Mikijen and led to the kamada's office where Alika and Kamada Enzi Soyinka waited. Alika greeted him with a smile; Soyinka scowled.

"You did a terrible job protecting Bwa Simba's daughter," the kamada said.

"She's alive," Omari replied. "I think that's well enough."

"I couldn't have asked for a better bodyguard," Alika said. "But my wellbeing is not why we came here. Do you know of the fire dhow?"

"We just became aware of it," Soyinka said. "We received a message from Tanza. A fleet is assembling now to find it."

"There is an easier way," Alika said.

"What is it?" the kamada asked.

"Put me and Omari on a dhow," she answered. "The fire dhow will find us."

Omari shook his head. "No."

"I agree with Ket," Soyinka said. "We cannot endanger your life again."

"It's worth the risk to restore the trade," Alika explained. "If trade dies, Kiswala dies."

Enzi scratched his left cheek. "I'm not sure about this."

"I am," Omari replied. "Let the Mikijen handle the fire dhow. We'll take the land route to Kabasa. The city lies on the Kamit Strait."

Alika's eyes shifted between Omari and Enzi before answering.

"So be it," she said. "It will add time to our safari, but it will hopefully be a safer route."

"I'll assign five of my Mikijen to you," Enzi said.

"Only if they'll take commands from Ket," Alika replied.

"He's not a Mikijen," Enzi protested.

"He is for now," Alika replied.

Enzi frowned. "As you wish, bwa."

"Excellent. We'll leave at first light."

Omari and Alika left the kamada's building.

"We have no idea if the land route will be safer," Alika said.

"True," Omari replied. "But I'd rather be stabbed than burned."

Alika laughed. "I agree. I pray to Eda that we don't encounter any more like our friends."

"Let's hope not," Omari said.

"Have you ever seen anything like them in your travels?" Alika asked.

Omari shook his head. "No. But Ki Khanga is a big place, and there are still lands I have not visited. I believe between the two of them it was the fisi that was the master."

"It seemed so," Alika said. "Fascinating. I've heard of sonchai of Zambululand that possess animal familiars, but they have control over them. This was the other way around."

"The world is full of mysteries," Omari said. "Too many for me to waste my time worrying about."

Alika gave Omari a sideways glance. "It's all very simple to you, isn't it?"

"Yes," Omari replied. "At least when it's allowed to be. But every now and then I meet someone like you or . . . well, let's just say some people have a way of complicating life. My mama used to say, 'life is hard if you make it hard."

They departed at first light. The journey across southern Ki Khanga took three weeks, twenty-one uneventful days. They arrived at Kabasa at midday, joining the throng of people traveling to the bustling port city. As the last port on the southwestern coast of Ki Khanga, Kabasa was a replenishing station before and after dhows rounded the Ki Khanga cape. For this reason, it was the Kiswalans most profitable port city, full of artisans and craftspeople and ringed by farms that supplied foodstuffs for famished crews. The crowds made way the best they could for the important looking woman and her impressive entourage of Mikijen. They were immediately allowed entrance to the Mikijen outpost. The kamada, a powerfully built woman with a stern face and close-cropped hair, met them at the stables. Her rank necklaces were impressive; even Omari raised an eyebrow. She helped Alika dismount.

"Welcome, bwa Simba," she said. "I am Kamada Tabia Mbuku. We have been expecting your arrival."

Omari and Alika were puzzled.

"Expecting?" Omari said. "We didn't send word ahead. How did you know?"

"The Kamite ambassador told us," Tabia said. "She arrived three days ago."

"Take me to her immediately," Alika said. "Omari, come with me."

Kamada Mbuku led them through the outpost to her office. They entered the room; the Kamite ambassador stood, a knowing smile on her face. She wore a simple dress, the hem and sleeves edged with hieroglyphics. Her garb and appearance reminded Omari of the people of Menu-Kash, as it should. The histories told that the people of Kamit were a Menu-Kash lost tribe that founded their own home on the island they now inhabited.

"It is good to see you again, Alika," the Kamite said. The ambassador looked at Omari and her smile widened.

"Omari Ket," she said. "You are more impressive than I imagined. Eda chose well."

Omari was dumbfounded. "What? How do you know about Eda?"

The ambassador winked then turned her attention back to Alika.

"I know what you want to ask, and I know what you suspect," she said.

"It's more than a suspicion Meresankh," Alika said. "The only way you could have known where we would be is if you were behind it all. The fire dhow, the fisi, it was all you."

"You are wrong," Meresankh replied. "We had nothing to do with what you have experienced. But we are familiar with its source. We suspected they would try to prevent you. We were not certain to what lengths they would try."

"Who are 'they'?" Omari asked.

"That is something we cannot discuss beyond Kamit," Meresankh said. "The sooner we return, the sooner we can share what we know."

"You will tell us now or we will not accompany you to Kamit!" Alika said.

Meresankh's smile faded, replaced by an expression Omari didn't think such a pleasant face was capable of making. He was afraid of this woman.

"This is not Shamsa, child," she said. "And even if it were, you have no power in my presence."

It was more than the emotions in her words. It was the underlying threat, a feeling that she was prepared to do whatever it took to get Alika to Kamit. Omari watched as Alika's shoulders slumped and she stepped away from the ambassador.

"I'm . . . I'm sorry," Alika said. "The stress of this safari has me on edge."

"That is understandable," Meresankh replied. The warmth returned to her voice like a roaring fire in a cold room.

"Thank you for your hospitality," Meresankh said to the kamada. "We will be leaving immediately."

"So soon?" Alika said. "But we just arrived! We've had no time to eat or rest."

"You will have plenty of time for both on our safari to Kamit," Meresankh said. "Please follow me to the docks. Our dhow awaits."

"Our gear?" Omari asked.

"Has already been stored," Meresankh said.

Omari and Alika followed Meresankh to the docks. Omari stopped in his tracks when he saw the Kamite dhow. It was the biggest dhow he'd seen his life, three times as wide as the largest bahglah and twice as tall as a warehouse.

"How does one make a dhow so large?" Alika asked.

"Very carefully," Meresankh replied.

Kamite baharia swarmed the docks, loading the massive vessel. As they approached the gangplank, Meresankh stepped between Omari and Alika. She placed her palm on Omari's chest, and his old wound warmed.

"She brought you back to life," Meresankh said.

Omari was no longer surprised by what Meresankh knew.

"Yes," he said. "Why, she would not say."

"You will play a part in what is to come," Meresankh said.

"What's to come?" Omari laughed. "I think you have me mistaken for someone else. What you're hinting at sounds like trouble, and I'm allergic to trouble."

As the last words slipped through his lips Omari felt a sharp pain in his chest. He dropped to his knees and gasped for air.

"It seems Eda disagrees," Meresankh said.

"Okay, okay," he said.

The pain subsided and Omari regained his feet.

"Let's go then."

"You will not come with us," Meresankh said.

"Wait. You just told me I have a role to play, and Eda emphasized your point," Omari said. "But I'm not to go with you?"

"It's time for you to return to Sati-Baa," Meresankh said. "It's time for you to go home."

Two bare-chested baharia appeared carrying a saddle bag.

"I think there is enough inside to pay for your services and get you safely to Sati-Baa," Meresankh said.

Omari knelt beside the saddle bag then opened it. He almost cried when he saw the contents.

"You just made me a very rich man," Omari said. "With this much I can live like a mansa in Sati-Baa!"

"Knowing you, half of it will be gone before you reach the city," Meresankh said.

Omari shrugged. "You're probably right. Stacks aren't worth anything unless you're spending them."

Omari picked up the saddle bag then threw it over his shoulder. He sauntered up to Alika, who stood at the bottom of the gangplank.

"This is where we part company," Omari said. "I hope you find what you're looking for in Kamit."

"Thank you, Omari," Alika said. "I have a feeling I will. Enjoy your new found wealth."

Alika hugged Omari, catching him by surprise. He returned the hug.

Omari grinned one last time then strolled away.

"Until we meet again, Omari Ket," Meresankh called out.

"I hope not," Omari yelled back. His chest wound itched.

"Cleave!" he said, then he shrugged. He couldn't change fate. This he understood. But he could determine how he spent his time until that day of reckoning was upon him.

Omari had plans. Wonderful outrageous plans. He shook the saddle bag on his shoulder then laughed out loud.

He was truly Eda blessed.

EPILOGUE

Daarila scratched his beard as he and Eda watched Omari saunter away from the docks. He turned to his wife with a frown on his dark face.

"This is your champion?" he asked.

"Yes," Eda replied.

"Then you will fail," he said.

Eda looked at her husband with a smile that would lift the dead.

"He's stronger than he looks," she said. "Besides, I am with him. The only thing that could bring his failure is if you interfere."

"I'm done with this world," Daarila replied. "Do with it what you want. But do not underestimate those who worship me."

Eda did not reply. Instead, she gazed upon Omari Ket.

Do not fail me. Do not fail us all.

GALLERY

Raiders of Kiwa Island

Road to Kamit

The Escort

Respite

ABOUT THE AUTHOR

Milton Davis is an award winning Black Speculative fiction writer and owner of MVmedia, LLC, a publishing company specializing in Science Fiction and Fantasy based on African/African Diaspora history, culture and traditions. Milton is the author of nineteen novels and short story collections; his most recent the Sword and Soul adventure *A Debt to Pay.* Milton is also a contributing author to the upcoming Black Panther: Tales of Wakanda, published by Marvel and Titan Books *and coauthor of Hadithi and the State of Black Speculative Fiction* with Eugen Bacon. He is the editor and co-editor of eight anthologies; *The City, Dark Universe* and *Dark Universe: The Bright Empire* with Gene Peterson; *Griots: A Sword and Soul Anthology and Griot: Sisters of the Spear*, with Charles R. Saunders; *The Ki Khanga Anthology,* the

Steamfunk! Anthology, and the *Dieselfunk anthology* with Balogun Ojetade. Milton's work had also been featured in *Black Power: The Superhero Anthology and Rococoa published by Roaring Lions Productions*; Skelos *2: The Journal of Weird Fiction and Dark Fantasy, Steampunk Writers Around the World* published by Luna Press; *Heroika: Dragoneaters* published by First Perseid Press, and *Bass Reeves Frontier Marshal Volume Two*. Milton Davis and Balogun Ojetade won the 2014 Urban Action Showcase Award for Best Script; Milton's story 'The Swarm' was nominated for the 2018 British Science Fiction Association Award for Short Fiction.

https://www.miltonjdavis.com/

Interested in more Ki Khanga Adventures?
Visit www.mumediaatl.com today!

What is Ki Khanga? The answer lies in the pages of this amazing anthology. Balogun Ojetade and Milton Davis define this fascinating world which forms the foundation of the Ki Khanga Sword and Soul Role Playing Game. Prepare yourself for stories of bravery, tragedy, love and adventure. Prepare yourself for Ki Khanga.

Omolewa lived a peaceful life in the Kiswala city of Nacala with her adopted family, giving little thought of her origins or the family she never knew. But one day a mysterious ship from Zimbabwa arrived in harbor and changed her life forever. Omolewa discovered not only that she was the long lost daughter of the rulers of Zimbabwa, she also discovered that she possessed powers that could change the fortunes of her family and the destiny of Ki Khanga. The Bene's Daughter is an exciting tale of action, discovery and revelation that will keep you riveted from beginning to end.

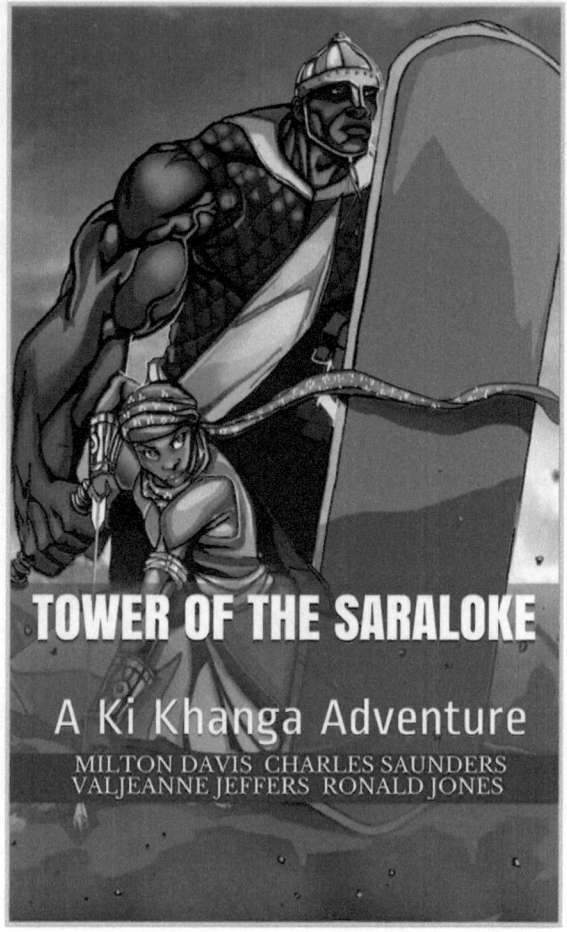

Kadira and Nguvu are captured by a mysterious and powerful being known as the Saraloke. While Nguvu is forced to fight to the death the Saraloke's champions as entertainment, Kadira is sent to a strange land to confront the Saraloke's enemy. How will they escape their dangerous circumstances?

Raised in the streets of Sati-Baa, Omari Ket is a man that gets by on his wits and skills . . . and the attentions of a god. Eda Blessed shares the tales of the man and the mercenary as he roams the roads of Ki Khanga bouncing from one adventure to another surviving with his skills, wits, and Eda's blessing.

www.ingramcontent.com/pod-product-compliance
Lightning Source LLC
Chambersburg PA
CBHW022220010726
47493CB00002B/534